Contemporary
Chinese Women Writers

II

Panda Books

Panda Books
First Edition 1991
Copyright 1991 by CHINESE LITERATURE PRESS
ISBN 7 – 5071 – 0079 – 0 /I . 73
ISBN 0 – 8351 – 2089 – 9

Published by CHINESE LITERATURE PRESS
Beijing 100037, China
Distributed by China International Book Trading Corporation
21 Chegongzhuang Xilu, Beijing 100044, China
P .O . Box 399, Beijing, China
Printed in the People's Republic of China

CONTENTS

Foreword

Li Ziyun

THE first of these collections was published in 1982 as *Seven Contemporary Chinese Women Writers*, and was well received by readers all over the world.

In the ten years since that book was published, women writers have emerged in great numbers in what seems to be a global phenomenon. In both the East and the West, they have become very active in many countries, including China. Therefore we are making another compilation of works by seven newly-popular women writers in a volume called *Contemporary Chinese Women Writers II* for the enjoyment of our foreign readers. In addition, for those scholars who are interested in Chinese literature, it offers new avenues of study.

In reading the present volume, those who have already read the first collection will find that the last ten years have seen great changes in the work of Chinese women writers.

The works contained in the first collection were produced during a period of transition in Chinese literature. Towards the beginning of this period of change most authors were not capable of completely shaking off the influence of past ideas. Almost without exception, they engaged in exposing social problems or political movements which caused great suffering. Though the seven authors' use of various literary techniques make them easily distinguishable, their approach to their subjects, the way in which they achieve their objectives, as well as their style and other aspects are all very similar. These works for the most part emphasize logic in the development of their plots and objectivity in their descriptions, though sometimes in individual works there is a kind of "time and space patchwork" approach in their writing or particular emphasis is placed on psychological description. Looking more closely at other aspects of their narration and overall structuring of language, we still find the works firmly rooted in realism. Thus one could say the differences among them are not necessarily immediately obvious.

The works in this collection, whether judged in terms of their origins or objectives, method or style, are all very different from each other.

I think the first thing that should be explained to the reader is that this is the youngest generation of authors to appear on the literary stage, all of them emerging in the last five or six years or so. Listed in order of the appearance of their first works, they are Peng Xiaolian, Liu Suola, and Can Xue, whose works first appeared in 1985; Fang Fang in 1986; and the rest, in just the last two or three years. From the time they first appeared, they demonstrated a completely different spirit. They were little influenced by the bounds of tradition and literary concepts popular in the last few decades. Much of the credit for this goes to the Chinese government's policy of opening up to the outside world. It is easy to see the influence of almost every style popular in Western literature in their works, though each writes in accordance with her own individual understanding of literature. From the subject matter to the style of narration, each author possesses her own characteristic features. Even the concept of value as expressed in each work illustrates differences among them. The result is that their works come in every shade and hue of the rainbow.

The seven stories in this collection abandon the conventional formula of exclusive reaction to important events in society and politics. They also do not limit themselves to writing about people's fate or the effect of changes in society on people's lives. Of course, China is presently experiencing the initial stages of reform and opening to the outside world. The problems of the new and the old society are intermingled and inevitably affect people living in these changing times. As a result, the characters' lives, fates and feelings unavoidably exhibit this influence. However, the stances they take and their treatment of narration have both undergone great changes. Some of the works in the collection also seem to touch on specific problems in society (such as Fang Fang's "Scenery"). But none of them addresses the problem directly or deals in moral judgements. Social phenomena are discussed in a calm manner from a neutral standpoint to objectively present some of the background environment of a character's life. Some works are primarily about the character's inner world, and some are about people's feelings and psychology. The immediate environment is pushed far into the background and is almost inconsequential. In some works the background is almost indiscernible and even disappears altogether.

These seven works may be roughly grouped into a few different types.

The vicissitudes of the main character's psychology in Can Xue's "The Mountain Cabin" and Jiang Yun's "Crucible" are actually both related to significant political activity, but both writers have moved away from earlier methods of writing. In "The Mountain Cabin", the reader is acutely aware of the problems, as the central female character is eccentric to the point of psychological abnormality. She is apprehensive of all other members of her family. she finds her mother's smile empty and hypocritical. Her young sister appears to have one green eye, her vision directly "focused on the small rash that appears on her neck, causing it to smart". Her father's eyes make her feel as though they run around her room every night, the eyes, she says, of one of a pack of hungry, panting wolves. In the paper window of her room she discovers numerous small holes made by someone's fingers poking through it. A large cloud of long-horned beetles descends from the heavens to bite people's toes. The house itself is soon to be destroyed by the rumbling tide of sand continuously pouring down from the mountain .... In the narrative there is not a single direct reference to society as a backdrop, but the piece does suggest the background. The fact that one finds the characters in such abnormal circumstances leads the reader to feel that something must be quite awry to bring about such an unsettling environment. If we look at Can Xue's other works in conjunction with this story, we can see more clearly her technique of highlighting the state of society through the characters' psychology.

In contrast, Jiang Yun's "Crucible" still retains certain direct references to the society in which it takes place. Yet the vast panorama of the "cultural revolution" only plays a small part in the story. Because of the movement to send middle school students to the countryside and remote areas to labour, the heroine has been sent to a factory in a small, distant town to become an apprentice. This then becomes the turning point in the characters' emotional changes. The small town is far away from the centre of political movements: the political atmosphere is hardly perceived there. It is also precisely because the town is small and remote that it is rarely visited by people from the big cities, and her arrival is like a pebble falling into a pool, generating ripples as it descends. The story describes the effects of her arrival on some of the people around her and the subtle changes she brings about in their feelings and reminds one of Turgenev's *A Nest of Gentlefolk*. It is only during a violent storm that the upper leaves of a tree come in contact with the lower ones. If not for the "cultural revolution", the protagonist would never have been thrown together in this small town factory with her apprentice master and the son of a family that has fallen on hard times. This young girl, with her headstrong, "citified" ideas, throws her master's slow, unemotional world into disorder and gives him extravagant hopes of love. At the same time he himself knows that his love will never be returned. It is only a dream. The appearance of this city girl arouses a certain tenderness and affection in the "son of a fallen family" and causes him to pity himself. In the end, when she returns to the city to attend college, everything that has happened in that place seems to dissipate like smoke in the air. This story's style is obviously different from the literature about "educated youth" of the past. Its focus is not on the difficulties encountered by young intellectuals but on what happens to the stagnant thinking and dulled emotions of the people in a remote, isolated crucible of a place when the young student arrives in their midst. This story leaves us with an unanswered question. Although she has left the place, will the lives of the people she has touched there ever return to their former state?

Fang Fang's "Landscape" employs still another style. She doesn't directly reveal subjective feelings and changes in psychology, and instead present an objective look at certain conditions in the lives of the characters. On the surface it appears that the technique is somewhat reminiscent of traditional realism. Looking more closely, however, we discover large differences. This style does not depend on stereotypes or heavily on plots as does traditional realism. Neither are the characters drawn in black and white. From Fang Fang's description of a noisy and confusing ten or twenty years in the lives of a destitute urban family of ten, we can see that the author has made every effort to show their lives as they are. She has given careful planning and consideration to the structure, narrative development, and selection of material. She consciously selects and carefully retains fragmented and seemingly disorderly detail to highlight the monotony of inconsequential people, and an exhausting, weary life. This style of writing appears to differ widely from Can Xue and Jiang Yun's style of concentrating on psychology, but they all use their work to stimulate thought in the reader in the same way, asking questions about the meaning and worth of human life — the same problems Western writers have been concerned with for a long time.

In comparing the present collection with the first, another difference becomes obvious: these new works all have a definite feminine character about them. Western readers may very well feel it strange to single this out, since it seems only natural for women authors to write from a woman's viewpoint. What is so peculiar about that? Those who have read *Seven Contemporary Chinese Women Writers* probably already know. Those works (indeed all works by women authors of the last 40 years) exhibit very little of that characteristic. With the exceptions of Zhang Kangkang and Zhang Jie's works, they were all relatively similar to works by male authors in terms of their vantage point and language. Only Zhang Kangkang and Zhang Jie touch lightly on the oppression of women via traditional moral standards and the indignation women have felt at such cruel treatment over the last few decades. The emphasis on the arts serving China and the political respectability of only one voice (a loud voice) presenting one subject (class struggle) with one type of character (heroes from among the workers, peasants and soldiers), made most works fairly similar. In this volume, on the other hand, with the possible exceptions of Fang Fang and a few others, who write from a neutral viewpoint, the authors take a distinct feminist stand. This feminism is different from Western ideas of women's rights, however, whose more militant ideas have already attracted the interest of scholars in China but haven't yet reached women authors. When we in China speak of a "feminist" viewpoint, we simply mean the author writes and examines matters as a woman, considering the real life situations women face and all the difficulties that trouble them. It also means that the language they use has a feminine flavour which expresses all their feelings and emotions.

Peng Xiaolian's "Hopes Worn Away" and Jiang Yun's "Crucible" seem to show that in some female authors this "feminine flavour" is gradually getting stronger.

"Hopes Worn Away" and "Crucible" are linked in two respects. One is that the protagonists in the two works are related in age and experience. When the main character in "Hopes Worn Away" returns from farming in the countryside, she has already finished college. Another is in the style of narration. The former carries the latter one step further. Although in "Crucible" there are two main characters — the apprentice and her master — the apprentice is really the key figure in the story. The whole story revolves around her arrival and ends when she leaves, so that the work bears mainly her imprint. The changes in her feelings bring out the development of the thinking and feelings of the other characters. The work clearly displays a feminist viewpoint. In "Hopes Worn Away" there is only one main character. The whole story is about her expressing all of the things which are troubling her. From the nature of her troubles to the style of narration she uses to describe them, the story represents an advance in Chinese feminist literature.

The female protagonists of "Hopes Worn Away" and "Crucible" are alike in that both are the luckier ones among the middle school graduates sent to farms and finally winning the chance to attend college. In "Crucible" the apprentice still hasn't resolved some of the problems of growing up, while the main character in "Hopes Worn Away" has graduated from college years ago. In China, once an unmarried woman passes the age of thirty she becomes an old maid. This story tells of an ambitious old maid, whose head is full of romantic ideals, alone, without a friend in the world in her loneliness. If "Crucible" depicts a female apprentice awakening the latent thoughts and desires of other people, then this story depicts an old maid's hopes for the future as they are slowly, little by little, worn away. She feels she can never get along with her small-town, penny-pinching brother, and although her sister is good-hearted, she is also shallow, uneducated and difficult to know well. She longs for a different kind of love — for the kind of mate who will accompany her hand-in-hand down the most difficult path life has to offer. But this will never happen. Even though she lowers her standards in the end, choosing someone only for his sincerity and goodness instead of looking for someone of similar intelligence, when she receives word from an American college that she had been accepted there, this young man throws in the towel. He believes he is not good enough for her, and they part. The story describes a woman's anxieties, hardships and disappointments in her search for love, and its portrayal of these carries the obvious imprint of a woman's hand.

Liu Suola's "Blue Sky and Green Sea" portrays China in the midst of economic reform and opening up to the outside world and changes in the lifestyles of some urban women, in their ideas of their own worth and in other aspects of their existences. They have quickly thrown off conventional ways of thinking and the limits of stereotypes. Their self-awareness has been awakened, and they are no longer so willing to sacrifice themselves unconditionally for other people. The main character in "Blue Sky and Green Sea", when faced with problems, continues to pace the floor, without being able to come to a decision about what to do. Outwardly she almost seems open-minded and modern. She ignores the objections of her family in taking a job that causes many people to look down on her. When she becomes a singer, or "star", her antics shake the world and mock convention. She rejects not only traditional norms but almost any standard of self-worth as well. Her heart, however, is full of paradoxes. Although she seems to deny the validity of orthodox music, whenever she goes into the recording studio to sing popular songs, she loses her voice and feels that her throat is riddled with cancer. She doesn't care what people think of her, but whatever she does she wonders what her deceased friend Manzi would think. Manzi is a symbol of the highest authority to her. Actually, what Manzi represents is orthodox music and the traditional way of expressing emotion. Though Manzi is only a spirit in the book, that spirit is always nearby, exerting its influence on her. She rebels against all conventional bounds but still gives in to the spirit of Manzi. These contradictions tend to rob her of vital energy. This kind of girl, her head full of such contradictory feelings and thoughts, has also emerged in China only in the last few years. In "Blue Sky and Green Sea", because of the female protagonist's many internal conflicts and lack of affection, the author has almost purposely used a tangled, ambiguous style of writ-

ing . In the development of the narrative we find constant repetition and confusion mirroring the character's
own depressed and confused mind .

Chi Zijian's " In the Vast Country of the
North" and Ding Xiaoqi's " Purple Asters" belong
to another category . Both use a strong lyrical flavour
to present an age-old theme — the tragic fate of
Chinese women for the last several thousand years .
These two pieces show the reader remote and isolated
areas in China where the situation seems to have
changed little if at all . These two women authors have
shifted their gaze from the city to the isolated, poverty-
stricken countryside, but this and the movement of
young intellectuals forced to go to the countryside are
completely different . The young female intellectuals retreat completely into themselves, too busy to think
about other concerns . The woman in " In the Vast
Country of the North" kills a cadre who has sub-
jected her to cruel treatment . She runs away to a remote, sparsely populated area in the far north of China, where a forester saves her life . Unfortunately she is
still not able to escape the fate of a captured slave . The
forester treats her even more badly than the cadre,
branding her forehead with two marks to make her a
lifelong captive, doomed to spend the rest of her life
ruled by the crack of his whip . The author chooses to
use a light touch to recount this soul-stirring story,
describing it through the eyes of the woman's little
girl: " Without warning, Dad pulled his belt from his
waist and struck straight out at Ma with it . She
didn't turn to run and hide, or cry ." With every
blow of the whip the reader feels a tightening of the
chest . The piece rarely indulges in describing the psy-

chology of the characters, but the reader nevertheless senses the quivering in their souls throughout. For example, after the "cultural revolution" has begun one young man happens upon this isolated place while fleeing from death. His appearance produces a distinct change in the woman, as her hardened heart begins to soften and awake. But a female slave doesn't have the right to fall in love. At the end of this sad tragedy, her captor burns her alive. The author speaks through her little daughter, and the narration is interspersed with thoughts of love for her father the forester. This lessens the terror in the tragedy and adds a more complex dimension to the work.

The woman in "In the Vast Country of the North" is a "captured slave". The sixteen-year-old "I" in "Purple Asters" on the other hand is being sold into "slavery" and taken to the northern border of China. Yet the tone used by Ding Xiaoqi is completely different from that found in "In the Vast Country of the North". Here we find warmth rather than bleakness. Because she goes to an area which is short of women and her "adoptive" family has sons and no daughter, she doesn't receive bad treatment at all. In fact she becomes the family favourite. In her real family she has always been left out in the cold, so that when she is sold, she is far from anxious: she is actually excited at the prospect of being an important member of a family. This is truly ironic. Her simple innocence and rare streak of luck together make the reader feel for the protagonist. One does not have to think too hard to imagine what fate awaits her in the coming years. Suppose the "husband's" next youngest brother's secret admiration becomes sexual: then what will happen? Although her happiness may only be temporary, at least she is certain of it. Her present overwhelming joy only comes from comparison with her former life, which was even more impoverished and gloomy. Chi Zijian and Ding Xiaoqi show us women's life and psychology in another corner of the world. Whether the plot leads the central character to great suffering or deep into an innocent happiness, her fate and fortune weigh heavily on the reader.

We hope the works in this collection will bring people in other countries to a better understanding of the true spirit of women in China and some of the predicaments they encounter. Perhaps it will also be of use to people in China as well as an aid to understanding the development of Chinese literature in the past few years.

Translated by Joe Adams

Landscape

Fang Fang

"BEHIND the lively facade of existence, in the darkest reaches of the abyss, I saw this strange world most clearly...."

— *Baudelaire*

1

Seventh Brother says that only when you realize that everything in this world, the very world itself, isn't even worth a cent will you finally be able to taste something in this life of yours. Then, like the heavenly stallion that trots across the skies you will be able to saunter, unfettered, down life's highway.

Seventh Brother says that lives like leaves are transient. The leaf that buds on a spring day only falls to the ground in autumn. In the end there are no exceptions, so why worry about robbing others of their nourishment to make yourself fat and green?

Seventh Brother says that most of the so-called upright citizens only live to establish good reputations for themselves; moreover, the ones who never harm anyone: what contribution have they ever made to society or to mankind? Meanwhile, those who are criticized for using questionable means to become rich may still donate large sums of money to renovate a hospital or a school and allow many others to enjoy these benefits. Can you say which type of person is better and which type is worse?

Whenever Seventh Brother comes back home, he acts like a mad dog, screams and yells uncontrollably, as if taking some sort of cruel revenge for having kept so silent as a child.

Father and Mother can't stand to listen to Seventh Brother when he behaves like that — they complain of "a toothache" and run outside. The Beijing-Guangzhou railroad just about scrapes underneath our house's eaves. A train thunders past every seven minutes with a shrieking wind and a deafening roar, so that every syllable that Father and Mother might have heard Seventh Brother utter is shattered beneath its huge rolling wheels.

Father is so hot-tempered that the first time Seventh Brother went on like that, he could have taken out a knife and cut out his tongue. But now he wouldn't dare. Now Seventh Brother is a somebody. Father must completely swallow his pride and adapt himself accordingly.

Seventh Brother is quite tall and well built. His face is flushed with a shiny red glow, and he has just the right amount of pot belly. It's hard to believe that supporting this fleshy body is that same old skeleton. I guess when he was twenty and went to have that operation, they didn't really take out his appendix — they changed his bones. Otherwise, it's hard to explain how he kept putting on weight. When Seventh Brother puts on a suit and tie, he looks just like the most dignified Hongkong businessman. If he puts on his rimless glasses, he seems very much like a professor or some sort of expert. On the street, there are always some girls who can't help but gaze lovingly as Seventh Brother passes. Away from home, Seventh Brother doesn't sound anything like a mad dog. When he shows off in that suave way of his, they say that you need at least ten years of schooling to understand what he's talking about.

Seventh Brother has stayed at the Qingchuan Hotel. At first Father wouldn't believe it. Every day when Father would stroll along the riverside, he could see that tall, white building. Father had lived in Hankou for so many years, and he had never seen such a tall building. He contended that only when you had attained the rank of a Chairman Mao or a Premier Zhou could you stay there. Mother said that Chairman Mao and Premier Zhou could never have lived there: they had passed away by then. But then there was General Secretary Hu and Premier Zhao, Father said: they would stay there. This was back in '84.

To convince him, Seventh Brother said that "Qingchuan Hotel" was written as "Anchuan Hotel" on the building's sign* — we could see it for ourselves.

Naturally, Father and Mother never dreamt that they would have a chance to go over and have a look. But the day after the newspaper printed the story of a stall-holder having stayed there, Fifth and Sixth Brothers, each with a thousand yuan, went down themselves.

---

*The Chinese characters *qing* "clear" and *an* "dark" look similar, especially in cursive script. *Chuan* means "stream".

When they came back the next day, they told Father and Mother that Little Seven must have stayed there — the way the character was written, it really did look like "Anchuan Hotel".

Seventh Brother said that he always went down "by cab" and that a red-suited attendant would open the car door for him, bow respectfully and say, "Welcome to our hotel."

Fifth and Sixth Brothers had gone by bus. They got off at the bridge and still had to walk quite some distance, so they had no way of telling if Seventh Brother was right. Nevertheless, Father and Mother didn't need any proof: they trusted him completely.

From then on, whenever Father met someone he knew on one of his strolls along the riverside, he couldn't help but say, "Yeah, Qingchuan Hotel is no big deal. My seventh kid has stayed there quite a few times."

"Oh, Little Seven, the one who used to sleep underneath the bed?"

"That's right," Father would reply. "He managed to sleep himself into a somebody." Father's face would glow with pride and affection.

In fact, Father suspected that Seventh Brother wasn't his son. By the time Mother's stomach began to swell, Father had it all figured out. Squatting in the doorway, he reckoned the timing. He counted and counted, then he grabbed Mother and slapped her across the face. Father said that was when he had taken the freighter to Anqing. A friend who was about to die wanted to see him one last time. All in all he had been away fifteen days, and it was then that Mother had become pregnant with Seventh Brother. Father knew that Mother had always been a bit of a flirt. He was away for a fortnight: how could she bear to be alone? Our neighbour, Bai Liquan, was Father's number-one suspect. Bai Liquan was a skinny guy whose slick, watery eyes harboured no good. Those thin lips could mouth just the right words to attract and seduce women. Most incriminating was Father's having seen, with his own eyes, Bai Liquan and Mother teasing each other. The more Father thought about it, the more he felt that he held the truth in the palm of his hand. Therefore, after Mother had given birth and was at home recuperating, Father never once looked at Seventh Brother. He would sit indifferently by the front door, drinking and chomping noisily on fried soya beans.

Eldest Brother took the responsibility for looking after Mother. By that time he was already seventeen. He cared for Seventh Brother, a soft worm of flesh, in the most dignified manner. It was six months later that Father took his first look at Seventh Brother. He scrutinized him. Then he tossed him, like a cloth bundle, on to the bed. Seventh Brother was scrawny, certainly not the flesh and blood of someone as tall and rugged as Father. Father grabbed hold of Mother's hair and demanded to know whose son he really was. Mother yelled at him until she was hoarse. She called him a wild pig, a rabid dog, a blind monster. How could he have the nerve to quarrel after he had gone to Anqing to see his old girlfriend before she died? Father and Mother's voices were so loud it was frightening. Even trains thundering past every seven minutes couldn't muffle the racket they were making, and all the neighbours came over to see what all the fuss was about. It was just dinner time; all the members of the audience brought their bowls, and they crowded together in front of the door. They chewed their food while chuckling and assessing Father and Mother's perform-ance. When Mother spat at Father, it was judged that her style wasn't as good as last time. When Father, so angry he couldn't contain himself, smashed a rice bowl, quite a few voices were in agreement — the sound of a bowl smashing couldn't compare with that of a thermos bottle shattering. Some who knew the in-side story added that our family didn't have a thermos bottle, otherwise Father wouldn't be smashing bowls. All of them could attest that Father was one of the noisiest good old boys in this district called "Henanpengzi".

This no one doubted. Father was a hell of a guy. All the family members respected Father, but Mother's respect was, of course, the deepest. Throughout her life, Father was her proudest possession. Even though during her forty years of marriage she had been beaten by him thousands of times, she was a hundred per cent satisfied with her lot. Father's beating Mother was practically at the heart of their relationship. When he had finished beating her, Father would become incomparably humble and meek and even act most warmheartedly. Therefore, had Mother gone for quite some time without being beaten, she would purposely provoke Father and send him into a fury. Mother was a beautiful woman, and she loved to put guys on, but she had never betrayed Father. It was her nature to enjoy teasing and showing off in front of men. But that was where it ended. Mother would ask if it was possible to find someone who was more of a man than Father. She said that if there was, it'd be the devil himself. She said that only if Father died first would she fall into another man's arms. She was only twenty-five when she said that, and now she was already over sixty. Father was still in good health, and Mother carried out her vow unfailingly. Therefore, Father's suspicion that Seventh Brother was actually neighbour Bai Liquan's bastard was obviously groundless. Bai Liquan was eighteen years younger than Mother. She couldn't help but flirt with him, and occasionally things got physical, but Seventh Brother was indisputably Father's son. In fact only Father could sire a son like Seventh Brother. It was only twenty-five years later, when Seventh Brother was transferred to the Provincial Committee of the Party Youth League, to become some sort of official, that Father finally appreciated this. Father had heard from Seventh Brother that members of the Provincial Committee of the Youth League were only a step below the Party Provincial Committee and that, with a little bit of luck, it wouldn't be hard to get to the Party Central. This was inconceivable for Father. He had never even seen the lowest level official. From his workplace the most official person he knew, and who knew him, was the shipping station's station master. He had once tried to say a couple of words to him, but before he could finish, the station master had to answer the phone. Now his Little Seven was so many grades higher than the station master and still only in his twenties. Therefore, when Seventh Brother bursts in and struts about the house like an arrogant cock, Father, nevertheless, behaves tolerantly toward him.

2

Father, along with his wife, seven sons and two daughters, lived in a thirteen-square-metre wooden-walled hut in the Henanpengzi district of Hankou. Father had lived there from the day he was married. In seventeen years he and Mother had produced their nine children. An eighth son had died a fortnight after birth. Father deeply resented the early passing of that little life. That year Father had turned forty-eight. Not only was the new kid also born in the year of the tiger like him, they were both born on the identical day, month and time of day. On each of those fifteen days, Father had held his little son with a crazy ecstasy. He had never shown such profound parental love to any of his other children. Then, suddenly on the sixteenth day, the infant's whole body was racked with cramps, and later that evening he passed away. Father's grief was so complete it nearly scared the life out of Mother. Father bought some wood, made a tiny coffin and buried the little one beneath the window. I was the little one. I was extremely moved that my father, who gave me this body of flesh, allowed me to remain with the rest of the family. Quietly I watched my brothers' and sisters' lives. I saw them grow up: how they struggled against dire circumstances and how they fought against each other. I heard each one of them say that it was Little Eight who was the comfortable one as they gazed beneath the window. I was uneasy that I had more happiness and peace of mind than each of them. That my lot should have been so good while theirs was so poor was certainly not my fault, yet I often felt guilty as I watched my parents and my

siblings. When their situation was at its most bitter, I
even thought of arising, giving up all of my good fortune and sharing in their hardships. But I never had
the courage to take such a step. The world they live in
truly petrifies me. I am a coward, and I often ask my
family to forgive my cowardice, to forgive my solitary
enjoyment of the peace and comfort that rightfully belongs to the whole family, to forgive my cold gaze as I
watch how bitterly they toil and how frantically they
rush about, as I observe their adversity and anxiety in
every detail.

That was in 1961. With nine hungry sons and
daughters craning their necks and watching them blankly, Father and Mother resolved to abandon the boast
of their youth, that they would produce a whole
platoon of kids.

In the little room were a large bed and a small, low
dining table. To store clothes, some wooden crates and
cardboard boxes were stacked in the corner of the
room. Father built a tiny loft for the two girls, and
come night-time, the seven boys would sleep, arranged
in a row, on mattresses on the floor. Every night before he went to sleep, Father would take count — if
all of his sons and daughters were alive, it was all
right — and then he would lay his head on his pillow and snore softly into Mother's arms.

Father said that the reason that this district was
called "Henanpengzi" * was that Grandfather and a
mass of refugees from the famine had pitched their
camp here. Today, Henanpengzi was, more or less, in

---

* "Henanpengzi" here means the shacks of the people from
Henan Province.

the middle of the city. To the south, across the Beijing-Guangzhou railway tracks, was Station Road. At the end of the road, like a gloomy cathedral, stood the Hankou railway station. Turning right off of Station Road was Sun Yat-sen Avenue. On this section of Sun Yat-sen Avenue, almost every door led into a business. The Tieniao Photo Shop, the Laotongcheng Restaurant, the Shoujia Clothing Factory, Yangzi Street, Jianghan Road, Liudu Bridge — this was Hankou's flourishing district. Every day Father would cross Sun Yat-sen Avenue and go straight to Riverside Park to practise Taijiquan. Father would boast to those he practised with that he was an old resident of Henanpengzi. Actually if old residents of Hankou didn't use a contemptuous tone of voice when they said "Henanpengzi", it was as if they had demeaned themselves.

Father said that in the twelfth year of the Guangxu Emperor of the Qing Dynasty, our grandfather had fled the famine in Zhoukou, Henan Province and come to Hankou. In Hankou, Grandfather had worked as a stevedore. Grandfather, Father and Fourth Brother — three generations in the same line of work. Third Brother always said that if Grandfather had joined the military instead, he might have taken part in the 1911 revolution, he might have been one of its leaders, and the family would have been much better off. All the brothers and the sisters would have been like the sons and daughters of Beijing's high-level cadres. Father called him a fool. He said that if one couldn't live like Grandfather did, then life was utterly meaningless. Grandfather was a round-waisted, thick-shouldered ox of a man whose heart was as big as his body. Grandfather had joined the Hongbang early on.* At that time the battles on the docks were very spirited, and Grandfather was one of the best scrappers. All the guys in the Hongbang really admired Grandfather. Grandfather always helped his friends. He didn't care if they were right or wrong; whenever there was a call for help, he'd be the first to answer. Father said that he was fourteen when he first helped Grandfather fight on the docks. He saw, with his own eyes, how brave and tough Grandfather was. Later on Grandfather was seriously wounded in a fierce battle. Many of his ribs were smashed, the blood just poured out of his body so it seemed as if he was wrapped in red cloth. By the time he was carried home, Grandfather was already breathing quite feebly. Even though he was in such a state, he still managed to smile. Father said that the boss, Yin Qizhou, specially sent someone with some powdered medicine from Yunnan Province. At that time, Yin Qizhou was Hankou's famous "Emperor of the Docks". To this day, whenever Father mentions his name, he's so moved he shudders. The medicine was not enough to save Grandfather. He put his hand on Father's shoulder, patted him twice and breathed his last. Father knelt in front of Grandfather with tears streaming down his face. When he saw Grandfather's head fall to one side, he let out a wail and fell on top of him. At once, everyone knew that Grandfather had gone. Their sobbing sounded like rolling thunder far off in a distant sky. There seemed to be no end to the mourners who came to pay their last respects. Father has never

---

*The Hongbang was an underworld secret society.

been able to figure out why this was so. He decided it must have been because Grandfather had been such a good fighter. Father was twenty at the time. Except for his being a little thinner, he and Grandfather were made from the same mould. Three days after he buried Grandfather, the boss called Father to help with the fighting. Like a tiger stalking his prey, he approached the station. Their opponents stared at him speechlessly. At last, in a quivering voice, one of them asked if he was a man or a ghost.

Whenever Father told this part of the story, he would tilt his head back and roar with laughter. Then he would take a big swig of booze, throw a dozen soya beans into his mouth and chomp on them noisily.

Whenever Father drank, he liked to go on and on about his fights. On such occasions, all of his sons had to dutifully sit by his side and listen to him practise ''traditional education''. Once Second Brother wanted to go over to his friend's house to review his lessons and prepare for the middle school entrance exam. To everyone's surprise, as soon as he got to the door, Father hurled the fried soya beans, plate and all, at him. Our sisters Xiaoxiang and Daxiang screeched. The soya beans scattered on the ground, and the plate cut Second Brother's face. The blood from his forehead trickled into the corner of his mouth. Father said, '' Your old man wants you to sit down and hear how he became a man.'' Therefore, when Father was like that no one would dare to even shift their bums. More than once, Seventh Brother couldn't hold himself back and wet his pants.

No one liked to hear Father talk about the past more than Mother. Her memory was a lot better than his. She reminded him of all the dates, places and names that he forgot. If Mother was also unable to remember, Father would pound his head and try to recall. He would think until his face was covered by the most painful expression. If he couldn't remember, Father would refuse to continue his story. Under these circumstances, it was as if all the kids were granted a big pardon. He once took an entire week to recall the date of the battle of the Xujiapeng Dock, which shook Wuhan in the thirty-sixth year of the Republic. When, a week later, he still couldn't remember the date, he reconvened his audience and used the season instead. Father said that it was in the winter of the thirty-sixth year of the Republic. The Japanese had just retreated, the Guangzhou-Wuhan railroad was reconnected, and working on the Xujiapeng Dock was extremely lucrative. The dockers were all mad with greed, and they fought among themselves without there being any clear winner. The head of the Hongbang, Wang Lisong, got someone to hire Father. Father's hands had been itching for the past few days, and he agreed at once. To win Xujiapeng Dock, Father had to get up at 3 a m. When he crossed the river, the sky was still pitch black, and the wild, frigid wind stung his face. Wrapped from shoulder to waist in his black jacket, Father was an awe-inspiring sight. Before getting on the boat, he had drunk eight ounces of booze. The alcohol fired his blood and sent rushes of tingling sensations through his body, so that he even felt a nameless sort of friendliness toward the frosty wind that pierced his bones. Looking out over the vast Yangtze River, his face had an expression of crazed fearlessness. Father clasped his shoulder-pole. He always used the same one, dark-brown and shiny. He was so good at wielding it that he felt not at all inferior to Guan Gong and his Black Dragon Moon-Stopping Halberd. Father's co-worker, Xiong Jingou, fidgeted noisily in the boat's hold. Father pointed at his legs and laughed until his whole body shook. "How I wish I could take you, you bag of shit, and throw you overboard to feed the fish," he said. The river was extremely dark and muddy. The little boat's squeaking as it rocked to and fro sounded like an entrancing song. In the grey morning light it appeared quite beautiful. Xiong Jingou never stopped trembling. No matter how Father cursed and insulted him, he never quit moving. This made the guys near him begin to fidget as well. Xiong Jingou had an old blind mother and three little daughters as thin and weak as straw. The fourth filled his wife's belly to the bursting point. It was not yet daylight when Father and the others reached the other side. Arriving before anyone else, they immediately seized control of Xujiapeng's upper, middle and lower docks. Father and the others were all brave and hearty men who frightened their opponents until their hands and feet went soft. When someone discovered that the Huaqing Street gang of deaf-mutes had come as well, they were even more frightened and almost shit their pants. As they ran away they wailed — why had their parents only given them one pair of legs? The Huaqing Street gang of deaf-mutes were thugs raised by Lu Old Ten. In those days, when someone mentioned the "Tiger of Huaqing Street", Lu Old Ten, it would make folks tremble uncontrollably. His gang had venom in their hearts and acid in their fists and they fought without asking why. Actually, they couldn't

have asked even if they wanted to . Father and Lu Old
Ten weren' t really friends, but among the deaf-mutes
there were a few that had respected Grandfather . Of
course, Father' s side was victorious . After the sky became light, they tied rocks to the fallen corpses and
threw them into the river . Father had bound a rock to
a guy named Zhang . He said that he had known this
guy . They had worked together on the same dock .
Father remembered how, once, when he had staggered,
Zhang had supported him . Father knew that Zhang
was an honest guy . What he didn' t know was why he
had to be killed . After mulling it over, he said that it
was his fate . Father' s leg had a triangular gash where
he had been hit with an iron bar . The blood poured
out of it . But Father was used to flowing blood; he
just rubbed his wound with dirt, and the next day he
was back at work on the dock . Even now, his leg has
a ridge-like scar the colour of earth . It was the tradition that the victorious leader would spend a night of
debauchery and toast his conquest repeatedly, while
people like Father went back to their huts to wash
their wounds, get medicine for their buddies or weep
over their fallen friends . The trembling Xiong Jingou
wasn' t even lightly wounded . He helped Father back
home and then left full of smiles . Father said it was
too bad he wasn' t killed, because two weeks later,
there was another fight and the gang' s boss had decided that he was to die . The boss, in order to use his
corpse and win a lawsuit, secretly sent one of his men
to kill Xiong Jingou in the midst of the fray . Father
saw the iron bar heading for Xiong Jingou and he
cried out, but since he was slow in turning his head
the iron bar broke through Xiong Jingou' s skull . He

fell to the ground without even as much as a groan. The gushing blood made his head look like a new variety of water melon.

That evening, Father drank himself silly. He beat Mother and then he swore he would never fight on the docks again. Father would, of course, eat his words. When it came to fighting, he was like an opium addict, unable to kick the habit.

Father had an excess of energy. If he didn't expend it in this way, it would stick in his body and torment him to death.

These moving scenes from the tragic past would drive Father into a frenzy. Sometimes he would gulp down his booze and shout, "When will my sons become like their old man and do something truly thrilling?"

3

Now Father's loneliness pains him, and it's not easy for a man like Father to let any sort of situation get to him. But without a doubt he's unhappy. Father still lives in the same old house, but his sons and daughters, one by one, have flown away. The sound of snoring rising and falling from the floor, the aggravating disturbances, even the silly giggling from the loft, have all been replaced by silence. The house seems empty. On New Year's Day, each son and daughter contributed ten yuan to buy him an easy chair. They placed it by the wall, but Father never sits in it. He says it freezes his ass. On clear days, Father plays cards by the side of the street, and when it rains, he lies on his bed moaning and groaning. "Only Lit-

tle Eight is here to keep me company," he says.
When Father says that, I feel quite touched for the
next few days. Later, he planted some red salvia on
the ground that covers me. He told Mother it was Little Eight's hair.

When the bleak winter comes, Father drinks sullenly
and silently. When the north wind blows, the door
and window rattle, and with the sudden noise of the
train, the whole place shakes so badly it seems ready
to collapse. Her eyes rheumy, Mother looks at Father.
Since he retired, Father no longer beats her up, and
she has aged suddenly. Father and Mother no longer
have anything to talk to each other about, they live in
silence. Words have become superfluous.

Of all of them, Seventh Brother came home the most
often. He hadn't married yet, and he would always
visit on Saturday. Occasionally, one of his brothers
and his kids would stop by for a chat. Father wasn't
interested in his grandchildren at all: little pink balls
wrapped in colourful clothing. Father said that
bringing up kids like this would surely turn them into
pigs. This sort of talk made all of his daughters-in-law
despise him. Father said that they didn't know shit.
"Look at our Little Seven. Wasn't he the product of
his old man's feet and fists? If you want to be a somebody, then you have to live through some inhuman ex-
periences."

When Father talked like that, it was as if a knife
twisted in Seventh Brother's heart. He never thought
of arguing with Father. He felt towards Father like a
domestic animal does towards its sire: Father had
given him this life, and compared to everything else,
life was the most important. Seventh Brother always

left early on Sunday; he hated being at home. He couldn't stand seeing Father drink and swear and then spit a dark green gob of phlegm in the middle of the room. He couldn't become accustomed to seeing his mother, whose limbs were as thin as kindling, start to act like a young girl every time she saw a man and begin to gossip about how so-and-so's father-in-law got on with his daughter-in-law and how someone else's mother-in-law tried to seduce her son-in-law. It was always damp in that little room; the air made Seventh Brother shiver.

When he left home early Sunday morning, Seventh Brother often took along his fishing rod. If acquaintances met him on the street they would tell him that he really looked "like a man of leisure". Seventh Brother would only laugh. As he wandered through the streets and alleys of Henanpengzi, he would affect a wealthy and elegant manner to show that he most certainly was not someone who was raised here. The change in Seventh Brother's appearance was so great it was as if the blue seas had turned to fields of mulberries. People couldn't imagine that this was the same little kid who, ten years before, had scavenged these streets for junk and old vegetables.

Seventh Brother appeared very composed. With his lips closed, he appeared calm and at ease. Yet his eyes were full of hatred. If you had observed him closely for a few minutes, you would have discovered that his eyeballs were like two bombs which could have exploded at any minute. Moreover, his whole life only existed for this explosion.

Seventh Brother was five when he began collecting junk. It was his own idea, and he started the day the twins, Fifth and Sixth Brothers, had eaten rotten apples from the fruit stand and had to be hospitalized with dysentery. Father had flown into a rage. Three months' wages was still far from enough to cover the hospital expenses. Seventh Brother squatted by the threshold and watched Father swear sputteringly. Seventh Brother felt something catch in his throat, and he coughed softly and, when Father heard him, was sent flying out of the door by a kick from Father, who said, " If you ever cough again, I' ll choke you to death ." " I wasn' t coughing," replied Seventh Brother. " I only wanted to say that I' m going out to collect junk ." " You ought to have done that long ago," said Father. " Your old man' s raised you for five years, and you' ve turned out worse than a dog ."

Seventh Brother was surprised that at five years old he had been resourceful and courageous enough to roam around the narrow lanes and alleys of Henanpengzi to collect junk. At five, his sister Daxiang' s kid still wanted to suck her breasts, and his sister Xiaoxiang' s kid couldn' t even squat down to pee. Seventh Brother could remember that the first thing he picked up was a ripped handkerchief. There was something sticky on it. He stuck out his tongue and tasted it — it was sweet. Then he licked at it until the whole handkerchief was wet. Seventh Brother believes that he' ll never forget squatting by the wall and passionately licking the handkerchief. He was a taciturn boy. When grown-ups pointed at his little basket and said something, he always ignored them. Every day he would stuff his basket so full that he almost couldn' t carry it. The junk he gathered was piled up underneath the window. There was room beside where his little brother was buried. He had seen his younger brother. When he saw Father kiss his little face, Seventh Brother touched his own face — he couldn't remember if Father had ever kissed him. He was extremely envious of his little brother, who would always lie there so peacefully. He had seen Father put him into a casket and then cover it with earth. How he wished that Father would give him a casket too and let him sleep in it restfully. However, he never dared to say anything about it.

Seventh Brother was often very hungry. When he saw other people eating, he couldn't stop the saliva from running down his chin. His chin became streaked by two white lines. One day, he walked over the platform bridge to the train station. A little further on he went into a children's store. Inside there were lots of little kids dressed like those in pictures. They were buying clothes and leather shoes. Seventh Brother didn't want clothes and leather shoes. He saw a girl in pink eating a walnut shortbread. She was munching away noisily. As he moved over next to her he could smell the cake, and its aroma made his intestines twist. Then he reached out and grabbed the shortbread. The little girl cried out "Mummy" and let go of the cake. And there it was, in Seventh Brother's hand. The little girl's mother glared at him. "Little beggar," she cursed and dragged her daughter away. Seventh Brother just couldn't believe that the piece of cake now belonged to him. He took a bite gingerly; no one interfered: it really was his. Then he gulped it down like a madman. Seventh Brother had never been so happy before; he wanted to run back and tell everybody at home. He began to go to the children's store regu-

larly. Anything that he grabbed out of the hands of
the other kids became his. He ate a lot of things that
he couldn't even name. The children's store gave Seventh Brother some of the brightest moments of his
childhood.

Seventh Brother began elementary school when he
was seven. Father was very much against it. Father
was illiterate, and he liked it. He said that there had to
be someone in the world who was illiterate, otherwise
who would there be to do all the hard work? Father's
words were meant for Second Brother. When he had
finished middle school, Second Brother had insisted on
going to high school instead of helping Father peddle
the freight bicycle. Second Brother said that it was a
complete waste of talent to work hauling merchandise
after having finished middle school. Father and Second
Brother fought for three nights, and when Third Brother supported Second Brother, Father finally gave in.
Since he had become an adult, he had rarely given in.
Father didn't understand how the government could
be so muddleheaded. Who would manage the docks if
everyone left to study culture? To be fair, Father did
have some insight. If the docks remained open, someone had to work there. And since educated people
weren't willing to take those sort of jobs, why not let
some people stay illiterate and have them specialize in
developing the docks? Father couldn't know that progress would make it possible to create the metal robot.

Because of government requirements, Seventh Brother
did, eventually, start elementary school. He wasn't interested in going to school though. When he walked
into the classroom in rags that first day, he heard someone ask who had let the filthy dog in. Later, everyone

began to call him filthy dog, so he abhorred the school and his classmates from that very first day. Seventh Brother stopped collecting junk. Mother told him that the junk didn' t bring in enough money and that he' d better start gathering vegetables at Black-Mud Pond. So he began gathering vegetables, skipping school every afternoon. After lunch he would walk towards the outskirts of town with a basket on his arm. He had to cross Huangpu Road and then walk over Huang Family Mound to the Liu Family Temple before reaching Black-Mud Pond. Here people were few, and land was plentiful; the farmers' vegetable fields were everywhere. Sometimes one could even find some nice vegetable leaves at the Liu Family Temple. In summer Seventh Brother had to take a fork as well. Father said that every day he had to spear him a bunch of frogs to have with his wine. Seventh Brother enjoyed spearing the frogs. When he jumped nimbly about the river bank and quickly speared a frog, he always wanted to laugh. He never laughed at home. Everyone who knew him said that the kid was born without a laugh nerve.

One day, Seventh Brother was out by the Liu Family Temple. He could see the farmers sitting on little stools thinning out cabbage seedlings. He quietly squatted behind a peasant woman. Whenever she threw a handful of seedlings into her basket, a few would fall to the ground. Those would belong to Seventh Brother. When he had collected a half basketful, a little girl also came up behind the peasant woman. Seventh Brother shot a disgusted look at her. She was quicker than he was, and whatever the peasant woman dropped, she would pick up first and

throw into her basket. Seventh Brother felt like cutting
off her hand. Just then the peasant woman turned
around. She asked them why they bothered about so
few vegetables. The little girl answered that if she
didn' t gather vegetables, she wouldn' t have anything
to eat. Seventh Brother said it was the same with him.
The peasant woman asked if it wasn' t very tiring
work. The little girl answered that it was better to be
tired than to be beaten up. Seventh Brother said it was
the same with him. The peasant woman sighed deeply,
then she pulled out bunches of fine seedlings and gave
them to Seventh Brother and the little girl. She filled
their baskets to the brim. The little girl was one big
smile. Seventh Brother didn' t smile, but he was
extremely happy.

Later, Seventh Brother got to know the little girl;
she was called Enough. Enough said that she lived
down by the Three-arch Bridge. She was her family' s
fifth girl. When she was born and her father saw that
she was a girl, he became furious and roared at her
mother,   " Isn' t   is   enough   now?'' " It' s
enough,'' her mother replied hastily. After the two of
them had quarrelled for a while, they gave her the
name " Enough". Although they already had
Enough, her father wouldn' t let her mother stop
having children. Enough now had two younger sisters.
She said that her mother was pregnant again. This
time everyone said that it would be a boy. There were
already seven fairy maidens in the family. Of the Eight
Immortals, one had to be of the opposite sex.

Seventh Brother often ran into Enough, and she
would invite him to walk with her. So they began to
meet by the railroad. Enough twittered excitedly, so

Seventh Brother suspected that she had once been a bird. She would prattle endlessly, and Seventh Brother would just listen silently. At first he was rather impatient with her, but after a while he got used to it, and eventually he came to enjoy listening to her. He thought how nice it would be if his sister Xiaoxiang was like Enough. They were the same age, both two years older than Seventh Brother. Xiaoxiang never paid any attention to Seventh Brother, but if Seventh Brother was on her mind, it meant trouble for him. One evening Father had been drinking and was rather tipsy. Xiaoxiang hurried over and told him that when Seventh Brother had met Bai Liquan he had wept, called him papa and taken a piece of candy from him. When Father heard this he flew into a rage, slammed his wine cup on to the table and roared at Seventh Brother, "Come over here!" Seventh Brother was so frightened he couldn't stand up. Like a dog, he crawled over to his father. Father raised Seventh Brother's chin with his big toe and cursed him, "You bastard!" Then he pushed him over with his foot. Father commanded Fifth Brother to pick Seventh Brother up and shove him against the wall. Then he ordered Sixth Brother to strip off Seventh Brother's pants and give him fifty lashes with a bamboo rod. Fifth and Sixth Brothers were only too happy to oblige. Father only let them do this sort of thing when he was particularly pleased with them. Xiaoxiang sat on the edge of the bed while Daxiang helped her paint her fingernails with mercurochrome. They were both shrieking with laughter. Seventh Brother put up with all of the pain as he listened to them laughing smoothly as songs flowing out. Father sat down and continued drinking. He slurped noisily . From beginning to end, Mother never looked up from trimming her nails and cutting off strips of callous skin from the soles of her feet . Mother liked to see people punish dogs, but since Seventh Brother wasn't a dog, she didn't lift her head once . The train roared past outside . The shining lights flashed by . These were interwoven with the bamboo rod and its whistling through the air . The whole scene made quite an impression on Seventh Brother's mind .

It's not clear where the railroad starts . It stretches out far ahead, but who knows where to? And where is Enough? Perhaps her spirit has been drifting around here all along . Seventh Brother is unable to control himself, and he starts walking over there .

To Seventh Brother these days are filled with beauty and kindness . In the countless days of gloom and darkness, they shimmer feebly like a sparkling star .

4

Whenever Eldest Brother was at home, Seventh Brother would stare at him with a confused look . Eldest Brother didn't beat him; Eldest Brother didn't fabricate lies which made Father beat him until he almost couldn't breathe . Eldest Brother didn't curse him with the meanest words . Eldest Brother didn't treat him like an idiot, like a toy, like a half-dead, loathsome creature . When Seventh Brother was a child, he used to think that Eldest Brother was his father; only later did he realize that he was just his oldest brother . Eldest Brother and Father were completely different .

It disgusts Eldest Brother to see Seventh Brother so insufferably arrogant today . Time is indeed a magician .

Little Seventh Brother, who used to sleep underneath his parents bed, has sloughed off his pitiable shell and now sits in the middle of the room and bitches about everything. Whenever he comes home and finds Seventh Brother flaunting his biting intellect, Eldest Brother is sure to bellow, "Little Seven, you say one more word and I'll cut out your tongue!"

What a pity that Eldest Brother spent so little time at home, so very little time! Since Seventh Brother could remember, Eldest Brother had never slept at home. Day by day, as the brothers grew up, it became impossible to squeeze seven guys together on the shakedown. Consequently Father kicked Seventh Brother underneath the bed, and Eldest Brother began the endless years of working the night shift.

When the stars began shining brightly in the sky, Eldest Brother would push open the door and leave with his lunch box in his hand. The box contained half a *jin* of rice and a small plate of salted vegetables. When he returned home early in the morning, Father and Mother would have already left for work, so Eldest Brother would fling himself on the bed and sleep soundly until sunset, when he would get up, and the family would eat supper together. When the stars began twinkling in the sky and Father started yawning, Eldest Brother would push the door open and leave with his lunch box in his hand. Day after day. Year after year.

Eldest Brother hadn't finished fourth grade when he began working in the factory. He had failed a year twice. After a year in the same class as Second Brother, he did another with Third Brother. Eldest Brother was four years older than Third Brother and almost a head taller. His classmates were all as small and weak as Third Brother. They nicknamed Eldest Brother "Uncle Liu".* At first Eldest Brother responded cheerfully, then Third Brother told him that they were mocking him for being as old as an uncle because he had failed twice, and from then on Eldest Brother would go crazy whenever someone called him that. Eldest Brother was uncommonly brave when he fought; his fists were quick and powerful, and if he got excited enough he'd pull out his knife too. This was what Father appreciated most about him. All of his classmates feared Eldest Brother as if he were a tiger. In fact he never beat up his classmates. They were too weak. He wouldn't stoop to raise his hands against the "little radishes", as he called them. Eldest Brother said that he wasn't like his father. He didn't beat up those who were weaker than himself. Father beat his wife and children as often and with as much excitement as he drank.

Eldest Brother had been thrown out of school. That day they had a phys. ed. class. The phys. ed. teacher was a bit of a dandy and wanted Eldest Brother to carry the box horse and the mat. The mat was for the girls to do somersaults on. Eldest Brother refused to carry the mat. The phys. ed. teacher said that if "Uncle Liu" didn't carry it, who else was there that could do it? Eldest Brother walked over to the phys. ed. teacher, lifted his upper arm, and gave him an elbow. In a moment, two streams of red blood trickled from his powder-white nose. All of the pupils were

---

*The surname Liu is pronounced the same as "failure" in Chinese.

dead scared, some of the girls were even sobbing. Eldest Brother swept his eyes over them and stalked off. At first the school didn't mean to throw Eldest Brother out. His classmates could attest that he had only struck the teacher because the latter had mocked him. That evening, the director, followed by the embarrassed teacher, came to Henanpengzi. Father stopped them in the doorway. The director said that they had come to apologize to Eldest Brother and he hoped that Eldest Brother would apologize to the teacher as well. Glowering, Father cursed them and their ancestors before saying, "It's lucky you came up against my son: he's no match for his father as a kid. Had it been me, aside from your nose, you wouldn't have any teeth left." When Father finished talking, his roaring laughter resonated like a large bell. The director and the phys. ed. teacher began to tremble. Then, step by step, they withdrew. Perplexed and alarmed, they gazed at Father as they staggered off.

Eldest Brother never went back to school. He had looked forward to this from the very first day he had shouldered his school bag. He had just turned fifteen. Father sent him to the ironworks as an apprentice, and Eldest Brother became a blacksmith. Father said that this trade paid high wages, and furthermore, it built up one's physique. And, true enough, Eldest Brother's arms grew thick, and his whole body became dark and shiny. At twenty, he was already as rugged as Father. A downy beard emerged on his chin. Sometimes he would prick Seventh Brother's face with this miserable beard. Seventh Brother was waiting for Eldest Brother's beard to grow long. He often wondered if it would be possible to braid it like

Xiaoxiang's hair.

After Eldest Brother turned twenty, he went through a remarkable change of temperament. At supper he flared up for nothing. When he entered the house, he kicked the door open with a crash. He quarrelled with both Father and Mother, and their quarrelling turned heaven and earth upside down. Seventh Brother would crawl underneath the bed and didn't dare move. He couldn't understand why Eldest Brother did it. One day Eldest Brother had a terrible fight with Father, after which things became much more peaceful at home.

Actually, it was all the neighbour Bai Liquan's fault that Eldest Brother fought with Father. During the day Eldest Brother came home to sleep. Mother would come home from her job at the baling factory to prepare lunch. At that time Fifth and Sixth Brothers had just started elementary school, and Seventh Brother was still engaged in collecting junk.

Mother was very good at baling. She was a pretty good talker too. The leader of the factory swallowed everything that she said. He made an exception and let her leave a half hour early every day to go home and prepare lunch. Mother had to go to the public water pipe to wash the vegetables. She often ran into Bai Liquan there. He worked shiftwork at the Wuhan Steel Factory, so it seemed like he was always at home. Mother liked to flirt with guys. When she twisted at the waist, she also wriggled her butt like a hen about to lay an egg. Mother's eyes were unique. Their radiance could infatuate all the men in the world. Mother had no scruples about Bai Liquan. His wife was beautiful and slender, like a jewel in his palm. This jewel, however, hadn't borne any children, and Mother had had nine in a row. Mother so ridiculed Bai Liquan because of this that he had no place to hide his shame and, as a result, he began to flirt with Mother. That day, Mother finished rinsing her vegetables and was giggling as she walked back to the house with Bai Liquan. He stood right behind her laughing and teasing. His fingers were long and thin and felt completely different from Father's short rough ones. When Mother bend over to cut up the vegetables, her breasts hung down like two cloth bags. Bai Liquan stood behind Mother and began fondling those two cloth bags with his long fingers. Mother didn't mind what he was doing; she just kept on calling him names like greedy pig, silly dog and so on. Bai Liquan suffered her scolding, but his fingers moved quickly and skilfully. As his hands became more and more lively and began moving in wider and wider circles, Mother couldn't help but laugh excitedly. At that moment, Eldest Brother, who was lying on the bed, woke up. He didn't say a word, he just yawned.

"You simpleton!" said Mother. "It's so late, and you still haven't got up?"

"A simpleton that you gave birth to," replied Eldest Brother. "That's not bad; we're all simpletons."

"Oh, do you sleep here during the day?" asked Bai Liquan. "Aren't Fifth, Sixth and Seventh Brothers awfully noisy during the afternoon?"

"With parents like these, who've only given us this much room, what can we do?" said Eldest Brother.

"If you don't mind, you can sleep at our house during the day," said Bai Liquan. "Both of us are at work, and if you sleep there, you'll be watching the house too. I've got a really good ghetto blaster, and I'm always so worried about it."

"That's not a bad idea at all," said Eldest Brother.

"Well then, thank you very much, Uncle Bai," said Mother.

For a change, Bai Liquan actually meant what he said, and Eldest Brother stayed at his place during the day. The first little while passed uneventfully. Then, on International Women's Day, Bai Liquan's wife, Zhijie, had half a day off and she spent the time at home. Suddenly the day took an unexpected turn. Zhijie wanted to use her half day off to rearrange the room, and Eldest Brother got up to give her a hand. After moving things back and forth for a while, Eldest Brother was streaming with sweat and took off his shirt. His dark shoulders were exposed, and his huge muscles bulged underneath his tanned skin. The sunlight shone obliquely through the window and fell on Eldest Brother's glistening shoulders. A couple of times he accidentally bumped into Zhijie, and it made her quiver inside. As they were putting up the bed, Zhijie's finger got jammed in between the boards; she cried out in pain and her eyes filled with tears. Eldest Brother rushed over, grabbed hold of her hand and put her finger in his mouth. He licked her finger over and over with his thick soft tongue. He said that it was a secret way of relieving pain that had been passed down from his ancestors. Zhijie believed what he said. From then on, her fingers got jammed all the time, and Eldest Brother always had to use his secret painkiller.

Zhijie was nine years older than Eldest Brother and

well past thirty, but since she hadn't had any children, she still looked like a blossoming young girl. Her black eyes sparkled, and her brows arched like a new moon. Naturally, the young, virile Eldest Brother was attracted to her like iron to a magnet.

From then on, Zhijie often worked half days. When she wasn't ill, she had switched her day off. Mother was the first to notice this. Mother can't read a single character, but her intuition is as perceptive as that of any gifted woman's. "You'd better keep an eye on that vixen. She's out to get you," she said to Eldest Brother.

"Maybe I'm the one that's out to get her," he replied.

"You son of a gun, you're just like your father."

"And that woman is just like you."

"How is she like me?"

"As soon as she sees a guy, she melts. She's just too willing to swallow the bait."

"You'd better be careful. That man may be scrawny, but he's not the type you'd want to provoke."

"Is he any worse than Father?"

"How much did you see that day."

"I saw everything. Women are worthless."

Mother leaned backwards and began to laugh. "Good boy! There's hope for you yet. Your mother didn't let him go much further though. You have to be a bit more brilliant than Bai Liquan to get anything."

Eldest Brother laughed too. "Sure. My son is probably in her belly already."

"Really?" asked Mother, pleasantly surprised.

All the neighbours found out about Eldest Brother's affair with Bai Liquan's woman. It was Mother who spread the word. When she met somebody, she would brag and say that though Bai Liquan's woman wriggled like a little tart, she was as affectionate as a cat in her eldest son's arms. Father only got wind of it much later. He couldn't believe that his son had reached the age of eating stolen fish.

Bai Liquan was the last to hear about it. He dared not act violently in front of Zhijie and so went over to Eldest Brother and swore at him. "If you swear again," Eldest Brother said, "I'll tell Zhijie to divorce you. She obeys me now."

"If we divorced, would you want her?"

"Of course."

"Okay," said Bai Liquan. "The house belongs to me. I'll keep that. Go ahead and marry her and let her live in that pigsty of yours with your father and your brothers. Let your whole family scrutinize her from the roots of her hair to the soles of her feet. And while they're at it, they may as well see how the two of you spend the night together."

Bai Liquan's words pounded like stones on Eldest Brother's chest. His face suddenly turned pale. His shattered expression was not only seen by Bai Liquan but by Father, who had just come home from work, and by all those who had come to watch the excitement. Bai Liquan laughed contemptuously. Obscenities kept flowing from his mouth. Eldest Brother fell silent. Father stepped forward and boxed his ears and cursed him for being even stupider than a worm: "That Bai Liquan's woman should even look at a thing like you just goes to show that there is no differ-

ence between her and the kind that takes in customers!'' When he heard what his father said, Eldest
Brother leapt like a fierce tiger and began grappling
with him. He cursed his father, saying that it would be
hard to find anybody in the whole world that was as
foolish and as degraded as he was. Muddling along
his whole life, he brought up his sons and daughters
like pigs and dogs, squeezing them into a little, wretch-
ed thirteen-square-metre room with nothing to eat and
nothing to wear. And this type of father had the nerve
to go on living in front of his children as if everything
was just fine.

They fought until the dust rose around them.
The spectators couldn't keep clear of it. Father's
face was all black and swollen from Eldest
Brother's blows. Eldest Brother's front teeth were
knocked out by Father, who used his knife to cut
a wound in Eldest Brother's arm — a fourteen-stitch
wound.

Bai Liquan didn't go to work the next day.
At noon he came over, very pleased with himself,
and said to Eldest Brother that he had taken Zhijie
to the hospital that morning. In just a
short time, they had destroyed the embryo in her belly.
Bai Liquan said that though he would have liked to
have a kid, he couldn't very well bring up a bastard.
Eldest Brother gave him a vicious look and roared,
'' Get the hell out of here!''

From that day on, Eldest Brother paid no more
attention to Zhijie. Whenever they met each
other in the street, Zhijie would look at him
anxiously, but he would straighten himself and walk
proudly by.

Ten years passed before Eldest Brother married Eldest Sister-in-law. During those ten years, he showed absolutely no interest in the women of this world, except for those of his own family. Once Mother had plans of introducing him to someone. "You bring her home, and I'll kill her," Eldest Brother said.

In the ninth year of those ten, a truck crushed Zhijie's legs when she was at work, and she bled to death. All those present heard her repeated cries for "Dagen". They thought it was her husband. In fact "Dagen" was Eldest Brother's name.

5

Seventh Brother hated his sisters Daxiang and Xiaoxiang more than anybody else. At far back as he could remember, he had never spoken to them. Seventh Brother recalls that one time, when he was very small, he wet his pants, and Daxiang kept pinching his bum as hard as she could with her long nails. Daxiang would let her nails grow long and pointy to imitate the girls from wealthy families. Xiaoxiang was even nastier. Whenever she was at home, she wouldn't allow Seventh Brother to walk normally. Xiaoxiang said that since he was the reincarnation of a dog, he had to crawl. Seventh Brother submitted to the humiliations; he didn't dare defy her. When supper time came, Xiaoxiang would point at his black knees and tell Father that Seventh Brother purposely crawled like a dog rather than walk like a human. Xiaoxiang resembled both Father and Mother. She had a glib tongue, was full of life and laughed a lot, but she was wicked and merciless. Father doted on her, and in order to please her, he did not hesitate to punish Seventh Brother. Xiaoxiang was two years older than Seventh Brother. She was born after the twins Fifth and Sixth Brothers — numbered eighth in the family. Therefore she was spoiled rotten. While Father would kick and punch Seventh Brother until he was barely conscious, she would just cover her mouth and giggle incessantly. She even mimicked Seventh Brother's expression of numb endurance for Daxiang's benefit. Xiaoxiang continued behaving like this right up until the time that Seventh Brother left for the countryside.

After Eldest Brother's fight with Father, Second Brother was the family member that showed a bit of warmth toward Seventh Brother. For a long time, Seventh Brother never had any impression of Second Brother, who always came and went with Third Brother. It seems as if he saw but didn't notice Seventh Brother. Before that episode took place, Seventh Brother couldn't remember if Second Brother had ever spoken to him.

It was in the summer: Seventh Brother had crawled underneath the bed after Father had beaten him up. Only in this pitch black place permeated with the familiar dampness could he at least feel somewhat safe. That day, Seventh Brother's whole body was seared with pain. He lay there on his stomach not daring to move. The pain from his injuries and the sultry weather made him feel as if he was about to die. He lay like that a full day and night. Every time a train passed by outside, it seemed as if it came rolling over his body. The rumbling sound pounded furiously on his head until it felt as if it was about to explode. He wanted to crawl out, but as soon as he tried to move, a sharp

pain stabbed inside his thigh . Just let me die, Seventh
Brother thought . Then, with a sigh, he passed out .

When he woke up, Seventh Brother sensed that someone was holding him in his arms . There was still a
stabbing pain in his leg . He opened his eyes and
stared into a stranger' s face . He was faintly aware of
the sound of dripping water . The water kept dripping
for a long time, until he came to realize that the
strange face was, in fact, Second Brother . Second
Brother was wiping his body with a towel . Seventh
Brother leaned meekly against his chest without
moving . For the first time, he felt safe being alive . For
the first time he experienced the warmth of a human
body . That evening, when Father came home, Second
Brother was still holding Seventh Brother in his arms .
" How come you' re treating him like the young master of the house?'' asked Father .

Second Brother put Seventh Brother down on the
bed, lifted up the piece of cloth that covered his leg
and said, " He' s still a human being . Don' t be ruthless . The wound on his leg is festering . Maggots have
got into it . If you want him to survive, you mustn' t
let him sleep under the bed any more . It' s damp and
stuffy down there, and there are all sorts of in-
sects .'' Father looked at Seventh Brother and said
coolly, " This old man has fathered him up . There' s
no need for you to come lecturing .'' " It' s because
he' s your son and my little brother that I ask you
to take good care of him .'' Father boxed him hard on
the ear . " I let you study, and then you turn
evil — waxing eloquent in front of your old man . Get
out of here!''

Second Brother gave Father a furious look and then

walked out stamping his feet. Naturally, Seventh Brother went back under the bed. He arranged his little quilt so that it curved, and he imagined that it was Second Brother's arm. Lying there it was just like being held by Second Brother.

From then on, Second Brother took especially good care of Seventh Brother. Every day at meal time, he purposely sat next to Seventh Brother. He picked up the vegetables with his chopsticks and gave them to Seventh Brother. Until then, Seventh Brother had been reduced to filling his belly with steamed rice, even though it was he who was responsible for gathering and bringing home most of the vegetables.

Seventh Brother was almost twelve that winter. Mother said that at that age Fifth and Sixth Brothers could dig up lotus roots to bring home, but as for Little Seven: "All he knows is how to gather a few rotten cabbage leaves." "Big deal! So we eat what he brings home, that's all," said Second Brother. "Mummy, I want to eat lotus roots," Xiaoxiang immediately cried. " I'll go and dig up some lotus roots tomorrow," said Seventh Brother in a thin voice.

There was a chilly wind blowing the next day. As soon as he went outside, Seventh Brother was bent by a strong gust. His body hunched over, he struggled forward. There was a canvas bag in his little bamboo basket. As he walked along, he tried to figure out which pond would be the best. The wind reddened his face. The chilblain on his cheek swelled up again. But Seventh Brother did not consider it a particularly miserable day. He was used to this life. Should it happen that he was left to enjoy a day of peace, he would, on the contrary, suspect that something unusual had hap-

pened. Seventh Brother ran into Enough by the railroad. She had just raised her voice to meet the wind
with a song. Seventh Brother could never forget the
words to that song:

> *Beautiful Havana,*
> *My family is there.*
> *The brilliant sun shines into the room;*
> *Red flowers bloom outside the door.*

Enough always sang that song; again and again she
would say to Seventh Brother how nice it would be to
have a new home in Havana, with brightly coloured
flowers by the door. It got to the point that they both
longed for Havana.

The lotus pond had been pumped dry. The grown-
ups had already been digging carefully through it. Seventh Brother walked around the pond and looked it
over, then he quickly pulled off his padded shirt and
pants and, before Enough could rush over to stop
him, he went down into the pond. In an instant, the
mud oozed up to his chest. Seventh Brother was too
short. There was a horrified look on his face, so frightening that Enough cried out in alarm and shouted for
people to help. A couple of middle-school students that
were passing by came over, pulled Seventh Brother out
and brought him to a cow-shed. In the cow-shed there
was an old one-eyed guy. He poured out a cup of
steaming hot water for Seventh Brother. Seventh Brother's whole body was shivering. Like an adult, Enough
told him, in a cross voice, to take off his mud-soaked
clothes. He put on his padded jacket and pants over
his naked body and curled up with the old guy in a

stack of hay in the corner of the barn. He watched
Enough take his dirty clothes down to the lake. In the
wind, she looked like a strange, huge shrimp as she
walked, bent forward, further and further away.
Enough rinsed out his muddy clothes for him, and
then she dried them in front of the brazier in the cow-
shed. Her face shone with a peculiar red glow, and her
eyes, embedded in this glow, looked like precious
stones. Seventh Brother stared at her blankly. Outside,
the dry, withered branches and leaves rustled in the
wind. Now and then the whistling wind sliced through
the vast sky. Seventh Brother suddenly felt his eyes
becoming moist. He thought how happy he would be
at this moment if he could only start crying. Enough
unwittingly cast a glance at him, and he immediately
changed back to his everyday expression. Seventh
Brother had never shown his feelings to anybody. He
didn't want other people to guess what was on his
mind.

It was completely dark by the time Enough had finished drying his clothes. When he put them on, he
told her that they felt cosy. He knew, however, that it
would be hard for him to avoid another thrashing today. As they were going out, the one-eyed guy sighed,
fetched two lotus roots from the shed and gave them to
Seventh Brother and Enough.

Seventh Brother didn't say a word all the way
back. When they parted, Enough gave him her lotus
root and said that her family didn't care for them. He
accepted it quietly and put it in his canvas bag. "Why
do you always look as if something is worrying
you?" she asked. Seventh Brother held back for a long
time before he said, "I'll tell you tomorrow."

As soon as Seventh Brother stepped over the threshold, Xiaoxiang shouted, "Pa, Ma, the bastard's back!" Mother rushed over, pulled his ear and roared, "You still know how to come home? While you were out having your fun, your second brother was so worried that he spent the whole evening by the Black-Mud Pond." Seventh Brother didn't have a chance to catch his breath before he got a slap in the face. It came from Father. "Why aren't you dead? Why did you come home? There are no guard rails along the tracks, are there? Because of you, you little stinking worm, the whole family hasn't been able to fall asleep. You think that we've all been as comfortable as you?" Father cursed and beat him again. Seventh Brother didn't utter a word. He never said anything when he got beaten. Normally, he would think about who to beat up first when he grew up, Father or Mother. This time all he thought about was Enough's face and eyes in the glowing light from the fire in the cow-shed. Thus his expression was unusually tranquil, and it made Father furious. "Look at him, pa. He's smiling," said Xiaoxiang. Father promptly kicked Seventh Brother's leg. He landed on the floor with a crash. The glowing red light turned into a red cloud that rose in a haze before his eyes. Everything — people, objects and sounds — rose into the air and dissolved in the red cloud. Indeed, Seventh Brother couldn't help smiling.

Seventh Brother's leg was so red and swollen that there was no way he could walk. He couldn't even take a single step. So he lay underneath the bed for almost three days. The red cloud continuously rose and drifted in front of him. He spent three days in utter silence. Second Brother asked him a number of times to come out and go with him to the hospital, but Seventh Brother wouldn't agree. "I'm taking a rest," he said.

Four days later, Father said, "Our sons are worthless. No one is sick for so many days at a time." Mother bent down and called under the bed, "You're behaving like a wealthy young master. If you don't go back out and gather vegetables, don't imagine that you'll get a single grain of rice."

When Father and Mother had left for work, Seventh Brother crawled out. With faltering steps he staggered outside. He walked over to the section of the railroad where he used to meet Enough. He sat down by the tracks waiting and thinking of how to tell Enough everything. He waited for a very long time, but she didn't show up. Seventh Brother had to go gather vegetables by himself.

On his way back, he happened by the cow-shed. He wanted to see the old one-eyed guy, he wanted to withdraw into the haystack and stare blankly at the red glow. When Seventh Brother entered, the old man looked a little distracted, then he asked, "Where's the little girl that was with you?" "She didn't show up. I waited for a long time," Seventh Brother replied. "Were you out walking with her in the last two days?" the old man asked. "I've been ill, and I haven't been out the last two days," said Seventh Brother. "The day before yesterday, in the afternoon, a girl was crushed by the train. I don't know if it was her," the old man said. Seventh Brother was struck dumb. Enough was the last girl on earth to be crushed. He gathered all of his strength and ran like mad to the railroad. His cries of "Enough! Enough!" sounded like the mournful howls of hungry wolves in the wilderness.

There weren't any traces of blood where the accident had taken place. At the foot of the slope, beside the tracks, Seventh Brother found the handle of a bamboo basket to which a little rope of white gauze was tied. Enough had braided this rope. He had watched her make it one day some time ago.

Enough had vanished forever. Because of this Seventh Brother became seriously ill. He remained unconscious for about a week, and his illness cost the family a lot of money. Money with which Father had promised to buy Daxiang and Xiaoxiang scarves, money with which he had promised to buy Fifth and Sixth Brothers sandals, money with which he had promised to buy Mother a pair of socks, as well as money which Eldest Brother had been saving for years to buy a watch — it all went to cover the cost of Seventh Brother's illness. Everyone pulled a long face and ignored him. Even Eldest Brother sulked and didn't say a word.

Afterwards, on his way to gather vegetables, Seventh Brother still walked along the same path as he had with Enough. Every single day, he sat down quietly for a few minutes where Enough had died. Sitting there, he earnestly told Enough everything about himself.

Those eight years of collecting vegetables left a deep impression on the now twenty-eight-year-old Seventh Brother. He remembered Enough fondly and had enjoyed the solitude that belonged to him alone. When he graduated from university, he returned home, and the next day he unwittingly went down to Black-Mud Pond. The changes there were astonishing. Various types of houses covered what had been vegetable fields. He couldn't figure out where the different roads led to. There was one spot that Seventh Brother was able to recognize at first glance, no matter how big the changes had been. He had been fond of sitting there all by himself. Enough would have been thirty by now, he thought to himself. Perhaps she would have become his wife, even though she was two years older than he. What did it matter anyway? Seventh Brother didn't care whether Enough was ten or one hundred years older than he was. She would always remain just fourteen years old.

The rails converged and then separated again. They wound and meandered far into the distance. Seventh Brother didn't know where they came from or where they headed. He often thought how much his life was like these rails.

6

Just when Seventh Brother began to feel that Second Brother was the only one in the family that he could talk to, Second Brother passed away. Whenever Seventh Brother remembered the cause of Second Brother's death, an ice-cold feeling of pity rose from his heart.

Father, however, was indignant about Second Brother's death. Every year, on the anniversary of his passing, Father cursed Second Brother for being the most useless man in the world. He was a wretch who pretended to be someone with sensibilities. Inevitably,

he would go on to curse books for having numbed
Second Brother's brains. If Third Brother happened to
be around when Father cursed Second Brother, the two
of them would get into an awful fight.

The relationship between Second Brother and Third
Brother was unbelievably good. Third Brother was
rough like Father, the kind of guy who just didn't feel
comfortable if he wasn't beating someone up, but
Second Brother was gentle and urbane, not at all like
one of Father's sons. Second Brother was only a year
older than Third Brother. The two of them slept on
the same pillow almost up until Second Brother's
death. Second Brother was scrawny and tall and not a
pretty sight. Father was terribly disappointed with
Second Brother's bony appearance, and he often sneered
that Second Brother didn't look like him at all, not at
all. Then, pounding Third Brother on the chest, he
would say that this was what the real stuff looked like,
just like this. This sort of talk hurt Mother. Mother
was more fond of Second Brother than of any of her
other six boys and two girls, because he had once
saved her life. Second Brother was only three at the
time and he had just learned to shuffle along. One day
Mother took him to buy salt. At the end of the road
they ran into some friends of Father's from his transport station. Mother began to fool around with them
in a provocative manner. The men and women from
the transport station acted shockingly with each other:
they pulled down each other's pants, or they reached
out to touch each other's crotches. Even though this
was obscene, it was nevertheless completely public.
Mother left Second Brother to himself and fooled
around with them by the side of a freight wagon. They

laughed until they were out of breath. Suddenly Second Brother trotted over unsteadily and in a strange tone of voice shouted, "Mama, I want to pee!" It was the beginning of winter. If Second Brother wet his pants, he wouldn't have another pair to wear. So Mother quickly grabbed hold of him and ran to a spot out of the wind. Just as she moved away, the rope on the freight wagon broke. A packing box fell and crushed three of the men. One of them had been calling Mother and was about to say something when his brains were splattered around him. When she heard the crash behind her, Mother was scared out of her wits. She held Second Brother and wailed hysterically. Just then, Second Brother said, "Mama, I want to go home, I don't want to pee." After the incident, Mother recalled that Second Brother had just peed before they went out. Normally he shouldn't have wanted to go again. His strange tone of voice still gave Mother the shivers when she thought about it. Father admitted that it did seem rather odd.

Second Brother was a man of few words. With his eyes sunk deep in his face, he appeared dark and gloomy. If it hadn't been for his nose, which was high and straight, and for the lines of his mouth, no one would have been able to stand those eyes of his. Appropriately, God had provided him with a nose and mouth that suited those eyes and gave him a singular beauty. The neighbours often praised the twins, Fifth and Sixth Brothers, as being the most handsome young men in Henanpengzi, but Seventh Brother and I were of a different opinion: Fifth and Sixth Brothers ranked below Second Brother. Their simple philosophy of life and the emptiness in their eyes gave a certain lifelessness to their beautiful features.

A look from Second Brother was enough to restrain Third Brother, whom Father couldn't even control with his fists. This had always humiliated Father. Even though he was humiliated he still couldn't accept it. Second and Third Brothers had entered into an alliance of steel. When Father wanted to beat one of them up, he couldn't help but hesitate again and again. Thus Second and Third Brothers rarely got beaten up. At first, Fifth and Sixth Brothers were envious, and then they tried to ingratiate themselves with Second and Third Brothers. Although Second Brother was noncommittal, Third Brother refused sternly. He said that they couldn't let little Seventh Brother suffer alone, they had to carry part of the burden. Third Brother was the "Second Dictator" of the family. Daxiang had given him that nickname. The "Big Dictator" was, of course, Father. Third Brother was two years older than Daxiang. Once, when they were having an argument, she blurted out the words "Second Dictator". Third Brother liked the sound of it. He didn't quarrel with her again but became like a guardian to her instead. For quite a long time, Third Brother became the "Brother Protector" of the kids in Henanpengzi. His reputation spread right over to the area around Stadium Street and West Road. Everyone who knew about him was very careful not to provoke him. He had a bunch of underlings to help him. In front of others, they were like wild beasts, but when Third Brother was around, they were as meek and humble as barnyard animals. They all knew how tough Third Brother could be. He had studied martial arts for some time with a master who wandered from place to place selling dog-skin plaster. The master was a blood brother of Father's from way back. He taught Third Brother very conscientiously. Third Brother could break three bricks with one chop of his hand; all the guys in Henanpengzi had seen it. If ten guys his own size attacked him, Third Brother could beat them all with his bare hands. Tough and crude as he was, Third Brother nevertheless yielded to a look from Second Brother. Second and Third Brothers were as close to each other as if they were one person. And yet, Second Brother was so completely different from Third Brother.

Actually, had it not been for a chance event which changed Second Brother's life, he never would have become so estranged from his family. That event steered Second Brother on to a path that was completely different from that of every one else in the family. Second Brother happily turned on to this path, one which drained the blood out of him, drop by drop, and eventually led him to his death.

That event, which happened so suddenly, took place the same year Seventh Brother was born. Every day, Second and Third Brothers went down to the other side of the tracks or to the freight yard to steal coal. Coal for the home had always been procured in this way. The thieves never bothered to consider whether this method was legal or not. When they needed coal at home and didn't have the money to buy any, it was only natural that they demand it, unconditionally, from the outside world. I can't remember exactly when Second and Third Brothers started doing this. I only know that to begin with, they only picked up partly burnt briquets. Subsequently, Third Brother implemented some reforms, and they progressed to using burlap sacks when stealing. During the winter, when the burning pieces of coal crackled, Father would praise Third Brother for being made of the right stuff.

That day, the train slowed as it crossed the Huangpu Road crossing. Third Brother reached out his hands and pulled himself up on to the train. Second Brother hesitated a moment and then followed. The train roared forward. The two of them stuffed their burlap sacks full of coal. Just before reaching the coal yard, Third Brother threw his sack down and then floated through the air himself. Second Brother hesitated once again. When he finally, very carefully, jumped off the train, there was no trace of Third Brother. Second Brother walked back along the tracks. As he approached a pond, he heard a girl's terrified voice: "Help! Brother, don't die!" Second Brother ran toward the voice. I know that it was precisely this terrified, trembling voice that changed Second Brother's life so radically. It ended his days abruptly at thirty — he who should have lived until eighty. The remaining fifty years turned into clouds of mist that silently drifted away before the eyes of his loved one.

The struggling arms in the pond resembled a magnificent dancer who moved and inspired his audience with his gestures. Second Brother jumped in without even taking off his shoes. He was an excellent swimmer. At most, it only took a half hour to go from Henanpengzi over the bridge to the bank of the Yangtze. In the summer, at noon and at dusk, Second and Third Brothers, along with their buddies, would go down there to swim. To swim from one side to the other and then back again for them was as easy as wiping their mouths after dinner. Even though every year one or two of them disappeared into its depths and turned into sons of the Yangtze, tragedies of this kind didn't affect the others' morale or damp their enthusiasm for a good swim. Second Brother wasn't the best swimmer among his buddies, but he wasn't bad either. The tiny pond was like a bathtub to him. With a few strokes, he reached the drowning person. The guy panicked and grabbed Second Brother tightly around the neck, so he had to knock him out and then held up his head while calmly swimming back. The guy's belly swelled like a pregnant woman's. Second Brother slapped him a couple of times, then he sat down on top of him and began pressing and releasing his chest. The girl shrieked, "Don't kill him! Don't kill him!" Then she started tearing at Second Brother's clothes. He had to slap her too. He hit her hard, and five red marks appeared on her pale face. She began to wail, turned around and fled, leaving Second Brother speechless.

When she returned, two frantic grown-ups followed right behind her. The girl said that they were her parents. By this time, their son had already regained consciousness. Utterly exhausted, he lay on the ground not wanting to move. The first thing he said as he saw his parents was, "Without him, I'd be finished." Then he looked at Second Brother. His expression was so grateful, so admiring, so sincere and so full of warmth that, all of a sudden, Second Brother felt his heart tremble. He had never seen an expression like that before.

Second Brother had become this family's benefactor

and was, naturally, very welcome in their home . The near-drowned boy was the same age as Second Brother . His name was Yang Meng . His sister was three years younger and was called Yang Lang . Their father was a well-known doctor at a big hospital in the city and their mother was a middle-school Chinese teacher, so their home had a very clean and tasteful appearance . They lived in a red storeyed building on Tianjin Road in the old British concession and occupied an entire floor of seven rooms . Even the room of their maid, Auntie Xu, was two square metres larger than Second Brother' s home . Each of the family members had their own room, and then there was a living room and a storage room . Yang Meng said that the house was left them by his maternal grandfather . His paternal grandfather' s home was even more beautiful — it had a garden in front — but his father had donated it to the state long ago .

Frankly speaking, to Second Brother, it seemed as if this family had come from outer space . Second Brother was brought up in Henanpengzi . He had been all but convinced that husbands and wives fighting, fathers and sons beating each other up and siblings quarrelling were normal events in all families . It was these disputes that made a family seem like a family, that made family members seem like family members . Otherwise a home wouldn' t be much different from a public place, would it? The Yang family, however, lived completely differently . Everyone was so intimate and kind to each other, so democratic and equal, so gentle and urbane, and so affectionate . The first time Second Brother entered the Yang home, he hardly knew what to do with himself . Two or three months later, he was slowly beginning to adjust. He was completely intoxicated by the atmosphere at the Yangs'. Only here did his heart sense that it was beating for a real human being. Unselfconsciously, he rushed to the Yangs' every other day.

Yang Meng was planning to take the entrance exam to the Number One Boys' High School where he wanted to go to senior high. He was the top student in his school, so he would certainly be successful. Second Brother, who went to the local public school, got grades that were only average. Yang Meng was very warm-hearted towards his benefactor. He was an easy talker and the two of them became very close friends. Second Brother gradually learned how to drink coffee. At first, he thought that this dark brown liquid that Mr Yang gave him was some sort of Chinese medicine for ridding the body of toxins. Later it dawned on him that this stuff was called coffee: all the upper class people drank it. At Yang Meng's house, Second Brother got to taste a variety of foods he had never eaten or seen before. Once they had tremella soup. Yang Lang didn't eat any because she had a toothache and there was one bowl extra. Yang Meng offered it to Second Brother. As a result, Second Brother couldn't fall asleep that night because his whole body was hot and dry. During the night, he began to suspect that there had been some sort of poison in the soup. When he asked Yang Meng about it, he just laughed out loud.

Second Brother also planned to take the exam to go to the Number One Boys' High School. After tutoring him a couple of days after school, Yang Meng said that with Second Brother's knowledge, it wouldn't be much of a problem for him to go on to Qinghua University. This suddenly provided Second Brother with a goal.

When they finished their homework in the evening, the Chinese teacher would bring out a book and softly read aloud with her beautiful, mellow voice. So relaxed and peaceful, as if it had floated down from the heavens, just like the voices of fairies in Second Brother's imagination. " If only Mother could be like her, things would be so much better," thought Second Brother. When Mother spoke, it was as if there was a hand in her throat doing its utmost to enlarge her voice. The saliva that splattered from her mouth forced the people around her to constantly wipe their faces with their sleeves. Mother never read books. She was very clever though. From the entire vocabulary, she was able to choose the wittiest and the most venomous, the cruellest and the funniest curses. Her victims would just stand there not knowing whether to laugh or to cry. But the Chinese teacher and her children never uttered even the commonest of swear-words. Once, when Second Brother was telling how someone had smashed the glass window at home, he threw in a "mother fucker" without thinking about it. Everyone in the room knit their brows. Yang Lang even covered her ears with her hands and said, "How ugly it sounds, just like a hooligan." Right away Second Brother turned so red it looked as if he had paint smeared on his face. For a long while, he was afraid to look up. No one made any further comments about it and, from then on, he dared not utter a single dirty word at the Yangs'. Second Brother listened to the Chinese teacher read from Gorky's *Song of the Storm Petrel*, from Zhu Ziqing's *Moonlight by the Lotus Pond* and from Dante's *Divine Comedy*. One Saturday, there was a beautiful moon. The moonlight shone through the shadows of the trees outside the window and projected a dappled light inside the room. Yang Lang made everyone sit beneath these fragments of moonlight and then she turned up the phonograph. The music rose gently, Yang Lang put on a white shirt and barefooted she floated through the air, chanting softly to the moon:

I can see those happy days, those sad days, my life, dark shadows that sweep across my body, one after another. And then, I can detect (I am crying now) a mystical dark shadow moving behind my back, grabbing my hair and pulling me back, a voice that cried (I am struggling), "Who had caught you this time? Guess!" "Death," I reply. Listen to it, that which sounds like a silver bell answering, "It's not death, it's love!"

Her last sentence exploded into a hearty laugh, then the light in the room came on. Everybody was touched by her beautiful performance; Yang Meng jumped up and cried, "Langlang, that was incredible!"

Second Brother was amazed by the white image that had drifted in the moonlight. Each line of the poem, layer after layer, twisted tightly around his heart. On the top layer, prominently displayed were the five words, "It's not death, it's love!" In the split second right after the enthusiastic applause, Second Brother was overcome by a limitless sense of grief. Up until his death, the source of his grief never stopped flowing. When Second Brother was about to breathe his last, "it's not death, it's love" were the last words he spoke before he lay his head down. It was Yang Meng who closed his eyes. Those profound depressions were filled with an incomprehensible sorrow.

Second Brother began to study very hard. He used homework as a pretext for going over to the Yangs' every other day. Once he passed through their front door, his restlessness gave way to a sense of peace.

Second Brother's behaviour upset Third Brother. Third Brother didn't want to study and felt that it wasn't worthwhile for Second Brother to do so either. "Father didn't have an education, but he's had a happy life, hasn't he?" Third Brother asked. "But his sons and daughters are hardly happy," Second Brother replied. "I don't think we're too bad off," said Third Brother. "I don't think that we're any better off than dogs — and even dogs are better off than little Seventh Brother." As Second Brother spoke, Seventh Brother, his face just filthy, was sitting on the door step, wiping his snot into his mouth and sucking noisily.

Third Brother felt a sort of natural disgust for the Yang family. He particularly disliked Yang Lang. He said that she must have been a witch in her previous life. The first time Third Brother said that, Second Brother just gave him a look. The second time was just after he and Second Brother had run into Yang Lang on the road. The two brothers had gone out to steal coal when they bumped into Yang Lang and Yang Meng. Yang Meng noticed the burlap sack in Second Brother's hand and he asked where they were going. Second Brother mumbled that they were going to get some coal. Second Brother avoided words like steal or

gather. "Do you want me to help?" Yang Meng
asked. No sooner had he finished speaking than Yang
Lang was pulling his sleeve and saying, "You can't
do that, it's so terribly filthy, so terribly filthy!" At
this point, Third Brother looked at Second Brother
sternly and said, "I'll just go on alone." Second
Brother uttered a quick, "I must be off" to the
Yangs. Then he hurried away with Third Brother.
"Stinking little witch," spat Third Brother. Second
Brother froze on the spot, his eyes full of rage.
Gnashing his teeth he said, "This is the second time
you cursed her. If I hear you do it a third time, then
I'm not your brother any more." Third Brother was
astonished and felt maligned. All he could do was cry
out, "What did I do? What did I do?"

Several days later, Yang Lang's mother, the
Chinese teacher, found out about her daughter's
having said "terribly filthy". The Chinese teacher
wanted her to apologize to Second Brother but, as
Yang Lang sincerely said, "Please forgive me," to
Second Brother, he immediately turned red. He confessed
to the Chinese teacher that he and his younger brother
had, in fact, been on their way to steal coal. The
Chinese teacher didn't say anything, she just sighed
deeply. The sound of her sigh weighed so heavily on
Second Brother's heart that it began to hurt under its
pressure. When they did their homework that evening,
Second Brother's mind kept wandering. When he was
about to leave, the Chinese teacher, for the first time,
saw him all the way to the street. The moonlight suffused the asphalt street in white. The language teacher
said, "I know that your family is quite hard up, but
poor people must preserve their integrity. You should

understand this much." Second Brother nodded emphatically.

He made the mistake of passing the Chinese teacher's exact words on to Father. Father became so furious that he smashed the bottle in his hand onto the floor and roared, "What does she mean by integrity? Let her come over and live like this, then she'll see what integrity really is." Second Brother was too frightened to say anything. Father continued, "You dare visit the Yangs again, kid, and you can bet I'll cut your legs off." "Ha! Those people, they depend on us workers, don't they? They've got fat from sucking our blood!" said Mother. "Their father is a doctor. They're not a family of capitalists," replied Second Brother. "You want to defend them, then call yourself 'Yang'," said Father. "Kid, I'll show you what integrity means. Integrity means not socializing with rich people and letting them think that you're drooling with envy over their lifestyle."

Second Brother was truly embarrassed by what Father had said. He felt that he was indeed someone who was drooling in admiration. For several days in a row he didn't visit the Yangs. He was very unhappy. He felt as if rocks hung from his heart and swung back and forth inside his chest. A week later, when Second and Third Brothers were returning home with coal on their backs, they ran into Yang Lang. She stepped out and greeted them: "Why don't you come round any more?" Second Brother opened his mouth, but he couldn't think of an answer. "You hate me, don't you? Haven't I already acknowledged my mistake?" asked Yang Lang. Second Brother gazed at her for a few seconds before hanging his head and despondently saying, "I'm not worthy of go-ing." Yang Lang followed Second Brother inside. For the first time she understood what kind of home he lived in. "You'd better come over this evening," she said, "otherwise my brother will blame me." "Tell Yang Meng that I'm busy at home and can't make it these days," said Second Brother. "All right," said Yang Lang. As she backed out of the door, her hand brushed against Seventh Brother, who was on his way in. She screamed and jumped outside. Then she took out her little handkerchief and wiped her hand vigorously as she walked away. She was still wiping her hand as her silhouette disappeared in the distance.

Second Brother didn't go back to the Yangs'. He also wasn't able to pass the entrance exam to the Number One High School. It wasn't because he didn't work hard. He would sit beneath the street lights for hours doing his homework and then, the week before the exam, it rained every day. He couldn't find any place to study. He had no choice but to sit at home among all his siblings and listen to his father tell-ing the stories of his youth over and over again. At eight o'clock he'd go to sleep with the rest of the family.

Second Brother was accepted by the Number Eight High School. He was our family's first high school stu-dent. Had it not been for Seventh Brother, who en-tered university under extremely fortuitous circum-stances, Second Brother's high school education would have been the most advanced in our family's history. Yang Meng, of course, got into the Number One High School. Second Brother knew he would. During the hol-idays, he came by a couple of times. He and Second

Brother would sit and watch the trains brush past one after another. The two of them talked and talked. After school began, Second Brother became increasingly distant from the Yangs, until eventually they weren't in touch any more.

Second Brother was a remarkable student. His bearing and speech became more and more different from the rest of the family's. One day he told Father that he wanted to go to university. He wanted to become an architect. He wanted to design the world's most beautiful house to accommodate Father and Mother. When he spoke, the radiance in his deep-set eyes could have shone into anyone's heart. As if struck by lightning, Father and Mother just stared at him blankly for a long while. Outside the steam whistle sounded and the little house shook as the train roared by; Father suddenly woke up to reality. He departed from his normal behaviour and, like a child wild with joy, he shouted, "My son's got a future. He's made of the same old stuff as me!" Then he looked Second Brother up and down and kept on patting him. The entire family was very excited that day, except for Seventh Brother, who, like a dog, crept under the bed as usual, and slept soundly.

Second Brother's dream of attending university, like those of so many other people, was, of course, destroyed by the "cultural revolution". Though his family origin was good enough for him to become a commander of the Red Guards, Second Brother still felt very downhearted. He didn't join any faction. Father instructed him to go to work. He had a whole set of half-grown younger siblings. He was obliged to work hard for a living. Father got a hold of a freight tricycle for

Second Brother, who went down to the Huangpu freight yard every day to haul goods down to the river. In this way he was able to earn quite a bit of money. In winter he made sure that all his younger siblings had cotton socks to wear.

One night after the whole family had fallen asleep — they always went to bed very early, not only because they had to get up for work the next day, but also because if they didn't the little room would get unbearably noisy — and the sound of snoring filled the room, suddenly there was the sound of someone hammering on the door. Everyone woke at the same moment. No one could remember that anything like this had ever happened before. At first Father swore, "What the hell! Is that any way to knock on a door?" They never expected to hear Yang Meng answer. Second Brother leapt up from his mattress on the floor. He seemed a bit anxious, as if he was expecting something. He opened the door and saw Yang Meng holding his right arm tightly around Yang Lang; her eyes were red and swollen. "What happened?" asked Second Brother worriedly. Yang Meng's expression was harsh, and his voice was full of sorrow. He said that their parents had gone out that afternoon and that they still hadn't returned. He and his sister.had waited until the evening, and they found it very odd, so they went into their father's bedroom to see if they had left any message. They discovered a letter to Yang Meng signed by both parents. The letter said that Yang Meng was not to be surprised by anything that happened to the family. His only responsibility was to take care of his younger sister. The last line read, "We're leaving now, dearest children.'' Yang Meng hadn't yet finished when Father yelled from inside, "Stupid pigs! Still gabbing! They've gone to visit the King of Hell. Quick, let's go find them!" "Yang Lang can't take any more. Auntie Xu was sent back to her home town last month. Please look after her for a while." "I'll go out to search. You stay here with Yang Lang," Second Brother said. "I couldn't," said Yang Meng. By this time Father was already out of bed. He kicked Third, Fourth, Fifth and Sixth Brothers, who lay motionless on the mattress listening to Yang Meng, and said, "Come on, get up. We're all going out to look for them tonight." He turned around and said to Yang Meng, "Let your sister stay here with the second son; the other guys are all at your disposal. You just go ahead and tell them what to do." "How can I thank you, uncle?" asked Yang Meng. "Just stop talking nonsense," said Father.

Second Brother practically carried Yang Lang home on his back. She was so weak that she couldn't walk, and he couldn't make out what she mumbled. For three days and three nights, Second Brother didn't get any sleep. Back in her home, Yang Lang developed a high fever. She had no more tears left, her face was burning hot, and the blisters on her lips completely altered her looks. Second Brother sent for the doctor, cooked rice gruel for her and helped her take her medicine. Then he leaned over her bed and begged her to get stronger.

After four days, Yang Meng returned, totally exhausted, and said that they had found his parents. The two of them had jumped into the Yangtze togeth-

er. They were bound at the waist by his mother's
white silk wedding veil. Their bodies were already bloat-
ed and deformed when they were pulled out of the
water at Yangluo. When he finished talking, Yang
Meng's legs failed him and, kneeling on the ground,
he began to vomit in agony. He hadn't eaten anything for quite a few days; he just threw up bits of yellow fluid. The blue veins in his neck writhed and
swelled so violently that Second Brother couldn't bear
to watch. Had it not been that Second Brother was quick-
witted enough to bend down and say to Yang Meng,
"For God's sake, don't go on like that. If Langlang
sees you, it's the end," Yang Meng might not have
been able to stop. Langlang was sleeping inside: they
must try to hide the truth from her.

One week later, because of the great help and efforts
of Second, Third and the other brothers, the funeral
was conducted rather smoothly. The ashes of the doctor and the Chinese teacher were placed together in a
tiny, white earthen jar. Father helped to find a plot on
Biandan Mountain, and on that solitary mountain
they were laid to rest. Second Brother stood next to
the grave and looked up the mountain, which was covered with trees full of green leaves and black graves
with white tablets, and suddenly he was overcome by a
feeling of despair. Alive, we're vermin. Dead, we're
dust. This was a description of how many people besides himself? And how big a difference is there between
the dead and the living? Is it possible that the dead, in
their own world, are saying that they are alive and
that all the living beings on earth are really dead? To
die: isn't that to reach a higher stage of life? Second
Brother had never felt such anguish. He couldn't free

himself from this suffering, which was rooted in his bewilderment and confusion. The suffering did not last long enough for him to become depressed, because it was just then that he began to love. His passion, the intensity of his love, changed his life. Under the sky of love he lived strong, free and easy. Then one cloudy day his love changed unexpectedly into a wisp of smoke and dispersed in the wind. His life began to harden again, and his anguish re-emerged and began pounding stubbornly on his heart. He recalled the sight of the green leaves and the black grave with the white tablet on Biandan Mountain, and suddenly he remembered his thoughts of reaching a higher stage of life. That same night, he used a razor blade to cut the veins on his wrist. He let his arm hang over the edge of the bed, and blood trickle on to the floor. Third Brother, who slept wedged in the same bed, only discovered in the early morning that his brother's life was like gossamer. Yang Meng and Yang Lang, who came by when they heard the news, looked shocked at the blood on the ground. "Why did you have to die?" Yang Lang cried out. At that moment, Second Brother opened his eyes and said clearly, "It's not death; it's love!" Then his head dropped to the side.

This took place on the northern bank of the Jinghe River on the Jianghan Plain, back in 1975, already ten years ago.

7

When Seventh Brother thinks back to when he received the news of Second Brother's death, it seems as if he had heard about the death of a stranger: he was indifferent, despite Second Brother's having treated him rather well for quite some time. Seventh Brother had been working in the countryside for a year. He lived up in the mountains in a little village densely surrounded by trees. He never went home. Eldest Brother scribbled a few characters telling him of the news of Second Brother's death. This was the one and only letter he received from home. He didn't write back.

It was very peaceful at home the day that Seventh Brother left for the countryside. He left quietly, by himself. As he reached the end of the alley, he ran into Xiaoxiang and a black-bearded guy. Xiaoxiang and the man were coming up the alley embracing each other. Seventh Brother couldn't keep track of the number of men that Xiaoxiang had had. Only recently he overheard Mother telling Father that Xiaoxiang was to be married off to this guy. For one thing, she wouldn't have to go off to the countryside; for another, she was already carrying his child. Xiaoxiang was not to have another abortion. If she did, she would never be able to conceive again. This was what the doctor had told Mother when she had taken Xiaoxiang in for a check-up. Xiaoxiang was as much of a flirt as Mother had been at her age. The only difference was that Xiaoxiang changed men several times, while Mother just had one man, Father. When Seventh Brother saw Xiaoxiang, he humbly stepped to the side of the road. Full of laughter, she walked past before he continued on alone. Xiaoxiang apparently didn't notice Seventh Brother; she never as much as looked at him. Seventh Brother hated the three women in his home, particularly Xiaoxiang. He had once sworn that if he ever got an opportunity for revenge, he would rape his

mother and his two sisters in front of his father. He
was fifteen when he took this oath, and he did so because one day, when he was underneath the bed, Fifth
and Sixth Brothers brought a girl into the room. After
a short while, he could hear the girl struggling and
weeping and the bed boards squeaking noisily over-
head. Seventh Brother didn't know what was going
on, so he stuck out his head. He saw that both Fifth
and Sixth Brothers were naked from the waist down.
Fifth Brother was on top of the girl while Sixth Brother was holding her legs apart. When he noticed Seventh Brother, Sixth Brother struck his head fiercely
and bellowed, "You didn't see anything, repeat
that!" "I didn't see anything," Seventh Brother
said haltingly. Then he shrunk back under the bed. He
could hear the girl groan and the torment in her voice
made his body ache. He felt that only someone who
was watching the destruction of the world could make
such tortured sounds. Immediately, he thought he had
to make the people he hated most, his mother and two
sisters, feel such pain.

Seventh Brother's oath later became material for his
self-mockery. He had plenty of opportunities later on,
but no desire whatsoever for that kind of revenge.

Seventh Brother arrived all alone in the little mountain village. He had chosen the place himself. To reach
it, he had to walk a whole day along a mountain road
after getting off the bus. This was exactly the sort of
place in which Seventh Brother wanted to live, a place
where he could be anonymous.

He slept in the same bed as his landlord's son. This
was the first time since he was born that he had slept
in a real bed. Underneath the filthy sheet, there was a

mattress of corn stalks and rice straw. The whole room had the sweet smell of plants. Behind the house there were three madder trees. Seventh Brother lay on his back. Two feet of space. No more dark mass of bed boards and creaking sounds when Father and Mother rolled over. There weren't the rolling sounds of snoring and sleep-talk from his brothers on the mattress three steps away. There was a lot of space. The mice brushed past along the roof beams. The pale light of the moon leaked down through the cracks between the roof tiles. As the clouds covered and uncovered it, it seemed as if the light danced about the room. Seventh Brother was suddenly attacked by an overwhelming fear. The landlord's son slept silently at the other end of the bed. It made Seventh Brother feel as if he was lying in a world separate from that of humans. That night he pondered many questions about death which he had never considered before. He wondered whether or not he was actually dead but didn't know it himself. People had buried him here and told him that he was out in the country, but in fact he was some place in the netherworld. For several days, Seventh Brother thought along these lines. He even tried to find me — his little brother — among the other males. He thought it was very likely that his little brother was somewhere in the crowd, but since we hadn't seen each other for such a long time, we couldn't recognize each other. Seventh Brother was happy that he knew something that the others didn't. He understood that the others around him were the spirits that had arrived before him. They didn't know that they were dead. They proudly maintained that they lived in the real world, and quite comfortably too.

Seventh Brother thought that one only had to see them walk in that sort of floating way to know that they had changed worlds.

Seventh Brother didn't associate with anyone else in the village. He never opened his mouth unless it was absolutely necessary to say something. He was like a taciturn dog. When its master tells it to lick something, it silently licks it a few times. At first the people in the village said that Seventh Brother was very well behaved, but later they said he was just morose. A dog that doesn't bark is the most dangerous kind, as everybody knows. Eventually they all agreed that Seventh Brother was an eccentric. Seventh Brother didn't listen to all the talk. He was convinced that normal dead people didn't speak.

Three months after his arrival, Seventh Brother heard that a ghost had begun to haunt the village. He thought it ridiculous: aren't we all ghosts? He ignored the ghost stories, which became more and more unnerving. He hoped that he would meet the ghost. Maybe it was little Eighth Brother, he thought.

Everyday, when the landlord's son came home for supper, he brought back more ghost stories. "It's a very skinny ghost. Yeah, just like him." He would point at Seventh Brother. "When it walks it's almost as if it's floating. Every day the ghost floats three times around the ginkgo trees at the edge of the village, and then it goes into the woods. In the woods the ghost turns white. It floats from tree to tree. Whenever it reaches a tree it makes a few sad, shrill cries. The sounds are really strange. From the woods it floats gently over the village, makes a turn and goes back to the woods. It goes on like that right past midnight, when it turns into a puff of smoke and disappears."

A few days later the landlord's son said, "Now the ghost goes somewhere deep in the woods and wails. The wild animals have all been scared away. The hunters can't even get a pheasant now."

A couple of days went by, and the landlord's son reported again: "The daughter of Old Fishhead was coming back to visit her parents. On her way over the mountain, she twisted her ankle, and limping along, she only got home at midnight. She ran into the ghost at the edge of the woods. At first she didn't realize it was the ghost who had floated up to her. Then she was so frightened she gave it a hard punch and began running away. Back home, she said that the ghost was slippery."

The ghost's shadow lay over the village, yet oddly enough it hadn't done anything malicious. Some people even discussed whether they should try to catch it and see what it looked like. This idea was of course brought up by the youngsters. Initially Seventh Brother wanted to go too to see what the ghost was all about, but he was too tired that day, and at dusk he crawled into bed and fell asleep.

The moon wasn't out that night. Seven or eight youngsters hid in the woods. The landlord's son was out there too. Each of them was trembling. They shook so much that the bushes kept rustling. At midnight the ghost began to circle around the trees. It really was very skinny, and it did almost float with each step. When it went into the woods, it sure enough did turn white. The youngsters were too scared to do anything. Finally one kid, who had done some hunting, threw a lasso and captured the ghost. The ghost cried out in a shrill voice, three cries in a row, long and clear. The people in the village all heard them. When it stopped crying, it fell to the ground with a crash. It made no more sounds. The youngsters tied it up with a rope. They touched it and found it was, indeed, slippery. They carried it over to a lighted spot at the edge of the village, and there they discovered it was a live human being. He was breathing heavily, as if sound asleep. The landlord's son lit a match and shouted involuntarily. Everyone recognized him. It was Seventh Brother. Seventh Brother was stark naked. His skin was shining white. He was still breathing calmly and even turned over once, very naturally.

Someone kicked him hard on his bum. Seventh Brother yelled and woke up with a start. Baffled, he looked at the rings of men and women around him. He blinked a few times, glanced down and discovered that he wasn't wearing a stitch of clothing. "What are you doing?" he roared in a powerful voice. His voice was deep and strong, as if it had come from the distant skies and had crossed countless mountain ridges before landing there. Someone asked if he had been sent by the Heavenly Spirit. Seventh Brother said he hadn't: he was a real dead person living in the netherworld. He answered according to what he believed, but everyone was absolutely terrified. The day broke, and everyone left perplexed and alarmed. The landlord's son fetched Seventh Brother's clothes. He was respectful and humble.

For a long time Seventh Brother wasn't able to figure out what had happened to him. Every night the ghost continued to float around the woods.

In 1976 Seventh Brother was unexpectedly recommended for university entrance. He was to attend a university called "Beijing University". He had barely ever heard the name of this university before, and he was even less aware that Beijing University is the best institution of higher learning in China. He was a lucky devil. Seventh Brother's father was a "long-suffering" dock worker — an unmatched class background. Furthermore the people of the village had been debating all along whether or not to send Seventh Brother away, since with each passing day the spooky atmosphere intensified, and it became harder and harder to bear. Beijing University wasn't scared of ghosts, and they coveted Seventh Brother's "long-suffering" family background. Father had been Seventh Brother's enemy since the day he was born, but this time he had inadvertently done Seventh Brother a good turn.

Seventh Brother sadly took leave of the little mountain village densely surrounded by trees. He felt that he had already lived there for a century, and now he was being reincarnated back into the world of human beings. As he walked on to the highway, the sun was already high over his head. The rays were so brilliant he felt dizzy. A gust of wind rustled the trees by the roadside. The birds were singing cheerfully. Seventh Brother took a breath. He rubbed his chest and felt that his heart was beating louder and stronger than before.

He was going to Beijing. Moreover he was going to Beijing full of dignity, by train. The train was going to roll triumphantly right by his house — the news infuriated his family. How could a loathsome creature like

Seventh Brother become the first member of the family to travel far away by train? The evening Seventh Brother returned home, Father was drinking and swearing. Seventh Brother crawled underneath the bed, his own territory, and put up with it all.

It was pouring the day Seventh Brother left. All he had was one pair of shining clean sneakers. He was afraid that he wouldn't have anything to wear once he got to campus, so he took off his shoes and went barefoot. Father and Mother both left for work early in the morning; they didn't say a word, as if they didn't even notice Seventh Brother. Eldest Brother walked Seventh Brother to the end of the alley and gave him ten cents. He said that it was pouring and to take the bus. Seventh Brother didn't take the bus. He walked along the streets and alleys in the pouring rain. His luggage got heavier and heavier. His clothes stuck to his body. The outlines of his limbs made him feel three-dimensional. His mind was clear. It didn't matter if his quilt got wet. The summer sun would dry it in an afternoon.

Seventh Brother didn't return home for three years. His family had no idea if he was dead or alive. Nobody inquired about him, and he didn't send any letters. So when he showed up on their doorstep three years later, healthy and full of vigour, everyone at home was flabbergasted.

"What are you gawking at? I still have seven openings in my head, just like the rest of you," Seventh Brother said.

But the Seventh Brother that returned wasn't the same at all.

8

With his wide shoulders and slim waist, Third Brother's upper body formed an inverted triangle, the kind of physique girls like the best. In the summer, when Third Brother took off his T-shirt and sat bare chested fanning himself by the roadside, the hearts of the girls who passed by jumped — they couldn't resist taking another look at him. The muscles on Third Brother's chest and arms were alive; they bulged to stretch his skin to its capacity. One day, when neighbour Bai Liquan came home from watching the movie *First Blood*, he commented, "Ha! That Yankee looks pretty good, almost as good as Little Third next door." This inspired many of the folks in Henanpengzi to see for themselves just how good Stallone's physique was. When they had seen the movie, they all said his body wasn't bad, just about as good as Little Third's. But Third Brother wasn't as good-looking as Stallone. On this they all agreed. Third Brother has grown to be as handsome as Father had been at his age. However, he always had a fierce expression on his face, and so gradually his features took on a ferocious aspect, something Father's never had. People weren't attracted to Third Brother, because of his ferocious-looking features.

Father said that only guys who don't think about girls end up looking like such tyrants.

Third Brother didn't think about girls. He had a hostile attitude toward the opposite sex. Even now that he's over thirty-five, indeed almost forty, he hasn't married. Women would often seek him out and do anything to endear themselves to him. He wouldn't reject them; he would even let them stay the night if they wanted to. He fooled around with them, nursing a desire for revenge all the while. He was venting his hate, not his love. As for the girls, they only wanted his body; they didn't care about the colour of his feelings. Third Brother was recruited by the shipping company after the death of Second Brother. His whole life long, Second Brother's death was the heaviest blow that Third Brother ever received. From the moment he had opened his eyes to the world, he had been inseparable from Second Brother — his dearest older brother. Third Brother loved him even more than he loved himself, because he remembered clearly how as a little kid, when he foolishly did a lot of bad things, Second Brother took responsibility for them. On his account Second Brother suffered many a beating, but as they grew up he never mentioned them to Third Brother. All of this was etched in Third Brother's memory. This was the type of person Third Brother was: when someone was truly good to him, he would go to extremes to repay them. Besides, Second Brother was his brother — of the same flesh and blood as he was. Second Brother was driven to death by a woman. From then on women were like daggers in Third Brother's heart: when he saw a woman his heart hurt until it bled. He often wondered, full of rage, how a woman could be worthy of a man's love. Had men become so foolish as to stoop to loving women? Whenever he saw a guy in the street humbly carrying a huge load behind an arrogant woman, when he saw guys meekly fawning on women on street corners, underneath trees and such places, he itched to rush forward and give the couples a thorough beating. He had done this before. One evening he saw his intoxicated captain home. On his way back he took a short cut over Guishan Mountain. Everything was bathed in moonlight. The silence was complete. Third Brother belched as he staggered along. Suddenly he spotted two human figures beneath a tree. At first he just walked by without paying any attention to them. By chance one of the figures threw itself on its knees. Third Brother could hear a man's voice. The man spoke pitiably: "I beg you to say yes. I can't go on living without you." The other figure just gave a snort. It was, of course, a woman. Third Brother flew into a rage. Without hesitating, he roared and rushed forward. He cuffed and kicked at the snivelling man. Then he turned on the petrified woman. He grabbed her at the chest and slapped her a few times in the face as hard as he could. "Pa! Pa!" rang his blows on her cheeks. It was a clear and pleasing sound. Third Brother felt much better. He finally left the couple behind and continued belching his way down the mountain.

Third Brother worked as a sailor on a barge. His captain thought highly of him. Third Brother enjoyed living on the boat and never felt it was disgraceful to be a sailor. He was tall and strong, and he never tried to shirk his duties. What's more, he made a great drinking buddy for the captain. This really delighted the captain. He said that in all his years he had never had a drinking buddy who understood him as well as Third Brother did. Together the two of them could polish off a litre bottle of sorghum whisky. When the summer came, the captain would often get crazy ideas. He would let the barge continue sailing, pull Third Brother into the Yangtze and the two of them would swim along. The captain and Third Brother swam equally well. They were very daring, like two brown dragons, in the Yangtze. The captain told Third Brother that if he ever got caught in a whirlpool, he should straighten his body and not move, and the whirlpool would automatically throw him out again. Third Brother teased him, "If you haven't been through it yourself, how do you expect to teach me?"

"Don't you believe me?" asked the annoyed captain. "All the old sailors know this trick."

"I don't believe what I've never seen," answered Third Brother.

The captain pointed at a whirlpool and said, "Well then, I'll have to show you."

Before Third Brother could stop him, he plunged into the whirlpool. Dumbfounded and sweating profusely, Third Brother trod water. He didn't dare advance. The whirlpool spun much faster than imaginable, and Third Brother couldn't see where the captain was. In a little while, he heard a shout. The captain was somewhere off to his side, chuckling and waving to him. When Third Brother swam up to him, the captain told him that he had nearly lost his life. Third Brother asked how. The captain said that it was as if many hands were pulling him down towards the bottom of the river. "I thought I was finished, when suddenly I was released." The captain said that merely straightening the body out and not moving was not enough: one had to judge just when to make a move. Third Brother was silent. Then he spotted a whirlpool and said to the captain, "Now watch me." He plunged head first into the whirlpool. In the middle of it Third Brother lost control of his body. Several gigan-

tic hands tossed him back and forth as if he was a
ball. A kind of magnetic force pulled at his belly,
pulled him into the depths. He cried out involuntarily,
"Help!" He had hardly opened his mouth when he
swallowed a few mouthfuls of water. For a split
second, Third Brother thought that it wouldn't be so
bad to end up in the netherworld, because he might
get to meet Second Brother again. Just then, he was
thrown out with a bang by an unseen hand. He was
in a daze and had lost his sense of direction. He only
came to when the captain swam up alongside of him.
The captain slapped him in the face a couple of times
and scolded him, "Do you think that your life's a little toy? If you get killed, I'll be the one who gets pun-
ished." Although his face was burning, Third Brother
felt good. "Whirlpool for a whirlpool," he said.

That evening, after they had cast anchor, the captain
and Third Brother sat on the deck and drank. The captain toasted Third Brother three times and told him repeatedly what a man he was.

When the captain drank with Third Brother, he
would often sigh how nice it was to have a woman.
The captain was married and had two kids. At night
he would think about them over and over. This was
the only subject about which Third Brother disagreed
with the captain. Third Brother said that wine was better than women. Even the cheapest wine was tastier
than the most beautiful woman. He smacked his lips
as he spoke and downed three cups in a row. A cool
breeze blew gently over the river. The moonlight enveloped the mountains. It was a perfect night. Third
Brother said that he was utterly content with life as it
was. The captain said that without a woman to build

a nest for you, a woman upon whose shoulder you could cry, you hadn't really tasted life. Third Brother was silent.

Third Brother thought that he preferred not to taste what life was all about. A woman had killed his Second Brother — how could he be intimate with women? What a joke! No one could imagine how much Second Brother had done for Yang Lang back then. Second Brother didn't have to go to work in the countryside, but when Yang Lang was sent down, he went with her. He left his freight tricycle with Fourth Brother. For Second Brother's sake, Third Brother also went down to work with Yang Lang's production team. Second Brother took upon himself nearly all the work assigned to Yang Lang. Even Yang Meng was no help at all. Yang Lang was all over Second Brother in those days, smiling and laughing. The two of them hugged and rolled around on the riverbank. Even Third Brother was too embarrassed to watch. Penny by penny, Second Brother saved his money. He wanted to buy the most beautiful furniture to decorate the bridal chamber. He wanted to make their home as comfortable as Yang Lang's had been. Third Brother helped Second Brother in his struggle. Time after time, when they came to recruit workers, Yang Lang's name wasn't on the list. Time after time Second Brother let good opportunities for himself slip by. Third Brother stayed by him. Every year, when he was off helping to repair the irrigation works, Second Brother would return to the village once a week. He walked dozens of li right through the night just to see his loved one. It went on like this year by year, week by week, until one day Yang Lang received an application form. She filled it out and went off to the county seat. She was gone three days. When she returned she told everyone that this time she was sure that they'd let her leave. She got a job as a nurse. Second Brother invited almost every youngster who had come to farm in the commune after graduation from middle school for a drink. When someone told him that Yang Lang had traded her chastity for the job, Second Brother was struck dumb. The bottle in his hand dropped to the ground. Yang Meng turned around and walked out. He grabbed his sister by the hair. She admitted everything, but she never told who the guy was. Third Brother was already holding his knife. He was ready to kill. Yang Lang said that since she had already given him her body, she was ready to marry the guy. Second Brother made Yang Meng loosen his grip. He couldn't bear to see his loved one being pulled by the hair. He tidied up Yang Lang's hair, lock by lock, and said in a trembling voice, "I know that you had no alternative. I don't blame you. I won't make a fuss over this. But you can't marry that guy. He's a beast." "You'd better drop your illusions," Yang Lang said. "I can't marry you now." Alarmed, Second Brother asked why not. "I have never loved you," Yang Lang told him. "I just felt sorry for you, and so I played along for a while. Don't be a fool." Second Brother's face went pale; he howled and rushed outside. Third Brother dropped his knife and went after him. He dragged Second Brother back to his room semi-delirious and made him lie down. And he lay down beside him. Third Brother was fuming. He wanted to teach Yang Lang a lesson, but he dared not leave Second Brother's side. He knew that Second Brother had received a lethal blow. He knew that Second Brother would not be able to go on living much longer. Despondent, Third Brother fell into a confused sleep. He never expected that without his love Second Brother didn't even intend to live through the night.

Yang Lang finally went away, and Yang Meng stayed behind. He put up a straw shack in front of Second Brother's grave. He said that he wanted to stay with his friend until his own death. He was going to atone for his sister's crime. Third Brother therefore threw away the knife with which he had planned to kill Yang Lang. He couldn't fathom how a brother and sister could behave so differently. All he could do was assume that women, by nature, were sinister.

The captain didn't comment on what Third Brother had told him. He just told him, " You wait: one day you'll meet a good woman. Then you'll discover that, compared to women, men are nothing but bedbugs."

Unfortunately, the captain never got a chance to see the day when Third Brother met a good woman. Not long after their talk, the captain's barge capsized in the strait at Qingshan. Everyone, including the captain, disappeared into the deep. Third Brother was the only survivor.

This was in the early spring of 1985. From then on Third Brother never set foot on a boat again. He dared not even swim any more. He quit his job and drifted around like a lonely spirit leaving neither shadow nor footprint. Some time later he applied for a licence and acquired a set of tools. Every day he sits by the entrance to the underground shopping mall, and when he sees someone with a pair of new leather shoes he calls out, " Hey, how about fixing those soles?"

9

Seventh Brother is busy all day long. He goes to meetings, drafts documents, receives progressive model workers and helps out backward youths. He goes to bed every night with his mind in chaos. He doesn't know exactly what it is that he is doing or what the point of doing these things is. He only knows that by working himself to the bone he will make a good impression on his superiors. A good impression leads to a promotion. A promotion leads to status and power. Power means higher wages, better housing, the good life and everyone's respect. Only in this way can one's lot be truly changed. Seventh Brother feels that his goal in life is to change his lot. He can't imagine what would have become of him had he not gone to university.

His first night on campus, Seventh Brother was caught sleepwalking by his roommate.

Seventh Brother slept in the upper bunk. When he climbed out of bed, he kicked over the square stool by the bed side. The guy in the lower bunk woke up immediately. When he saw Seventh Brother take off his undershirt and shorts and then walk out stark naked, he was utterly astonished. When Seventh Brother had gone out, he woke up everyone else in the room, and together they trailed Seventh Brother. They followed him out of the dormitory. When Seventh Brother saw a tree, he began to circle it. After a few circles, he let out an absolutely terrifying shrill howl. The students went from fear to bewilderment. Someone eventually figured it out — he must be sleepwalking. They stepped forward, grabbed a hold of Seventh Brother and shook him violently. Seventh Brother opened his eyes, blinked a few times and woke with a start. "What are you doing?" he asked. "You were sleepwalking," one of the students said. "We want to take you back." Seventh Brother looked around dully, then he saw his own naked body, and his head cleared. He freed himself from the hands of his fellow students, ran like mad back to his room, crawled up into his bed and stayed there motionless. He recalled the ghost stories that had been going around. That white, slippery ghost that they had been talking about: it must have been him.

Seventh Brother had been used to being humiliated since he was a little kid. When he entered university he still had that timid look in his eyes and a rather faded appearance. The sleepwalking incident made him the laughing stock of the whole student body, and this made him feel even more afraid and inadequate. His day was like three points on a line: the dormitory — the classroom — the dining hall. No one took any notice of him, and he took no notice of those around him. In this way he co-existed with the others peacefully and uneventfully for almost a year.

Campus life was of course difficult. To Seventh Brother, however, those days were absolutely wonderful. His thin, pointed face grew mellow and full. He was after all his father's son. Among all of Father's sons, there wasn't one who didn't have a fine build, good posture and balanced features. Despite Seventh Brother's faded appearance, the features were still evident. The pretty, vivacious girls in his class sighed that if only Seventh Brother could take it easy, he would be the most handsome guy in their department. But Seventh Brother stuttered, and he was nowhere near being able to take it easy. The title of most handsome guy therefore fell to the one in the bunk below Seventh Brother.

The guy in the bunk below Seventh Brother came from a village in Subei, the northern part of Jiangsu Province. The guy from Subei had been a very good writer at his commune's high school. He had written quite a few of the commune secretary's achievement reports, which were widely circulated, and the secretary's name became known to everyone in the county. When he finished high school a year later the famous secretary gladly recommended him for university. At the farewell party before his departure the guy from Subei also took the Party member's oath. That's how, as soon as he got to campus, he got to be the class's Party branch propaganda committee member. The guy from Subei had the fair complexion of young male opera singers from the southern reaches of the Yangtze. In addition he had big eyes and a small mouth. He was gentle and cultivated, so all the female students had crushes on him. Almost all of the female students in the class were high-ranking cadres' daughters or cadres themselves. They were bold, capable and aggressive by nature, and yet they were attracted to the more docile and delicate males. This of course was a very odd thing. The guy from Subei was pursued like a fox by a couple of the most uninhibited girls, and still he didn't appear to show any interest in them. His fortitude left the female students with tearful eyes and the males with jealous hearts.

One day everyone in the department was unexpectedly told to attend a meeting. A letter was read aloud. It was a letter full of genuine emotion. The author was a female sanitation worker. The students were told that since she suffered from bone cancer she had given up all hope for life until she had met Tian Shuisheng. "But wasn't Tian Shuisheng the guy from Subei?" thought Seventh Brother. It was Tian Shuisheng's sincere urging that made her abandon her plan of dying. Later he often came to see and encourage her. He took her to the Great Wall to enjoy the panorama of mile after mile of rivers and mountains. He took her to Xiangshan to enjoy late autumn's red leaves. He taught her a great deal about the meaning of living. And the two of them fell in love. Their love for each other was very deep. But in the last six months her condition had worsened considerably. The cancer cells had already spread all over her body. But Shuisheng had remained loyal and devoted, and he looked after her in every way. He had already promised to marry her, so that she might enjoy life's happiness. The letter said, "I'm about to leave this world and start on my way down the path to death. Before I step on to that path, it is my responsibility to bring this young and beautiful soul to your attention. I wish to announce to the whole world that my husband is a truly incredible person."

Like a bomb detonated in a library, the letter reverberated through the school. The guy from Subei instantly became a hero. The newspaper reporters came in an endless stream. Each story was an absolute tear-jerker. The guy from Subei often went out to speak. They said that his talks always had an exquisite impact.

These stories, which tugged at the heart, set a gorgeous garland upon his destiny. The guy from Subei had married the sanitation worker. She had died less than six months later. But the garland she gave him remained fresh and stunning.

Seventh Brother, however, could see the traces of a peculiar, treacherous smile behind the guy from Subei's sincerity and emotion. The smile became more and more apparent after the woman's death. One morning the guy from Subei was combing his hair in front of a small, round mirror, humming a cheerful tune all the while. All the roommates had gone out to do their morning exercises. When Seventh Brother returned from brushing his teeth and heard this tune, he couldn't help but stare. The guy from Subei put down the mirror and saw Seventh Brother; he also noted his stare. Embarrassed, he cleared his throat and hurried out. The sanitation worker had died only twenty-three days ago. Seventh Brother arrived at this figure after reckoning it on his fingers.

The guy from Subei knew that Seventh Brother had uncovered his true face. He suddenly became Seventh Brother's best friend. When Seventh Brother got appendicitis and had to go in for an operation, he went to visit him every day. Seventh Brother had never experienced someone else's constant concern. As a result of his eager attentiveness, Seventh Brother's pale face began to shine with gratitude. The guy from Subei would smile indifferently and say, "It's nothing; it's nothing."

Seventh Brother was almost healed, and he was reclining in his hospital bed reading a book. The guy from Subei had brought a bunch of books to kill the boredom. Seventh Brother had never really read any literature, so this hospital stay turned out to broaden his horizons quite a bit. Outside the window the dry wind stirred in the tree branches. Seventh Brother was so astonished that someone who had cut wood for railings had actually become president of the United States that when the guy from Subei entered the room, his forehead was covered in sweat, and his fingers were still trembling.

The guy from Subei sat down by the bed and looked at Seventh Brother silently. Seventh Brother felt that his soul was being drawn out by this look.

"I understand you now," he said suddenly.

"As long as you understand," said the guy from Subei.

"What should I do?" asked Seventh Brother.

"Change your way of living."

"How should I live, then?"

"Do something that changes your lot. Don't think about ends and means."

"I've got to be ruthless, right?"

"Every night think about all the hardships you've been through. Think about how others looked at you with contempt because of your menial status. Think about how your children and grandchildren will follow in your footsteps, staggering along at the bottom of society."

Seventh Brother thought about it the whole night long. Past events rose like the tide and ebbed away again. He cried out with terror. When the nurse came, he was trembling and bathed in sweat. His incision had burst open, and blood was dripping out of it. "Had a bad dream?" the nurse asked. "Yes, it was a bad dream,'' he answered.

The nightmare had already passed. By the time the sun was high in the sky, Seventh Brother felt that the motive forces of life were gathering in his body; his blood coursed smoothly and quickly, and his bones hummed in their youthfulness. He felt utterly relieved and at peace.

That year Seventh Brother turned twenty. Two years later he was assigned a job back in Wuhan. He taught in an ordinary middle school in Hankou. Seventh Brother realized he wouldn't remain there for long. He was fed up with living in silence. He longed to go out and conquer the world. He only had to look for and take advantage of the right opportunities.

10

Fourth Brother is the one that Seventh Brother sees the least of now. He neither likes nor dislikes Fourth Brother, who feels the same way about him.

Fourth Brother is a deaf-mute. When he was six months old, he developed a high fever, but that same day Father was wounded in a fight on the docks, and Mother was busy taking care of him. Though Fourth Brother survived the fever, he lost the ability to hear and speak. Still able to eat and drink, he grew up happily in the family. He was the only one who was never beaten by Father. Thus Fourth Brother was unusually affectionate toward him. When Father came home from work, Fourth Brother would rush out to greet him with a muddled "Pa — Pa". He only knew this one word. He couldn't say "Ma", so Mother didn't show him any special kindness because of his handicap.

When he was fourteen years old, Fourth Brother started as a casual labourer. First he worked as an assistant to a bricklayer. Later on, when Second Brother went down to the countryside with Yang Lang and left him the freight tricycle that was registered in his name, Fourth Brother became a stevedore. He's been working steadily right up until today.

Fourth Brother's history has been uneventful. At twenty-four he married a blind woman. Fourth Brother had eyes and she had acute hearing and a quick mouth. They were a complete family. Fourth Brother was allotted a room of sixteen square metres. It was slightly bigger than the room in which Father and Mother had lived their entire lives. Here Fourth Brother and his wife had their children. First they had a girl, then they had a boy. Fourth Brother's son was born just before the one-child policy. His children were as handsome as their father and as smart as their mother. Each day they gave him endless hours of excitement. Fourth Brother had already added a TV and a washing machine to his possessions. Fourth Sister-in-law said that they would soon have enough saved up for a refrigerator too.

Seventh Brother had been to Fourth Brother's place once. He saw that the walls were covered with all kinds of certificates of merit. They belonged to Fourth Sister-in-law, the nephew and the niece. None was Fourth Brother's. Seventh Brother asked his sister-in-law why there weren't any for Fourth Brother. She said that he couldn't say all those honey-sweet phrases. He didn't understand what went on when they selected the advanced workers. Fourth Brother and Sister-in-law invited Seventh Brother to stay for dinner. Fourth Brother brought out a bottle of Yanghe liquor. In that respect he was like Father. Only he didn't beat up his kids when he'd been drinking. Seventh Brother thought it was because Fourth Brother had never been beaten up himself.

How many people live in such peaceful self-sufficiency as Fourth Brother? Was it because the sounds of the world's commotion never entered his consciousness that he was able to live such a tranquil and harmonious life?

Fourth Brother was, after all, both deaf and dumb.

11

When Seventh Brother reached the age of falling in love, he naturally fell in love. The girl was two years younger than him and had very delicate features. Even Father was surprised. He said that Little Seven had really played his cards right to get a girl like that. This was the first time Father ever praised Seventh Brother. The girl was an English teacher, a graduate from the foreign languages department. Her father was a university professor. The girl came from an educated and refined family, and she was gentle, graceful and unaffected. Seventh Brother really admired these qualities. After he'd been going out with her for two years, he too adopted the gentle and cultivated manners of a professor's son. He had already spoken to his girlfriend about buying furniture. However, there wasn't enough housing on campus, and they had to put off the furniture shopping and the marriage for the time being. Given his seniority and rank, Seventh Brother would have to wait another three years before he could even get a tiny room. There was no one to blame. Even the senior school teachers didn't live any better, let alone the junior ones. But Seventh Brother was losing his patience.

During the summer holidays, Seventh Brother had to go on a business trip. He went to Shanghai for twenty days on a practical course. On the way back, the boat sailed against the current, so the trip was slow and unbearably dull. Seventh Brother got to know the person in the berth above him. It was a woman who already had a few wrinkles in the corner of her eyes. She dressed fashionably and had a refined style of speech revealing her upbringing in a respectable family. Seventh Brother got along very well with her during the trip and when they got off the boat, she left him her address and telephone number. As Seventh Brother watched her write the characters "Fruit Lake", he knew that this woman wasn't from an ordinary family and when she wrote down her phone number, it was as if lightning flashed across his mind. The shock of the lightning made his heart ache but, when the pain passed he suddenly felt very excited. "Would it be all right to come by some time?" he asked with a smile. "The door is always open for a gentleman," she replied.

Three days later Seventh Brother phoned the lady. She said that she had been waiting for his call. He felt his heart jump. Thus Seventh Brother began asking her out for a walk or out to eat, and she in turn would invite him to see a movie or go to a play.

Seventh Brother already knew what kind of a person her father was. She was eight years older than Seventh

Brother, graduating from middle school during the "cultural revolution". When her father got into trouble during the "cultural revolution", she went down to work in the countryside. She worked so desperately to atone for her "sinister" background that she ended up getting sick and lost her ability to have children. One stormy day she insisted on rushing out to help with emergency repairs on the big dyke even though she had her period. When the dam cracked, she plunged into the water with the guys, and arm in arm they blocked the surging torrents. Eventually she fainted in the waves. After they pulled her out she stayed in the hospital for a month. When she was released, the doctor told her the news - the worst possible for a woman. She was twenty-two at the time; she hadn't yet thought about finding a boyfriend and even less about the problems of having children. So she just smiled coolly. It was only as she got older that the problem appeared more and more serious. Whenever she got to know a guy, she would be honest and tell him about her condition. Most of them sighed and broke up with her. After she turned thirty-five, the wounds in her soul were beyond healing. She thought that if, at forty, she was still living like this, she would go back and kill herself on that same dam that made her lose her most precious quality. She was in the midst of considering this course of action when she met Seventh Brother. At first she had only intended to get to know Seventh Brother for the same reasons as any woman had for getting to know a handsome and apparently knowledgeable man. She liked to talk about her private thoughts with someone of the opposite sex. However, she never imagined that half a month later

Seventh Brother would be pursuing her so vigorously. When she told him about her inability to have children, Seventh Brother never even expressed surprise. As usual, he was there by her side. He went shopping with her, had coffee with her, and he accompanied her to visit friends and relatives. When there was no one around, he put his arm around her waist and, sometimes, he smiled and kissed her on the forehead. In her room, which was permeated with woman's smells, he held her so tightly that she would gasp for breath. Big, tender hugs like this made her giddy, and yet deep in her heart she felt an unbearable pain. When her feelings settled slightly, there was a voice which cried out to her like an alarm bell that this man is not interested in you but in your father. She wanted to turn off this alarm, but the voice just rang out more and more frequently.

One day she couldn't stand it any longer and asked Seventh Brother, "If my father had been like your father, would you still have courted me so eagerly?" Seventh Brother smiled coolly and said, "Why must you ask such a foolish question?" "I'm aware of your ambitions," she said. Seventh Brother calmly looked into her eyes for a few seconds and said, "If you were a complete woman, would you still accept the love of someone with a family background and a position like mine?" She lowered her head.

A couple of days later Seventh Brother brought her to Henanpengzi. He took her to his home. He lifted up the bed planks and, pointing to that damp, dark spot, told her that he slept there up to the day he went to work in the countryside. He pushed aside the newly acquired easy chair, and with his foot he outlined an area and said that it was where his five brothers used to sleep. He said that his oldest brother worked the night shift for years because there wasn't enough room for him.

Everything was the same in the room except for the easy chair and the black-and-white TV on the little square table. The window in the little room had been sealed, because they had added a kitchen. All that was left now was the pane of glass embedded in the ceiling. That was the room's only source of light. The walls were still covered with newspapers. The yellow newspapers still revealed interesting articles from days gone by. Seventh Brother said, "If you lived one year in a place like this, you'd understand how important the things that I do are. Your father's power was, in fact, eighty percent of the reason I chose you. Twenty percent was because of your honesty and your good heart. I need your father as a bridge to reach my goal. I can also tell you that before meeting you I had another girlfriend. Her father was a university professor. Our relationship had already become quite serious. I was about to get a marriage licence when I met you. You and your father are more important to me than she and her father." Seventh Brother said that professors weren't worth anything here in China. "They are of as little help to me as these outdated newspapers. Therefore, I decided to break up with her. I pursued you with full confidence and courage. I am determined to get you." Seventh Brother spoke with certainty and eloquence. She was so stunned that her no longer youthful face looked twisted. She tilted it in a frightening way. Then she stepped forward and boxed Seventh Brother on the ear and fled the room.

Seventh Brother smiled calmly and didn't say a word. With limitless confidence, he waited for her to change her mind. He knew that she needed him. Someone had once written a novel with the title *A Tragedy Is Better Than No Play at All*. Seventh Brother hadn't read that novel, but he thought the title was excellent. It's better to have a monster than to have no one at all. Seventh Brother thought that she would eventually come to this conclusion.

Seventh Brother's judgement was as good as a wise man's. Just three days passed before she came looking for him, her eyes all red and swollen. She had no other man to go to but him. All she had was him. Besides, Seventh Brother wasn't that bad a character. She told him that she had acted on impulse, that she tried to see things from his point of view. She begged him to forgive her. Seventh Brother didn't say anything; he just went up to her and kissed her. She was so moved that tears filled her eyes. True enough, Seventh Brother used her to reach his goals, but she used him too, to get a full, new life. That day Seventh Brother gave her what she had been longing for. Life's most thorough feeling of happiness made her waning looks shine once more. When she appeared before her friends glowing with youth and vigour they could hardly believe she was the same person. Seventh Brother had restored her youthfulness. She was, therefore, all the more intent on having Seventh Brother, and she watched him jealously.

In fact Seventh Brother wasn't at all the type that chases women. He never gave those matters any attention. To not have realized that was really to belittle Seventh Brother. He felt that those who took lust too seriously were on the same level as animals. He wasn't among them. His goal was to reach the top of society. He wanted power. He wanted the whole world to watch him. He wanted hundreds of people to obey his orders. Seventh Brother wanted to rid himself of his pauper's roots, to completely turn his lot upside-down. He wanted to rescue himself. He felt that he had a responsibility to give himself the kind of grand, upper-class life that others had. Otherwise, feeling so abused by the world, his soul would refuse to depart his body.

Seventh Brother was transferred to the Provincial Youth League Committee. It was his own suggestion to go there. He had seen a statistical chart which listed the progress of former Youth League cadres from Liberation onward. He didn't remember the exact position of each of them, but one thing impressed him: almost all of those who passed through the Youth League Committee door had advanced to higher positions and were still on their way up. The high-ranking positions, arranged in order, crept, one after another, across Seventh Brother's heart like an ice-cold snake. A shiver ran through his body, then he felt utterly exhilarated. He knew that he had found his path to success.

Seventh Brother was allotted a spacious house. Back on his old campus even the teachers with thirty years of teaching experience weren't senior enough to live in such a house. Seventh Brother's house was decorated like a palace. Lined curtains that reached to the floor, the most advanced stereo system, a remote-controlled colour TV and a soft, wide bed with a spring mattress. The night before Seventh Brother's wedding, Father and Mother went over hand-in-hand. Father insisted that the bed was bad for one's bones, and Mother angrily scolded that the curtains were a waste of material that could have been made into several gowns.

Seventh Brother spent his honeymoon in Guangzhou and Shenzhen. The few nights that they stayed in Shenzhen's Wanda Hotel he hardly got any sleep. He felt as if his whole body was burning with pain and yet scorched with excitement. After his wife had already fallen asleep, he couldn't help but bury his face in her chest again and again. He cried tears of gratitude. Seventh Brother had a premonition that the good fortune she had brought him would some day exceed his expectations.

Seventh Brother enjoyed those days immensely. He was as happy and full of laughter as if he had entered the gates of heaven. But there was a girl who wept until she had no tears left, who bit her lips until they bled. Her dad and mum cursed "the bastard" by this and other useless names between their teeth, and then sighed deeply with their broken-hearted daughter.

12

When Fifth Brother quit his job to go into business for himself, he wasn't aware that Sixth Brother had done the very same thing. They ran into each other on board a steamboat. When Fifth Brother entered the dining room and saw Sixth Brother carrying a plate of food, he let out such a cry that Sixth Brother's hand slipped and his plate fell to the floor. As soon as they saw each other, they were both roaring with laughter. Fifth Brother was on his way to Nanjing to place an order for a batch of T-shirts and Sixth Brother was going to Nantong to stock up on cotton knee-socks.

Fifth and Sixth Brothers are twins. It was as if they were connected by the heart. Whatever Fifth Brother thought about, most likely Sixth Brother thought about too. When Fifth Brother caught a cold, Sixth Brother's nose would surely be running as well. The strangest thing happened during a language test in elementary school: everyone had to compose three sentences, and the two of them wrote exactly the same ones despite their sitting far apart. Since they were little kids, Fifth and Sixth Brothers had been a couple of troublemakers. They fought, they swore at people, they stole, and they fooled around with girls. There wasn't anything that they hadn't tried. It was only after both of them were married and had kids that they got on to the right track and started living decent lives.

The first time Fifth Brother brought his fiancée home, Father and Mother were in the middle of a fight. It started when Mother bought some wine which had been watered, and in a fit of rage Father had thrown the whole pot out on the tracks. At that moment, the train passed by, and the wine-pot was flattened into two thin, iron sheets. Mother began screaming and fighting with Father. Fifth Brother's fiancée acted like a high-ranking official on a tour of inspection. She didn't take the least notice of Father and Mother. She just looked around the room disdainfully and said, "So this is it, this shitty, dilapidated room?" Fifth Brother never got a chance to answer, because Father turned away from Mother and began bellowing at the girl. "So you find this place dilapidated? Well, there's no room for you here." The fiancée didn't take it lying down: "The old guy must be on the wrong medication. How come he howls at everyone he sees?" With this she swaggered off. Fifth Brother was furious. He leapt up and shouted a bunch of things at Father before stomping off after his fiancée. Father remained speechless for a moment, then he shook his head and said, " Life is upside-down." He found an empty bottle and, sighing, he went out to buy some more wine.

The result of all of this was that Fifth Brother's fiancée refused to go to his home again, so he had to go live with *her* family. Fifth Brother's fiancée was from Hanzheng Street. Since Sixth Brother often accompanied him there, he also ended up with a girl from Hanzheng Street. Sixth Brother was sensible; he dared not bring his fiancée home. On his own initiative, he told Father that he wanted to move in with the girl's family. Father waved his big hand: " Go ahead, go ahead; just stop babbling. The two of you are twins anyway." Sixth Brother felt like he had been given an amnesty. Greatly relieved, he bade his home farewell and moved in with his wife's family. Fifth and Sixth Brothers both became fathers at almost the same time (in fact there were only three days in between). The babies were chubby, and the in-laws were overjoyed. Fifth and Sixth Brothers were much more comfortable being sons-in-law than being sons, and they gradually seemed to forget old Papa and Mama back in Henanpengzi.

Since old times, Hanzheng Street was the gathering place of merchants. With the Qianxiangyi Shop at its centre, it stretched up to Wusheng Road in one direction and down to Jijiazui in the other. There are already more than two thousand private stalls by the side of the streets — a long street with small stalls and merchandise of all varieties. When Fifth Brother found out that nearly a thousand stall-holders had already a capital of ten thousand yuan, his heart started to palpitate, and his head began to spin. Fifth Brother was a bricklayer with a construction company; his salary wasn't bad. But if you considered it, even if his salary wasn't bad, he could sweat a whole month and still not earn as much as the stall-holders did in one day. Fifth Brother felt that his life was worthless; he had to earn big money and live in style so as not to have wasted his life. He never even thought of talking it over with his wife; he just went and handed in his resignation that very same day. Sixth Brother was only one day ahead of Fifth Brother. Sixth Brother's neighbour had gone into business with just 150 yuan in capital; he had ten thousand yuan less than a year later. Sixth Brother had seen this change with his own eyes — and his eyeballs nearly popped out. After thinking it over one night, he quit his job as an auto repairman with the transport company.

The T-shirts that Fifth Brother had ordered were surplus stock. He ordered 10,000 of them but was only able to sell 1,500. He didn't make any money, and every night Fifth Sister-in-law would point at his nose and curse his ancestors. Fifth Brother was afraid of his wife. In this respect he was completely different from Father. Day after day he ran back and forth trying to sell his stock, but his face became drawn, and the shirts remained piled up.

One day, when Fifth Sister-in-law was smashing cups and throwing around bowls while cursing his ancestors, Fifth Brother sneaked away. He wandered aimlessly until he came to Hangkong Road. This stretch of Hangkong Road down to the market was the "Flying Tigers'" territory. The "Flying Tigers" was what the townspeople had nicknamed the itinerant vendors. One could call the way the "Flying Tigers" did business underhanded. Their trademark was raising prices and shorting quantities while making it seem as if you still got a good deal. Fifth Brother saw a few women standing around a vendor arguing loudly over the price of a woollen sweater. He could see right away that they were all together. They pretended to be buying and selling in order to coax a few real customers over. A woman in red kept sweeping her eyes over the passers-by. She spotted Fifth Brother and cried out, "Ooh, if he was to wear this sweater, it would make him the best looking guy in these parts." Fifth Brother smiled, walked over and asked the vendor, "How much does it cost?" "I can see that it really fits you," the vendor replied. "That makes me happy, so I'll give it to you for 26 — everyone else pays 30." Fifth Brother rubbed the sweater between his fingers. He knew that there were more acrylic fibres than wool in the yarn. He smiled again and said, "The wholesale price is 16, that I know for sure." He walked off smiling knowingly. He could hear the voices of the vendor and the women cursing him behind his back. Fifth Brother was not the type to swallow that. Outside of his home he had yet to lose a fight, and this time wasn't going to be any different. He chuckled to himself, found a place that was a bit more quiet, and then cleared his throat and bellowed, "The officers from the Bureau of Industry and Commerce are coming!"

It was as if someone had dropped a bomb. Everyone Fifth Brother could see was scattering: vendors gathering their clothes, people fleeing in disarray, pretend-customers mixing in with the crowd, everyone warning each other, just as Fifth Brother had expected — utter chaos. In an instant the "Flying Tigers" had vanished, and there were only a few empty cardboard boxes left on the road. Fifth Brother was very amused. He had to lean against the base of a wall, doubled up with laughter. He laughed until he was gasping for breath, then someone tapped him on the shoulder. Fifth Brother turned his head, and he recognized the woman in red. "How come you're not running?" asked Fifth Brother. "I want to see what other tricks you have," the woman in red said coldly.

"It was just a joke; no need to take it seriously."

"When you fool around like that, you better watch who you're dealing with."

Fifth Brother laughed. "You attract customers and then curse them. You didn't watch who you were dealing with."

The woman in red sized up Fifth Brother. "You look like you're someone special."

"Of course: Henanpengzi's son, Hanzheng Street's son-in-law; I *am* someone special."

"Hanzheng Street? A ten-thousand yuan household?"

"It'll still be a couple more years before I'm one."

"You mean to say that we are in the same business? Why have fun at the expense of your own kind? Aren't we all just trying to make a living?"

"Well then, I'm sorry. Let's go to the Cloud and Crane, and I'll buy you something to take the edge off that fright."

"Sure. We' re buddies. You ask, and I' ll go ."

Fifth Brother and the woman in red went up to the third floor together. The woman in red took the menu and began ordering. Cold and heartless, she didn' t consider how much money Fifth Brother might have brought with him: stewed soft-shelled turtle, sauteed sea cucumber, stir-fried shrimp, chopped chicken breast, a bowl of three-delicacy soup and four bottles of Qingdao beer. Fifth Brother groaned to himself.

The woman asked Fifth Brother how business was going. He poured down a couple of mouthfuls of beer, sighed deeply and said that he was having a bit of trouble. The woman in red asked why. Fifth Brother told her all about his unsaleable T-shirts .

"When you' re having trouble selling something," she said, "you just have to come up with a good angle, then you can always make money ."

"What' s your suggestion?"

"Do you think that I' d give it to you for free?"

"Of course, I' ll make it worth your while ."

"Can you be more specific?"

"Half a grand ."

"Five hundred yuan, you call that money? If you earn one yuan on every shirt, how much are you going to make? And you' re only prepared to give me that much? That' s really cheap!"

"Do I have to give you a thousand?"

"Again, to be fair, I might not ask for that much . In business you have to look at the long term ."

Fifth Brother was silent. He noticed that they had almost finished the beer and said, "I' ll go and get a couple more cans of beer ." He had just taken the

beer from the counter and was about to return to the
table when he noticed that the woman in red had her
back to him. He got an idea. He put the beer in his
pocket and mumbled, " I' ll go get a couple more cold
platters ." Then he leisurely went downstairs. When he
got to the street, he ran straight to the number one
bus stop and took the bus all the way to Liudu Bridge
and went off, burping, to his friend' s place, where he
played mahjongg the whole night long, and only in the
early morning hours did he finally stagger home.

Immediately after she opened the door, Fifth Sister-
in-law slapped Fifth Brother in the face. He didn' t get
angry. " I' ll tell you something funny," he said slowly. Then he told her all the details about the free meal
the day before, adding colour and emphasis to his
narration. Fifth Sister-in-law collapsed on the bed with
laughter. She cursed the woman' s stupidity and the
man' s cunning, and in the midst of cursing she
couldn' t help but feel proud that the man was her husband. Fifth Brother just slumped into the easy chair
and fell asleep wheezing loudly.

The next morning, before Fifth Brother had got up,
Sixth Brother came running over dripping with sweat.
Sixth Brother shook Fifth Brother and shouted angrily,
" No matter what, you' ve got to help your brother today ." Fifth Brother quickly asked what had happened. ' ' This morning," Sixth Brother said, " as
soon as I had set up, a woman came over with a
bunch of guys and, for no good reason, totalled my
stall. There were so many of them that I didn' t dare
fight back. Finally the woman threw down this T-shirt
and said when the thousand yuan were ready she' d be
back ." Fifth Brother jumped out of bed, grabbed the

T-shirt and examined it carefully. The outline of Huo Yuanjia, in a fighting pose, was drawn on the chest with a ballpoint pen. Fifth Brother brightened up, his brows smoothed out, and he said, " Excellent, excellent" over and over again. Sixth Brother was completely confused. Then Fifth Brother told him what had happened the day before, and thumping his chest he said to Sixth Brother, " I' ll make sure that you get double compensation for what you lost today. And that' s not bullshit."

Fifth Brother took the near 10,000 shirts he had left in stock and had a Huo Yuanjia figure printed on 5,000 of them and a Chen Zhen figure printed on another 3,000. The TV series had just been aired, and people were still quite familiar with both of them. Fifth Brother gave 20 shirts to the boys practising martial arts, and within three days the customers were swarming in front of his stall. Fifth Brother quietly raised the price three times, and the shirts continued to sell well. He made a bundle. Every day when she saw him, Fifth Sister-in-law was all smiles. She served him tea. She fanned him. Like a spoiled child, she pranced back and forth in front of him. Fifth Brother on the other hand couldn' t get the woman in red out of his mind. All this time she hadn' t even shown up once.

Three months later Fifth Brother was returning from a trip to Guangzhou, and just as he walked out of the Hankou train station a woman gave him a sweet smile. He suddenly realized it was the woman in red. The red dress had been replaced by an olive green one. Fifth Brother walked up to her. " Well, well, you recognize me?" the woman said. " You are after all my benefactor. How could I forget you?" Fifth Brother replied.

"I live around here. Do you want to come over?"

"I sure do. That is, if you think enough of me."

The woman in red smiled. "You're a good-looking guy, smart and competent, too good for the likes of me."

"You're the only woman I admire."

The woman in red tilted her head. "Really?"

The look in her eyes stirred Fifth Brother's heart. He felt that comparing his wife to this woman was like comparing a beggar-woman to a fairy. If only he could enjoy this woman once, thought Fifth Brother, he'd become an immortal too. "Who else is there at your place?" he asked. "I'm alone. My husband has gone to Shenzhen." "I've just come back from the south. I'm two days early. My wife is expecting me the day after tomorrow." The woman in red smiled. Fifth Brother seized the opportunity and put his arm around her waist.

He followed her around corners and through alleys. He was ecstatic. In this sweet mood he inspected the woman by his side: her eyes, brows and mouth as well as her breasts. He almost lost control of himself.

Just as Fifth Brother walked in the door with the woman in red, a few burly guys stepped in behind them. Fifth Brother felt that something wasn't quite right and quickly forced a smile. "You did me a big favour," he said. "I have decided to reward you with 2,000 yuan." The woman in red laughed coldly, "I asked for 1,000, so I only want 1,000. I've already collected the money from your brother. But it's not all that simple." Fifth Brother started sweating. "What do you want? Just tell me."

"I'm not a lady to let people play games with her," said the woman in red. "Pretending that officers from the Bureau of Industry and Commerce were on their way: that was the first game. Slipping away from the Cloud and Crane: that was the second game. And today having all those dirty ideas: that was the third game. I'll be frank with you, I want someone to teach you a lesson to help you remember that when you play a joke, you've got to watch who you're dealing with."

Fifth Brother had nothing to say for himself. And of course he couldn't easily beg for mercy. He was after all Father's son. Father said that a real man would tough it out, even with a knife thrust against his throat. When Fifth Brother watched the husky guys take off their jackets and saw that each of them wore one of the T-shirts he sold with Huo Yuanjia printed on it, he felt his heart sink. Suddenly he said, "Friend, I'd like to say a few words." "Spit it out," said the woman in red. "An eye for an eye, I'll take my licks," said Fifth Brother. "If I'm hurt, I'll go see a doctor. If I'm crippled, I'll lie down in bed. If I die, I won't complain. However, when this account has been settled, I'll mind my own business, and you mind yours. There's no need to remain enemies. A prosperous business depends on friends. If we pull the rug out from under each other's feet, we'll all end up falling." "You're some tough guy," said the woman in red. "Don't worry. You won't die, and you won't become a cripple. As for pulling the rug out from under each other's feet, I don't do that sort of thing, but I can't speak for anyone else."

With these words, the woman in red left. Fifth Brother was immediately engulfed by fists and feet. In no time, he lay immobile on the ground, unaware of anything around him. When he came to it was already dark outside. A lamp was lit in the room. The woman in red was clicking away on her knitting machine, knitting a sweater. Fifth Brother got up with difficulty and without a word walked to the door. As he was about to step outside, the woman's soft voice suddenly wafted through the air, "Please apologize to your brother for me. Tell him we mistook him for someone else that day."

Fifth Brother took a cab home. When his family saw him in this bloody condition they cried out in alarm. Fifth Brother was so embarrassed he dared not explain what had happened. He just said that he had got into an arguement with some hooligans on the bus and they had ended up fighting. Fifth Brother remained in bed for a week. When the news reached Father he sneered with contempt and said that Fifth Brother was an idiot and a loathsome creature rolled into one. What an idiot to let someone beat him up so badly! And how loathsome to lie quietly in bed for seven full days! Indeed, Father sighed, young people were going to the dogs.

It all seemed like a dream. When Fifth Brother had recovered from his wounds he continued doing business as usual. He was worried that someone would try to provoke him again, but it turned out that everything remained peaceful for months. He couldn't stop thinking about that woman. He had been all over to inquire about her. He wanted to be her friend. Unfortunately he still hasn't been able to locate her.

Fifth Brother is now one of those with a capital

of over 10,000 yuan in Hanzheng Street. And so, naturally, is Sixth Brother. They say that there are about 1,000 ten-thousand-yuan households on Hanzheng Street, but in fact there are many more. There are at least a few hundred hiding underground. When people like Fifth and Sixth Brothers make it big one of the first things they do is take up gambling. They started with mahjongg. Later they decided that mahjongg was too much trouble and too hard on the brain, so they began throwing dice. Some of their friends had read Jin Yong's novel *Story of Luding Mountain* and knew about the expert gambler called "Wei Xiaobao". As they shook the dice they'd shout out loud, "Here comes Wei Xiaobao!" Neither Fifth nor Sixth Brothers knew who Wei Xiaobao was, but when it was their turn to throw, they'd still cry, "Wei Xiaobao!"

When Fifth Brother went home to Henanpengzi to visit his father and his mother he would occasionally find his father sitting on a little stool playing cards for a few *jiao* with his cronies, cursing and swearing at the cards, all red in the face from the excitement. Fifth Brother would sneer contemptuously at his father, as his father had at him. Fifth Brother said that when his bunch gambled they didn't even count the bills any more. Unconvinced, Father would ask condescendingly how they were able to settle accounts. Fifth Brother answered that they just stacked up the money and measured the thickness with a ruler. He said that once, when he was playing a wild game, he put down ten centimetres worth to up the ante. Father asked how much ten centimetres was worth. It couldn't be more than a hundred bucks, could it? Fifth Brother replied that if you pressed them together a bit it was just

about a thousand. "Ptooh!" Father sent a mouthful
of dark spittle in Fifth Brother's direction. "You
wanna brag, go tell it to your grandchildren; don't
come to your old man," he said angrily. Fifth Brother left swearing loudly that Father was a real son-
of-a-bitch. When Fifth Brother was completely out of
sight Father's card-buddies were still stupefied.

Then Father began to wonder if Fifth and Sixth
Brothers were really his sons.

13

Seventh Brother's contempt for Fifth and Sixth Brothers is extreme. In his heart he often curses them most
bitterly and maliciously. Seventh Brother could never
forget all the abuse he had suffered in his childhood at
the hands of Fifth and Sixth Brothers. However, when
Seventh Brother organized an informal discussion
among the stall-holders he would always proudly mention that his two older brothers were stall-holders too.
He said that he had a lot of respect for these brothers
of his, because they had created lives for themselves by
relying solely on their own hard work and intelligence.
Seventh Brother encouraged the young stall-holders not
to feel inferior but to have self-confidence. They had to
recognize the loftiness and importance of their work.
He also said, jokingly, that those who do political
work, like himself, could only wag their lips and had
no skills at all. "If one day I got fed up with my job
and resigned, I would start up my own business," said Seventh Brother. "That way I might at
least get in a couple of trips to Guangzhou and
Shenzhen, two places I'd love to visit." Seventh

Brother made the stall-holders, who went south regularly, laugh. They all praised him and said that it was hard to find another like him. They thought of him as a friend, someone who could really appreciate their talents. In fact none of them could have known that Seventh Brother had spent twenty days in Shenzhen on his honeymoon.

Seventh Brother went home for New Year's. By coincidence, Fifth and Sixth Brothers had come home too, bringing their sons. Since they were kids, Fifth and Sixth Brothers had never paid a lot of attention to Seventh Brother. It was still like that. They ignored Seventh Brother's special friendship with the stall-holders. They ganged up on Seventh Brother and mocked him. They said that his efforts to get ahead didn't pay off like working to make a bit of money. Then they kissed their pudgy sons' cheeks, purposefully making loud smacking noises. The sound was like a hammer pounding on Seventh Brother's heart, and he suffered at every stroke.

Father was dissatisfied with Seventh Sister-in-law. He thought that she must be a sorceress. How else could she have seduced Seventh Brother at her advanced age and with the unforgivable defect of not being able to bear children? Father thought that no man would want to marry a woman who wasn't able to have kids. And if a woman wasn't able to have children, thought Father, what else was she good for? Father said that there are three unfilial acts, of which the worst is not having any male offspring. He said that these days no one could have a concubine, and what would Little Seven do in the future? Father said that he should cast off that wife of his and find another who was younger and more beautiful. Seventh Brother said that there was no point in arguing: Father didn't understand shit. Seventh Brother's words choked off Father. He humbled himself in front of Seventh Brother. He remembered that Seventh Brother was in the provincial bureaucracy.

A few days after New Year's Father rushed off to Wuchang to find Seventh Brother. Father said that Daxiang and Xiaoxiang wanted to invite him to dinner to have a sisterly chat with him. Seventh Brother was shocked. He was no less astonished than if he had heard that President Reagan had invited him to a banquet. After a moment he gave a cold laugh: "The weasel wishes the hen happy New Year; what can his intentions be?" "They aren't weasels," said Father, "and you're not a hen either."

"I have never had any sisters."

"All of you were raised by me. You've all made your way out of the same mother's belly. It's not up to you whether or not you have sisters."

Seventh Brother laughed coldly again. Seventh Sister-in-law said that as he'd been invited he might as well go, not to mention that Father had travelled such a long way. Seventh Brother listened to his wife. "An invitation's an invitation. There'll be food. I may as well enjoy it," he said indifferently to Father.

Xiaoxiang lived by the Huangxiao River. The black-bearded guy that she married turned out to be a vagrant. After they'd been married for three and a half months, Xiaoxiang gave birth to a baby girl. The black-bearded guy had wanted a boy, but Xiaoxiang hadn't been able to accomplish that. She could do what ever she liked to Seventh Brother, but she couldn't handle her husband. The baby girl wasn't two years old when the the black-bearded guy, on the pretence of going back to see his family, sold Xiaoxiang to a peasant in Henan Province. Life in the Henan countryside was tough, and Xiaoxiang tried again and again to escape. Finally, three years later, she made it back home with a little baby boy in her arms. Mother took her for a beggar. Only when Xiaoxiang wretchedly called out "Mama!" did Mother realize that this was her youngest daughter.

In less than a year Xiaoxiang remarried. She couldn't survive without a man. And with only one man, she felt life was still pretty miserable. Xiaoxiang bore her new husband a son. Her husband was a vegetable farmer. He had divorced his previous wife in a fit of anger because she had given birth to a girl. This time Xiaoxiang fulfilled his yearning. Now he let her have her own way with everything. Since he already had a son, a wife wasn't so important any more. As long as his son was happy, he didn't even mind if Xiaoxiang brought her boyfriends home and flirted with them. He would cook for Xiaoxiang while holding the little boy in his arms and would even ask the guests if everything tasted Okay.

Xiaoxiang now had a daughter and two sons. The one that she had brought from Henan still wasn't registered anywhere. Then she thought of Seventh Brother.

Just about the same time, Daxiang was also thinking about Seventh Brother. She had married long ago. Her three sons were like tiger cubs. The youngest had already graduated from junior middle school, and the oldest was waiting for work. Daxiang was eighteen when she married. Her husband was a carpenter, and he was ten years older than she. Daxiang lived comfortably with her family. On holidays she would sit on the doorstep and enjoy the sun. Munching on sunflower seeds, she would pass the time of day with a gang of elderly ladies. On Sundays she would bring a little food or some wine with her to Henanpengzi to visit Father and Mother. Daxiang lived by the Sanyan Bridge, in another area of Hankou where the poor had lived for ages.

Father informed Daxiang and Xiaoxiang that Seventh Brother had agreed to come for dinner. Daxiang said that they should go to her place. Xiaoxiang said no, no, no, they had to go to her place. Daxiang asked how Seventh Brother could set foot in that miserable place of Xiaoxiang's. Xiaoxiang said that Daxiang needn't get the best of everything; her life was already quite comfortable. Daxiang said that was true: her life was comfortable, and now she had to think about her children and grandchildren. Xiaoxiang said that she only wanted what was best for Seventh Brother. Daxiang said that if she was so kind-hearted, how come she never worried about Seventh Brother when they were kids? Xiaoxiang said that Daxiang was so much older than Seventh Brother, but she never looked after him. Daxiang and Xiaoxiang argued so heatedly that they ended up cursing each other's ancestors. One would have never guessed that they were the descendants of the same forefathers.

Father said that arguing wouldn't solve anything. "Let's just have it here at my place. You two can both act as hostesses. The old man will join Little Seven for a drink, and you two can spit out whatever's on your minds." Father's two daughters were delighted by his suggestion.

When Seventh Brother walked in and saw Daxiang and Xiaoxiang's smiling faces he nearly threw up on the spot. Like in the old days, the train came rumbling by, and the little house shook slightly. They had put the small table in the centre of the room. A round table top had been added. Several cold dishes like sausage, braised beef and roasted peanuts were arranged on the enlarged, round table top. The wine was Yellow Crane Tower. With narrow eyes, Father smelled the food and smacked his lips. There were three cups of wine on the table. Father had sent for Eldest Brother too. Seventh Brother, Father and Eldest Brother, the three men, were seated by the table, while the women — Mother, Daxiang and Xiaoxiang — were busy by their sides modestly asking Seventh Brother how the food was and how the wine was. Seventh Brother didn't know what they were up to. He felt like a guest in a stranger's house.

With three cups of wine already in his belly, Father's tongue was lubricated. Father said, "Little Seven, you mustn't go through life just the two of you alone."

"What do you mean?" asked Seventh Brother.

"You must have a son. Otherwise who will there be to continue the life that you're working so hard for?"

"Little Seven," said Eldest Brother, "Father is right. No matter how high you rise in society, once you're dead, everything's finished. It would be better to bequeath everything to a son."

Seventh Brother was silent. He felt that there was, in fact, something to what Father and Eldest Brother were saying. He thought that he was busy trying to change his lot, but then what? He had no sons or grandsons to take pride in his efforts. No sons and grandsons to enjoy his achievements. Wasn't it a bit futile? "Little Seven," said Father, "you could adopt a son."

Immediately Xiaoxiang said, "My second son — you know him — he's very strong and not bad looking either — I am willing to take the chance and give him up to you, someone for my little brother to rely on in his old age."

Seventh Brother was stunned. "Your son?"

Xiaoxiang gave him a chicken leg. "Yeah. He's a fine boy."

"Don't listen to her," Daxiang said. "She had that kid with a peasant from the Henan countryside. He's an idiot. That third son of mine — now he's a handsome boy. Although he is a bit older, he's still suitable for you to adopt."

Seventh Brother was stupefied. "You mean Sanmao?"

"Yeah. Sanmao always says the person he admires most — well, it's his Seventh Uncle."

"Sanmao is fifteen years old: how can he be suitable?" asked Xiaoxiang.

"He's certainly more suitable than a bastard," said Daxiang.

The sisters had another fight. Seventh Brother was terribly upset and had completely lost his appetite. The food and wine on the table made his hair stand up on end as if it were all poison. He got up from his chair and said to Father and Eldest Brother, "I'm not having any more." Father shouted at Daxiang and Xiaoxiang to stop fighting and then said to Seventh

Brother, "Come on, stay a bit longer, if not to keep your old man company then at least your Eldest Brother."

"If Seventh Brother wants to go, let him," said Eldest Brother. "However, I want you to be clear about this: when you were little you suffered enough at home, I know that, but that misery has made you a strong person. Today you have a future. Anyone with a promising future must have a son. Daxiang and Xiaoxiang's sons are your nephews. You're tied to them by blood. You can choose between them to adopt. It is best to adopt a blood relation, otherwise the family won't recognize him as a grandson."

"I'll have to think about it," said Seventh Brother. As soon as he stepped outside, Daxiang and Xiaoxiang's voices exploded behind his back. He walked quite some way, and he could still hear them shouting. This all made Seventh Brother feel as if he had returned to the old days. Horrified, he quickened his step. Finally he couldn't stand it any longer. He rested his hand against a tree, bent his head and threw up all the food he had just eaten. He wanted to throw up all the fear and iciness that was inside of him too. When he was done he gazed into the overcast sky and thought, "Since when did they recognize me as a son at home?"

Three days later Seventh Brother returned home again. He told his father that he had already taken home a little boy from the orphanage. The child had just turned one. "Regardless of whether you recognize him as a grandson or not, I'll tell you this: he is my son!" With these words Seventh Brother stalked off. Father was completely taken aback by his behaviour.

He wanted to curse him, but he didn't. Father didn't dare curse Seventh Brother. In his heart he knew that Seventh Brother was the government's son, not his.

14

A lot of new houses have gone up in Henanpengzi. The scattered, old-fashioned wooden ones seem like waifs in rags among the buxom young brides. A new train station is apparently going to be built somewhere over by Jianshe Boulevard. Then the cathedral-like Hankou station will have completed its mission. The rails that run through the city will be changed into high-quality avenues. The old houses on either side of the avenues are to be demolished. New high-rises and sky-scrapers will take their place.

The neighbours are all overjoyed. They are busy try-ing to figure out how much their old houses are worth and how to bargain with the government so that they may be allotted a couple more rooms. Only Father wears a worried frown. He says that he won't be able to fall asleep without the train. He says in a high rise, with-out the feel of the earth, one can't live very long. Fath-er worried what would become of Little Eight. He sat for days beneath the window mumbling, "Only Little Eight is here to keep me company."

I know that I will never be with Father and Mother again. For twenty happy years I enjoyed the incomparably warm love of my parents. My tiny, frail body was wrapped in layers of warm, cosy earth. A beautiful cluster of fire-red salvia bloomed over the warm earth. The train rumbled by majestically, and the rays of light, white as snow, illuminated Father's little house. It is hard to imagine what the world will be like without that little house of Father's.

The sky was a deep blue the day Father dug me out. The sun shone dazzlingly bright over the earth. Father had sent for Third Brother. Third Brother placed the casket in a big cardboard box, which he tied up with a rope and said, "I'll bury him next to Second Brother. That way he'll have a companion." Third Brother attached the cardboard box to the back of his bike. He stepped on to the pedal with his left foot and swung his right foot over the cardboard box and on to the other pedal. Father and Mother watched, hand in hand, as Third Brother's bicycle bell jingled and we drove far away. They looked just like an affectionate old couple as they stood there for a long time, looking off into the distance, with tender expressions on their faces. Then the two of them sat on the door step, feeling dejected. That day I realized that Mother and Father had become very, very old, very, very withered and very, very weak.

Third Brother buried me right next to Second Brother, then, with his hand resting on Second Brother's grave and a sad expression on his face, he heaved a deep sigh. It was dark before he slowly started walking, with heavy, lonely steps, down the mountain. One by one his footsteps knocked on the crust of the earth as if to tell his friends in the mountain how extremely tired he was.

The stars are out, but the resplendent night isn't able to alter the stillness of the mountain. The moon sadly shines and illuminates this ever-gentle, peaceful land of ours.

I recall Seventh Brother's words. He says that lives

are like leaves . All growth ends in death . There are no exceptions to this rule . Seventh Brother says there is never any way to determine whether someone is truly good or bad . He says that only when you've seen through this world and right through its very essence will you be able to decide what sort of life to lead . I have given a lot of thought to what Seventh Brother said, but I still haven't understood exactly what it is he has seen through, what sort of decision he has made and, finally, whether he has chosen growth or death . As I see it, Seventh Brother is, after all, as naive and as shallow as anyone else alive .

But I am not like Seventh Brother; I don't say anything at all . Solemn and eternal, I just watch the endlessly fluctuating and most beautiful landscape at the foot of this mountain .

Translated by Anne-Marie Traeholt
and Mark Kruger

Fang Fang was born in 1955 in Jiangxi Province . Since graduation from the Chinese Language Department of Wuhan University she has been working at Hubei TV . She has publish-ed stories and novellas . Her "Landscape" won a literary award in 1987 .

Dialogue in Heaven

Can Xue

LAST night I went out again. You warned me not to wander about at night for fear of an accident. And I remembered your warning, but still I slipped out like a wraith, rising in the air to flit downstairs. Before my eyes was a vast expanse of white. I crossed tower-blocks, soughing woods and old cliffs from which emanated a cold, colourless light, as if these were forgotten places, hoary and illusory. Beside me flew a pale grey night-bird, but I knew this was no bird, it was a paper crane I had made long ago in the kitchen, which would accompany me till the end of my life.

I have been a good flier since childhood, a secret known only by me, because no one can see me flying. If I'm chased by something scary, I have only to rise lightly on my toes and I'm up on a telegraph pole. I kiss the roof-tops, afraid yet pleased, and if I want to change course that's very easy. I have only to raise or lower an arm and it's done. I am so nimble that I've never been caught, not once! Last night something went slightly wrong; I hadn't been gone long when it started to drizzle, and though the sky was still white my view was blurred, no doubt because of my tiresome cold. I grabbed hold of the branch of an old tree and perched there for a while to catch my breath. I

thought of you. Lying in your arms that day I'd
sighed as I stroked your hair and face, till I suddenly
saw you hide in a distant wood. Actually what I saw
was simply a coloured photograph, very big and stere-
oscopic, in which you appeared, disappeared and
moved about, hiding behind first one tree then another. Your face kept changing too, first into that of my
uncle, then my cousin, then into what seemed —   yet
wasn't — your real self. I've heard that nowadays
there is a kind of photograph that's like a video cassette. I heard that one day in an imaginary empty
room, and it made an unforgettable impression.
Maybe this was a photograph like that. I was meaning
to tell you what I'd seen as you held me in your
arms, but as I opened my lips I found you'd gone
and I was lying on the grass playing make-believe with
myself! But that coloured photograph really exists.
When the fallen leaves rustle in autumn, you sit on
that high pile of logs, your chin in your hands, and
your whole body enclosed in a bell-shaped glass globe.
Once I butted my head against the wall, which
sounded like a bomb exploding. Another time I made
up my mind to find my uncle and ask him to tell me
the truth: Does this type of photograph actually exist?
Why had I been seeing it as far back as I could remember? I'd tell him: This is an extraordinary riddle;
each time I see it I find the correct answer, but as soon
as it disappears it becomes a riddle again, and the answer I'd found has completely slipped my mind. The
problem is: it won't come when called; only when
completely forgotten will it appear imposingly before
you. And the people in the photograph are definitely
not the ones you'd choose. It may be him or someone

you hadn't been thinking of, with whom you'd long
lost touch. Whoever appears it has nothing to do with
my longing. He comes without being called. I asked
my uncle, but I had no proof, speaking incoherently
with endless irrelevant comparisons, so that he was as-
tounded —   that was all.

This tiresome drizzle is freezing. I dare not go back
like this, because wet weather throws me off balance.
Each time you impulsively kissed my lips, I said,
"Darling." And then I promptly turned pale and icy
cold, looking right and left to avoid imaginary wasps.
So later I took care not to say "darling" again. I
swallowed it back, silently smoothing your hair with
my fingers. But you could sense it all the same, you
knew what I had in mind, and you still turned pale
and trembled, your expression frozen like a mask. And
wordlessly you said: "My left leg is atrophied, yet
you've mistaken me for a man crouching by the river
at dusk to play ducks and drakes. You've made this
mistake more than twice." You implied that I
shouldn't imagine that by flying I could penetrate
through anything —   I couldn't. Take yourself for instance. Because you were a much bigger riddle than
the photograph, and as even your existence was in
question I shouldn't be so sure that you existed; for
one morning you might vanish into the   crowd,
becoming one of countless strange faces; and I might
not go away, just realizing that you weren't the man
playing ducks and drakes at dusk. Then I'd go, well
aware of my own flightiness and laughing foolishly.

This rain wouldn't be stopping yet awhile; I remembered a stone tower outside the wood where I could go
and rest. "An orange pleasure-boat cruises over the

sea, trailing a thin red thread, and an old man coughs. Your conviction is really strange." Sitting in a bell-shaped glass globe you spoke impassively. After leaving the wood I realized that there was no tower; it wasn't by the wood but in the sea, with a green light on top. I had seen it when I was ten and found it as hard to forget as that coloured photograph. The first photograph had appeared on the cabinet by my bed when I was eight; in its background was a green meadow; in the middle a boy in sky-blue embroidered shorts was playing football. When I flicked the picture he winked and kicked out mischievously. I couldn't take my eyes off him. I circled round and round the open ground because many little creatures were moving to and fro there, among them boars and panthers, and I didn't dare alight rashly. Gliding hastily up and down, I recognized the cliff where the two of us had lain. Seen from above it was a round black splodge, like gangrene on a pale grey body.

As I lay on the cliff I felt your palms, soft and warm. The sunlight had turned your moustache a reddish brown. Tossing heavily about, you made cracks in the cliff, and countless sparrows soared up in fright to the clouds. When I told you my feelings you were so startled you snatched up a pebble and crushed it into pieces. "Nothing exists." You raised one arm and swung it in an enormous arc, while transparent butterflies, one after another, fluttered lazily, slantingly, from behind your back. "I can fly." I aroused myself again to debate with you. "Your hands are really beautiful. When I made paper cranes I cried." You winked cryptically and said, "It's the same. Many man-made things confirm that we don't exist, we're simply butterflies flitting about at random. When you feel the palms of my hands, they may actually belong to someone else who has long since disappeared into the crowd. That feeling stays for a long time on your face, but this has nothing to do with that man. You may search for him but can never be sure you've found him. Sometimes he plays ducks and drakes by the river at dusk, sometimes appears on a tower, sometimes casts his net from the prow of a boat — each time it's someone different. You have to attach the image which captivates you to one person after another, and each time it is realistic and moving. Those men give their flesh, blood and spirit to this model, so that it is soul-stirring, forever young. But you...." "Why kiss me?" You didn't answer; your delicate fingers on the palms of my hands gripped them like rubber bands till an angrily pulsing blood-vessel broke, and blood trickled out to crawl slowly like a bright red leech over the back of my hand.

The year that I was fifteen I fell and injured my leg. While in bed I folded several thousand paper cranes. One morning I stuck my thin, greenish neck out of the window. The frosty wind pierced me to the bone, but the noisy bustling crowds outside kept me watching until dark, and ice and frost riveted me to the window sill. I nearly had to have my arms amputated. I remembered those paper cranes were of various lovely colours (my imaginary colours), dainty and stylish. Finally one day a young man looking like you came into my room, saw the paper cranes tossed on the floor and after a long silence bent down as if he wanted to pick them all up. I hastily trod on the one he was reaching for. Our glances, clashing, sparked off a row of stars, and I saw a scar at the corner of his temple. He was me: how well I knew that scarred face. All I've said is your past history; we've met many times; I was the girl who made the paper cranes; of course this isn't in the least apparent.

The rain has stopped; I must fly back. I shall meet you again by chance in an imaginary empty room or on the gangrenous cliff. You will impulsively kiss my lips, and next time I shall certainly say:

"You are he, I am that girl, on the river bank, the light-house, the prow of a boat, on the beach under the fierce midday sun, or in the grove of fragrant osmanthus at dusk. In the warm drizzle of the south red rosebuds will open, a snow-white figure will stand in the smoke-coloured mist."

Translated by Gladys Yang

Can Xue, born in 1953 in Changxue, Hunan, began to publish stories in 1985, and her works have been translated into English, French and Japanese. This is her third story.

Blue Sky and Green Sea

Liu Suola

> *When I find myself in times of trouble,*
> *Mother Mary comes to me,*
> *Speaking words of wisdom:*
> *Let it be.*
> *And in my hour of darkness*
> *She is standing right in front of me,*
> *Speaking words of wisdom:*
> *Let it be.*
> *Whisp' ring words of wisdom:*
> *Let it be.*

— The Beatles

I quote this passage from a Beatles lyric not to show that I know English, only a friend of mine gets drunk one day and translates it into Chinese and reads it out, and I' ve never known what it' s about before. But he reads it so choppily, the way drunks do, that I' d never be able to reproduce his original, so I might as well keep it in English. Everyone argues about how really to translate " Let it be", and I' d be the last person to know: I *want* to explain it the way my friend does. He says it' s " bloody well leave off" .

You might well tell a friend to " bloody well leave off" if he got drunk again and told you that listening to " Let it be" lying in a recording studio was almost like listening to it in the bath, because that's where I am at the time, in this massive recording studio flat out on a deep purple carpet, with a cold draught creeping quietly up and down and the drummer asleep hugging his beloved tape recorder as it moans on and on, " Let it be, let it be ."

I'm a female vocalist, and I might be on my way to stardom . There are a lot of singing stars in town, even more than there are poets . Fling a stone anywhere, they say, and you'll crack a poet on the skull, but to be a singing star all you've got to be able to do is cough and there's hope .

I've lost count myself of the years I've been singing . I probably wanted to be a singer at birth, but I never could make it . This is the first time in my twenty-four-year-old life of song that I've been in a recording studio, where I've longed to be, like a serious star, with earphones on and a mike in front of me and all this bulky recording equipment on for me . I've always thought it must be even more fascinating than the stage . But once inside the big studio, I find the whole band browbeaten by the sound man and all their usual swagger and sparkle gone . That's why I'm left all on my own in the corner listening to " Let it be" on the carpet .

They tell me at the record company that my picture's been taken to Hongkong to be made into a tape cover, and the band say that I'm set to take the music business by storm, leaving everyone else at a loss like a new sun bursting out of the sky, and all that goes with it: continual performances, recordings, discs, tapes, flowers and money . No doubt if Manzi was alive she' d say I " wasn' t up to it" , because she never thought of flowers and things; she just went at it and sang and sang for all she was worth, and her songs could make me cry just like a Christian with a vision of God .

I have to laugh at myself whenever I think of her, which I know is doing myself down . It gives me stage fright to think of her, especially when I' ve signed a contract . Sometimes I sink into a limbo as if I was just singing to her, without knowing what I' m on about . The critics say I' m the " dreamy" type . I know half the house don' t know what I' m really singing or why or what the song' s *actually* about, not even where to applaud and where to keep quiet . They never know that I don' t need the applause at all . I' d be infinitely grateful for even five seconds' quiet during the interval . Yesterday at a university concert I sang for the first time the song I wrote for Manzi, a hard one that had the sweat pouring off me and ruined my voice . All I wanted was for it to touch her, not for her soul to up and abandon me to the audience' s cheers . When I got back to the hotel at night I lay on the bed just wanting to pull out my vocal cords and throw them out of the window, hoping I would turn into a mute, a real mute, and stop fussing about talking and talking . I wondered if they' d get cancer one day from exhaustion . I opened my mouth wide, imagining I really had cancer in there . There was an empty feeling in my throat . I coughed as hard as I could and actually still made a noise . I switched on the table lamp, took a small roll of adhesive tape from my vanity case, snipped off a long strip of it and stuck my lips together with it . If my vocal cords wouldn' t come out, I' d just have to seal my mouth up to stop any noise slipping out unawares. I sealed it up then lay down and went to sleep. I dreamt vaguely all night and waking in the morning saw a telegram stuffed under the door: " Come record soonest ."

2

I was told ages ago that a recording session's nothing like a stage performance. You can sing until only your tongue's moving on stage, and there'll still be people to go wild about you. Here you can put all the expression you've got into it and still get just a " One more time" from the sound man. Nobody's going to tell you one more time for a quarter tone sharp on stage. Here, with gadgets of all sizes staring at you, you can't even breathe wrong. This could be the one place you get real " art" . I doubt if I'm really an artist, because I sing until my voice cracks up .

The studio's paint scheme, all deep purple, black-green and dark brown, makes it specially conspicuous with the drummer lying on the floor clapping in his pale yellow sweatshirt. I was wearing a yellow top in the photo that was going on the tape cover too, with blue sky and green sea in the background. Manzi took it one evening of non-stop laughter on a summer holiday at the seaside, which is why I'm grinning from ear to ear in it. The cover designer wants a new one done of me on the same lines, but I doubt if I'm up to laughing like that any more. I'm a stickler about friendship, inflexible you might say, and I've never had anything like it with anyone but Manzi. No doubt the word " love" can be abused, but *friendship* is

much more sacred a thing. I just couldn't laugh, let
alone all over again for a tape cover, in that top, in
that place; I couldn't stand that. I nearly went crazy
the first time Mr Ding my teacher took me along to an
"artists'" salon, when all I knew was singing, not
"stardom" and I still imagined watching a real
"star" magically retail cliches. Having life's simplest
truths sung by a star is much more comfortable than
reading a novel. I'd never seen any "star" but
Manzi. I felt that one day I'd smash all the tape
recorders in the world when I finally came up against
great   "stars",   but   the   memory   of   that
"artists'" salon is one of shame. There was a man
there with fifteen years' vocal training behind him, who
roguishly murdered *Traviata* and then went on to a
rendition   of   "Green   Grass   and   Sweet
Wildflowers" that had everyone blushing: he'd have
been so much better as a shoeshine boy. When he was
through he announced that he was giving up opera for
pop, because there was more money in it. He was obviously trying to do a Sada and hadn't got one note
right. It was all I could do to hide my face behind my
glass. Hard upon this came an effeminate man with a
guitar, swooning with enthusiasm in the manner of a
Hongkong female vocalist to the bravoes of either sex
all around. Mr Ding, blushing, tried his best to avoid
my eyes. Manzi, looking at me through the glass,
waved her long fingers at me expressionlessly, without
once winking. I smiled at her rather awkwardly, and
she lowered her eyes.

3

I put my coat over me, because my back's cold. I've

hardly lived anywhere long for years. I long to settle
but never can. Lu Sheng has had God's own patience
with me over that. He never objects to anything I do
and never encourages me to do anything either.

He grew up with me, and we know each other like
the backs of our hands. He isn't a great talker. He
hasn't wanted to talk for years and has just ended up
not doing. He's a great guitar player. A guitar in his
hands seems to have a soul, and a splendid one too.
He accompanied me without a word when Manzi died
and I signed my first performing contract. I couldn't
have sung to anybody else's guitar. Thoughts of
Manzi forced us to avoid the topic of marriage: both
of us wretchedly clung to friendship instead.

I clamber off the floor and go to the telephone
booth, for some reason feeling a desire to make a
phone call, without knowing who to. Listlessly I pick
up the receiver. Dialing a number will bring any familiar voice, but Manzi isn't on the phone. I hang up,
then lift the receiver again. Maybe I should call Mr
Ding, as this tape is the result of his dashing about on
my behalf, but I'm afraid of botching the whole thing.
I suspect that instead of the splash hit he expects I'll
be a flash in the pan, because I can't get a sound out.

The sound man tells the drummer to turn off the din
of his tape recorder and then has him go to the drums
and play with no let up, until he throws his sticks on
the floor streaming with sweat and yells at him. Not a
man to take directions, he'd play *Ten Gongs and
Drums* if you asked him for country rock.

4

I was born in a big city, where you could go for a

year at a stretch without bumping into anyone you knew. I've been singing all my life and only came across Mr Ding after Manzi died. It was his doing that my singing career saw the daylight. He wanted me to be an actress when he met me, not a singer at all. I failed in every part, and then my singing voice surprised him. He had a police dog's nose for "artists". He was a bit off, though, because Manzi died. On her deathbed, in that pale yellow top like mine, she looked every inch the film star. She gave me a merry laugh, and I laughed too. The top suited her to a tee, needless to say. I'd always thought of her as dusky, not realizing how pale she was. Lu Sheng played the guitar nonstop up to the cremation. It was covered with blood from his fingers. The expression on her face was as if she'd signed a contract, and death doesn't seem frightening now.

It was exactly as if she'd signed a contract. She hadn't a care in the world. Once she cut the back of her hand climbing a wall, and a soft tendon poked out of the wound. I went white, but she laughed fit to burst. Manzi and I were a headache to my parents, who thought we were a "distracting influence" on each other. I never saw them sorry for her until the day after the cremation. They needn't have been.

I waved at her and ran like the wind out of the crematorium, racing alongside a bus, which didn't take too long to leave me way behind. I swore as I ran, all the way to my room, where Lu Sheng was already sitting. I wanted to sing, but the sight of his guitar made me sick. The way it was splotched red and brown just turned my stomach. I looked out from the twelfth floor, where we lived, into the distance, where a factory chimney belched livid smoke. The sky, the buildings, the smoke, everything was such a clean grey, so bloody clean. I sang *Yesterday*, a global hit then.

No doubt if everybody knew my mother was a serious contralto and my father just as serious a pianist, they'd all be going on about how my present success was inevitable given their patronage or about how utterly I'd let them down. Decades ago — I can't really remember how old I was — somebody asked me, "Do you want to be a musician?" I remember saying I'd just "give it a go". I adored the first prelude and fugue in Bach's *Well-tempered Clavier*, not entirely for its own sake but because a singable melody had been put to it too, which I would launch into whenever my father began it, and when he changed to the first movement of Beethoven's *Moonlight* I'd launch into the main part of that. I'd make any piano piece into a song, and if it didn't have an obvious melody I'd fit one to it, like Gounod. Equally talented composer and singer, you might think, but I never tried to make my voice come out of the top of my head. I preferred it to flow out along with the words. If everybody else was moved by my singing, my mother told me with a dismissive sneer to get on with my school work. I had a gift for mathematics, she said, whereas all I would ever achieve with music was to shame her. For me with my lack of musical "schooling", she said, it was as "brazen" as wanting to write novels without knowing any grammar.

5

Perhaps I really ought to put a call through to Mr

Ding. My throat's as dry as if it was cancered all up now. I definitely won't be able to sing, because I've never felt this listless before. If I told Lu Sheng what happened last night he'd be off to the bus without a word, with his guitar on his back and my bag in his hand. Certainly he'd get his fingers all bloody if I mentioned Manzi. One word from her, if she were here, and I'd be singing like a river in spate. She wouldn't believe me for a minute if I told her I was going to fail. With the preposterous confidence we built up since we were small, I wouldn't hang back for a minute if she told me I could blow every mind in the world. That's what I must do now, imagine as hard as I can what she looked like when she told me how great I was. That'll boost my confidence. If I don't believe it, it may still calm me down. God, every second from now on I'll suspect cancer cells spreading.

I dial Mr Ding's number and get through. No one answers for a very, very long time. The *brring-brring-brring* makes me think of a ship about to sink. Why that is I don't know.

"Hello."

"It's me."

"Mm."

"I'm at the recording studio."

"Great. Are you singing *Yesterday* to the original tune?"

I nearly wail.

"Are you still there?"

What's to say? The one song that I'm not up for singing, that I couldn't sing, that I'd do badly even if I did it better than anyone else, which I might, with John Lennon killed and Manzi dead.

"My daughter says you could do with some more forceful songs." He underlines "forceful" with a laugh.

His daughter's the type that makes the coarsest vulgarity sound like sweet, angelic song.

"There's *Ho-ha, Ho-ha*. That's disco."

"Any that you've written?"

"Too many to count."

"The tape'll be a big seller. Work hard on it."

"Thanks."

"That's all?"

"— "

"Do your best, now."

"Thanks."

He's hung up. I suppose I'd better sing, just sing, and make it more disco, then.

6

I slouch back to the sound room, where the guy on the synthesizer's losing his temper with everybody. Someone's messed up the electronic drum sequence he's just worked out. They take him a day to do, and everybody will wait till he's done a new one.

"Meteoric rise" is an overworked phrase. Almost everybody's complimented by it. If anyone used it on me, I'd fight to the death. I daresay a lot of people already know that the tape I'm doing will be quite a sensation, because I'm not run of the mill when it comes to dealing with music and the songs I write for myself. If I really make a go of it, I'll be set up for life, until the cancer really does for my vocal cords. Mr Ding thinks highly of me more for my "feeling" than my "voice". As far as voice goes, a mere nod from my mother would be fine, but that she is not going to give, not for my singing. She considers that my loose performances and their style demean me and art, whereas I get delirious with joy at the "public spirit" of my own art, knowing for sure that audiences go as wild as I do. I've sung in dark, sumptuous grand hotel bars with a few ladies and gentlemen sitting here and there who couldn't care less whether you sang or not. The most pitiful sight is singers who pull out all the stops to pander to the people with songs that are an offering of "art" rather than a part of themselves; what is thoroughly sad is that whether their faces are wreathed in smiles or a picture of suffering the people out there won't let it deflect them one little bit from their drinks and their chitchat. My mother calls it greedy of me. If I had wanted only to earn my daily bread I wouldn't need to be so serious. I met a singer on a train once who said he could record three cassettes a day with a minimum of ten songs on each, right through with his eyes closed in one breath and never mind any artistic mishaps, and earn a few thousand a tape. "Real cognac, real 555s and a dab of Paris scent on the collar, aah!" Luckily this was said to me and not to my mother, who would have had another example of art demeaned to berate me with. Quite where things went wrong is hard to say, but I doubt if an operatic diva could even sign a contract in this town: she would have to doff her crown to cognac.

The critics have appraised me far too highly. In fact not a lot of people know what I'm singing about. The critics are forever giving my pieces a high rating, like novelists, who will fabricate. If doctors said the human body only absorbed two eggs a day no one would touch a third, but nobody can make head or tail of what an artist really thinks. I'd be loath to offer a single word of explanation whether they called me a classic angel or a classic shit. I'd rather jump off a high roof than explain everything I sang. Manzi once said to Lu Sheng, "Why be so serious? Ease up," which had him dancing for joy. But he still ended up with bloody fingers. You have to understand a lot of things you don't and not understand a lot you do. Ease up.

7

I walked into Manzi's room mindlessly one afternoon and trod a chick to death. The way she burst out crying scared me out of my wits. We were both at primary school. She didn't like going, because she wasn't from town but came from a remote border area, which to me was as great and mystical as if she'd been from abroad. Her clothes and her satchel were different from mine, and she spoke with a lovely brogue.

She didn't like school, and the teacher would send me to activate her into coming with "thought work". I would make up a heap of lies to tell her about how wonderful it was at school, how happy I was playing football with the boys on the team (when in fact they'd beaten me up for losing points for them in the running races), how I'd had an essay up on the notice board (when in fact mine had been the only essay with top marks not to go up, because it had been about "villainous" flies) — but all the stories I'd made up to jolly her into school were forgotten the minute I trod on her pet chick, I was so frightened, and I told her in tears how I'd been beaten and how the teacher had singled out just my essay not to go up on the board — and when we'd had a cry together we took the chick outside and buried it, while a boy who lived nearby came up and told us how "stupid" we were. He became a writer of popular songs eventually, every one of them so indescribably common that I could never stand to hear them — ugly and vulgar — but practically every studio records them. I happened to catch one once that was so nasty as to verge on crudity — it practically turned my stomach — and I'm talking about composition so crude that no language has the words to describe it. It's a game beyond tears or laughter, but the great writer pushes his songs on everyone in a welter of enthusiasm, and if you aren't interested he gets out the music and sings you one, jigging for joy. He once gave Manzi and me a personal performance, with a mock trumpet trill followed by facial contortions, and we buried our mouths in our teacups so as not to let him see how we were laughing, which hid our mouths all right, but we were shaking. Even our eyes were running. I'll never again put up with a dabbler of a songwriter after that.

Manzi and I became best friends after we'd buried the chick, and I hung around her place daily during the holidays. She told me her big sister had a song book in her room "with all foreign stuff in it", and we decided to steal it. One day the sister was installed with every evidence of comfort at the desk reading a book with her legs up and her feet in the open treasure drawer, rocking back on the chair. She was really skinny, and try as I would later I could never get both feet in the drawer the way she did without falling off the chair. The song book was in a corner of the draw. Manzi went up to her and dropped a teacup. It broke, and the sister screamed, whipped her feet out of the drawer and scrabbled after the pieces for her. I ran up with a washbasin to collect the shards but slipped and fell on top of them, and while I howled and her sister comforted me, Manzi contrived to manoeuvre herself in front of the drawer and "steal" the book. We fell about afterwards, and Manzi ran and stole two ciga- rettes of her father's too, which we puffed at, pre- tending to be street boys. She was superb, actually gulping down the smoke and letting it trail out of her nostrils. She buried her head in the bed and shouted that it ached. I opened the book, and every song in it was about "love". I tried to sing one but dried up when I got to the word, and she grabbed it from me and started again, but she got no further than I had. Then we sang "love" together softly and went as red as beetroots, as fidgety as if we'd committed every crime there was. Two days later her sister demanded the return of the book. She'd seen through the ruse at the time, she said: "I knew the kind of shit you were up to the minute you tilted your arses." Manzi begged for another two days, and her sister said scorn- fully, ''What the hell do you know about it, kid?'' But she gave her the book. That got us busy. We managed to learn at least three a day and sang them wherever we went, even out loud on the streets and the buses eventually, and I can confidently claim we were one of the best duos in the world, because an old fellow walking past us called us idiots.

8

The drummer's in a fight with the synthesizer guy, who insists on dragging hundreds of electronic percussion rhythms into the accompaniment: it wouldn't sound anywhere near as good as if he could play it himself, he says. Boring, says the synthesizer guy: you couldn't do rhythms that complicated to save your life. I wouldn't want to, says the drummer.

Our neighbours are all "musicians". The minute you walk through the main entrance you see shades of Bach and Mozart, for whom I have always been filled with reverence, to the point of utter disbelief in such divine music having actually been written, of feeling that no human could have composed it and that neither Bach nor Mozart ever existed as men.

The smell of the people in the corridor hits you whenever you walk into it. Any inhabited building has a smell. Mother's frowns began when Manzi and I started going in and out all the time with a guitar singing foreign pop songs with no temperance, discrimination or sense of occasion. She would send me off to bed before nine-thirty. "You go home now!" she would say to Manzi if she was there, not giving ground. She got quite mad at me once for belting out a pop song I'd actually written and set to music myself about the cigarette incident. "What's wrong with you?" she said, storming in.

"Wrong?"

"What's that you're singing?"

"I'm learning composition, aren't't I?" I looked at her over the guitar.

"What was that about cigarettes? Have you ever

smoked one? How do you know what it's like?''

"It's art, isn't it?''

"Art! It's crap!''

Fancy: "crap'' from mother!

I got up and took the guitar on to the balcony without a murmur. I was in junior high school, and songs of love — whatever that might be — no longer raised a blush. I swore because of that "crap'' to write two hundred more songs about cigarettes and love, though the vow got forgotten because of Manzi.

Manzi's face came out in spots in the third year of junior high. She was restless and excitable. She scared me by suddenly announcing one day that she had a boyfriend. "Are you afraid?'' She shook her head. "Is it fun?'' She laughed out loud. I twisted my head away when she came to kiss me. For some reason I felt sick to think that her mouth and face had been kissed by a man I didn't know. Still, I wrote her a love song. I couldn't bear to watch the way she always sang it with her eyes closed. "Why aren't you happy?'' she shouted at me. "Why aren't you happy for me?''

9

The very thought of Manzi and the love she bore to all and sundry makes me suspect all the more I have cancer. No one can see Manzi still loving now; the living are always thoughtless. No one will notice that gorgeous yellow top of hers, or that she and I once wore the same, and even the blue sky and green sea on the cassette cover will change with reproduction into a kind of publicity shot. I suppose I shall look affected, grinning at everybody out of that cover in the yellow top. The same photo feels very different in an advertising frame or on something for sale than in my collection. A writer I knew once told me that he was never so hurt as when he was called a writer, as if it was a synonym for bastard or lout. He played a game with me by producing a photograph of a woman and saying, "Put a job to her." "Film actress," I said, from which angle she had a distinctly pensive air. "Writer," I said next, and that made her patently pretentious. It's sad. I wonder if a synonym for pop star is idiot. And it occurs to me to wonder whether a cameraman lighting the face of the androgyne mimicking a female vocalist would weep.

The synthesizer guy's having a go at the electric bass player now, who has a hard time keeping up with the rhythms programmed by the former, the difficulty of which strikes terror into his heart and which the synthesizer guy can't keep on playing. The bassist mops his brow and pounds the fingerboard as the spots on his face get redder. The band has sworn to make this a quality tape in order to smash the opposition, who are as numerous as matchboxes. Almost all the band are bachelors, those with wives having got shut of them and those with girlfriends having broken with them, except for the band leader, who's been thrown out by his old lady. They do gigs all over the place and never stay anywhere long. All they ever do apart from daily rehearsals, performances and recordings is sunbathe, joke around and eat well, like overgrown kids. Mother sniffs at the very mention of people like that, as if they were an offence against decency. I really can't see why people who aspire to be thought civilized pour the utmost scorn on the likes of us and people who don't aspire to be thought anything worship the first Tom, Dick or Harry of a pop star that comes along. There was one performance where the star gulped for breath twice a line like a hooting owl, but the folks went wild, and the applause raised the roof. Our electric guitarist said it was spring in the air, a figure of speech I had to ask three people about before I understood what he meant.

Manzi and I gave a little concert one evening with Lu Sheng accompanying us. She was in the worst of moods. She'd broken up with the boyfriend, but she was pregnant. She sang in floods of tears, often couldn't get a sound out. I'd never heard such moving singing in my life and almost wanted to sing everything the way she did, suddenly discovering that random silences were more moving than sounds. It would never have occurred to her that I harboured so base a design while she sang. She was doing a number I adore to this day, with words by her and music by me. None of us knew where to put ourselves when she'd done. I hid my face in tobacco smoke, terrified she'd see my eyes. She was the only one among us who would expose her very self, and it made other people feel awkward by contrast when she did. She looked at all of us and just said, "I know what everyone needs." There was nothing but tobacco smoke in the room for a long while, till I gave them the Beatles' *Yellow Submarine* to perk things up, thinking blue skies and green seas would be diverting, but I stopped short. Suddenly I wasn't in the mood, and I couldn't forgive myself. Forever sticking my nose in to perk people up is my worst failing.

10

I must tell Mr Ding there's no way I can sing. Seize the hour. I clamber up from the carpet, go to the telephone booth and actually get through as soon as I dial. "Hello?"

It's him. "It's me."

"What, again? Aren't you recording yet?"

"They're quarrelling."

"What did you all have for lunch?"

"Beef."

"Don't drink too much water while you're singing."

"I won't."

"Any mistakes in the part scores?"

"Tons."

"Tell your band leader not to use that copyist any more."

"Mm."

"He's too easily led, that leader of yours."

"Yes."

"He'd do better spending more time and keeping up quality, tell him. I've just been sent a sample tape by another band. Shoddy, quite shoddy."

"Mm."

"I'd sing along while they're recording the band if I were you and get you used to each other rather than moon around."

"Um — "

"That all?"

"Yeah."

"Good luck."

"Thanks."

I go back to the studio, and the last thing I want is for me and the band to get used to each other. It's far too late to get any more acquainted than we are.

We'd a date to see a film the day Manzi had her accident. Lu Sheng and I had the fright of our lives when we went into her room. She was lying pallid on the floor in a pool of blood. I ran to her and held her; she was calling out. "Get me to a hospital. Get me to a hospital." We carried her out, into the street, where the only thing we could hire was a flatbed trike. That trip to the hospital was the longest I've taken in my life. She huddled on the flatbed, and the blood kept coming. Neither of us liked to ask her what had happened, and when the nurse in casualty did ask I said, "Something gynaecological," and she wheeled her off to the emergency gynaecology ward. She was back in a bit, asking, "Does either of you know what she's taken?" Lu Sheng and I just stood there. "Honestly, you young people! Time's running out!" "What's happened?" I shouted. "Don't you know?" "Tell us!" "She tried to give herself an abortion. She took something for it." "Is she in danger?" I wailed. "It's hard to say." The nurse was grim. "You young people don't use the brains you've got. You're degenerate." I could have gone up and punched her.

Manzi'd lost a lot of blood. The hospital sent for her whole family, while Lu Sheng and I watched the life ebbing out of her body. He went home specially at her request to fetch his guitar. She was too weak to sing by then, but she opened her mouth to demand I sing *My Heart Belongs to Me* for her. I was choked, not in imitation this time but for real: I couldn't get a

note out. The mere act of singing repelled me. We'd
been fooled. What the hell did they mean, "My Heart
Belongs to Me"? We've no way of completely
stopping our hearts belonging to someone else.

11

I doubt if anyone else in the world understands
singers. Certainly not all singers understand each
other. I expect most only think of the competition and
the money. I find it very moving the odd time I see
singers quite engrossed in performing their own music,
not that it happens often; more frequently they're like
actors in a play, woodenly going through the motions
of the worst heartbreak. I truly marvel whether they
have souls in there or not. "Degenerate" the nurse
would have called them, but I know what
undegenerate people are like. I was watching an im-
ported war film when at a shot of a woman stark naked, though they only showed her from the waist up,
a middle-aged man in front of me got up out of his
seat as if the shot was a window at home — a
suave, middle-aged man in spectacles, definitely not the
sort to sing his heart out in the street to a guitar, let
alone throw all up for love.

Neither the dilettantes that ordinary people call us
nor the pop artists that other artists call us quite gets
it: no one knows but yourself what you are. I'm seldom comfortable in the company of artists. Manzi and
I once went to a young painter's place to see his
work. "See," he said in subdued tones as he took
out his most recent masterpiece: "Humanity can never
ascend." It was of a man standing on a high cliff

with his hands raised to the sky but a black thread wound fast round his foot. This "sable vine of worldliness", as the painter called it, extended downwards right into a woman's hand. There was a butterfly in the bottom left-hand corner and a patch of red in the top right. At the top was a white circle, the sun, he said, as white stood for infinity, just as the butterfly and the red stood for sex. It would have been perfectly admirable as a pretty abstract needing no explanation, but it was intolerable that what seemed a collage of shoddy publicity pictures should claim to stand for a philosophy. On the subject of music he expatiated on Richard Strauss, would you believe? Anyway, we were not about to launch into *Thus Spoke Zarathustra*.

If I have one secret wish, in fact, it would be to share a stage with a real singer, to cooperate, not compete. Something like Domingo and Denver. Far from resenting them, I get quite carried away, but the eternal problem is they would be ashamed to appear with me. I envy them the breathing that holds the melody on and on and the mastery of musical cohesion that I'd like to use in my own songs. I think all mankind has the same reverence for music. The only difference is God's gift of a voice. I want my songs to shake off the inferior pop style, but I doubt if most musicians would ever make allowances for my voice. I write for the kids and for the adults like them, telling them to walk slowly in the snow, telling them not only birds fly, telling them of sorrow and joy, telling them my love for them is free.

Manzi would look so dreamily into the sky that she'd drop what she was holding. She'd go that way during a meal sometimes, mouthing her chopsticks

till I rapped her over the skull with mine. She sat by
me once with a picture book held up to the open
door, eyes front and the book cover straight in her
hands as if she was showing it to someone in the doorway. I looked at her, and I looked out. There was no
one there. I laughed out loud and hit her. "What are
you looking at?" All at once she laughed too.
"Don't know." "I suspect," Mother used to say,
"that that child is not quite normal in the head." I
disagree. During a meal at home, after Manzi's death,
I once burst out laughing, on and on, and couldn't
stop however I tried, because the girl in my mind
laughing at me wouldn't let me and made me want to
laugh whenever I saw her. Mother was scared to death
and slapped my face hard, which only made me worse.
I was frightened myself but couldn't stop for the girl
laughing on and on in my mind. At last I burst into
tears, and Lu Sheng came up and handed me a glass
of red wine, which made we cry all the harder, and
Mother could never work out whether we were not
quite normal or she was.

12

Manzi became timid after she got pregnant. She was
afraid of anything, and though she seldom said so, the
tiniest noise had her trembling. I wanted her to go to
the hospital, but she wouldn't. She was frightened of
doctors. She'd been for a checkup and lied that she
was thirty; the doctor hadn't believed her and had
shouted at her like someone abusing a dog, and she
hadn't dared go back. She was for ever singing *Help!*
and *Don't let me down!* Her man went off with anoth-

er woman, and I hated all the men and women in the world, because we were girls. I even wanted to stay a girl all my life and never be a woman. She took me climbing with her and ran up for all she was worth to try and lose the child, then when she'd got to the very top she'd walk out to a cliff, to see if she'd slip and fall, I think, because she wouldn't have dared just jump. When we listened to music she'd sometimes dance madly until she threw up. One day she ran out into the rain with her guitar and held it up to the sky to be watered, held it up in both hands till the soundbox was full to the brim and then came indoors, solemnly and silently. There was nothing I could say. I knew she probably hated me for the unfairness of it.

I discover my tears running down the corners of my eyes and on to the carpet; my back is frozen. I know Manzi hates me. I in my entirety lie on the stuido floor preparing to sing "I love — ", and she, fragmented, surveys it all. She lives so far away now, through a pitch-black tunnel and then over thousands of miles of uninhabited desert. There are lots of stone steps up the mountain, and all the trees that aren't just a splash of colour have circular leaves with holes in the middle. The house she lives in only has two windows made of three slats and nestles against a hill where nothing but black and white shadow grows. Further up is a mountain with only half left, whether the rest has been eaten by clouds or was never there, and nothing but black and white shadow on it too. All you see when you go into her room are unintelligible lyrics. Perhaps Manzi's in love with another man. Perhaps she's pregnant again.

Whatever you do, Manzi, don't take any more of that medicine.

Don't forget the song you liked Manzi *My Heart Belongs to Me* don't forget telling fortunes by stripping hibiscus petals when we were young don't forget disbelief isn't your forte don't forget the other things you'll never think of —

13

"You'll catch cold like that." The band leader comes across, and I turn over and sit up. "Tell me, are you interested in going on working with the band?" I laugh. "You'll be surprised when we've done recording. Is that me singing?" I simply turn my laugh into a grin without moving. His aim is after all to make me laugh. "I'll tell you a joke. It's the entrance exam for the ballet school. The examiner calls 'One-eighty-five!', and in comes a fellow with bow legs." The band leader does a bowlegged walk. "The instructor frowns when he sees him and says, 'To dance ballet you have to point your toes out with your heels together. Can you do that?' The fellow turns round" — The band leader sticks his arse out at me with his toes together — "and says 'like thith, thir?'" I start to laugh, but he does three more turns and still has his toes pointed in. I have no idea why I'm laughing. "Anyway, the instructor tells him he can go and calls, 'One-eighty-six!' and the same fellow comes back in. 'What are you doing back?' He says. 'I didn't think I'd path,' says the fellow, 'tho I put me name down twithe.'" I roar. "That's all for now, folks," says the band leader and walks off cockily. I'm still laughing. I feel like it, but I'm frightened I won't be able to stop. I hug my knees against my forehead. That damned exam with the toes turned in has my shoulders shaking with laughter, when all of a sudden the drummer sings "Never forget!" into the mike in English like some foreign star, and it brings me up cold as I manage to understand the phrase.

I run to the hamper, open some braised chicken and tear off a thigh, which I throw into the waste bin after just one bite. I realize I haven't made a sound all day and should run to the microphone for the feeling, should at least get Lu Sheng to play along with me, but I'm a bit scared of him at the moment, scared he'd play without being sure about me, try to smile and not feel sick about my recording, scared he won't blame me at all for putting the yellow top on the tape cover. But I have to be estranged from myself before I can be a stranger to all feeling, to all people, and do this blasted thing in cold blood. I'll be able to forget about myself and everyone as long as I sing, seeing nothing, whoever my eyes may be on, able to go wild, an image almost of terror in the song, I'm sure, as long as I sing.

"Never forget!" intones the drummer into the mike again.

"You eat pretty fast," says the band leader; "You've had practically nothing."

"I don't want anything, just some hot water."

"Over there."

I go and pour myself a cup from the thermos.

"Guess this one," says the electric guitarist. "Half a dozen brothers, sitting round a stake; if they let go hands, their coats all break. What are they?''

I watch them carefully as they all try to guess, but I don't understand a word they say.

"Garlic!'' The synthesizer guy gets it quickly, and everybody sees it at once except me. I still don't understand.

"Smart lad!'' says the electric guitarist.

"Why?'' I ask dully, still turning over "Never forget'' in my mind.

"You are stupid if you still don't get that,'' says the synthesizer guy.

They must think I'm a blockhead. I pour myself another cup.

"You can't say that about the star of the show!''

I smirk amusement.

"How much are you getting for singing on this tape?''

I blush and smirk again.

"You know the great Mr Bei? He's due to sing once, the audience all applauding the minute he's announced on stage, and he just sits backstage not moving a muscle. 'Mr Bei,' says the manager, 'you're on.' He holds out one hand: 'A hundred.' The manager's thunderstruck. 'I thought we said fifty.' 'A hundred, or no performance.' 'Sixty?' 'A hundred!' More applause from the front of the house. 'Please, seventy.' 'A hundred.' The audience is crying out. 'Eighty.' 'A hundred!' The manager — ''

I'm back in the studio, not knowing whether this Mr Bei sang or not. I freely admit to not being disgusted by money, and I might have liked it even more if I'd never known Manzi, but we'd have been the last of the big spenders if we'd been big spenders at

at all. We split whatever money either of us had evenly, and one of us always found a way to make it up if
the other one was short. If we only had enough for a
pair of the slacks we'd decide it was better spent on a
meal for two, and if we didn't even have enough for
that we'd both go through our wardrobes for clothes
worth something second hand and spend what the
shop gave us on a meal. We used to fantasize, when
she was alive, about having enough money one day to
go on a grand tour, just the two of us. She never put
her boyfriend in these fantasies, yet a couple of days
away from him and she'd be in a state of collapse. I
don't think I had her back under orders until the day
she died.

14

I try opening my mouth, but I can't make a sound. I
try again, but nothing comes out. That's the end, I
think, and good riddance too. People do sink low
enough to hope something'll happen to them, and
then they break down when it does. When Manzi and
I left middle school we dressed to catch eyes. If everybody else was in fashion gear, we wore what they
didn't wear any more or didn't dare, totally convinced that weird garb on us had charm: old men's
hats and shoes, old women's jackets and suchlike. We
floated down the street on the consciousness of our
own beauty, not deigning to notice everyone's eyes on
us, even thinking vocal duets on buses perfectly natural. Our spring blouses were of the material other people made quilt covers out of. Mother would scold me
for lack of dress sense. On holidays we would go out

to the park in patched (or quite unpatched) rags. Mother railed at me and said I was a "disgrace to the city". We sang a song we made out of Burns' "Integrity there's ne'er a whit in/propriety though ne'er sae fittin'". Whitman was just fantastic: "Whether or not I wear a hat indoors or out is entirely a matter of my own happiness." In fact Manzi stopped doing herself up when she got pregnant, and she lost her complexion, as if she had turned into an old woman all at once. She smoked doggedly, and she kept saying I'm old, I'm old. Why do they never talk about those things in the songs?

Where I once thought that legitimate music was heavenly and pop music was earthly, I now detect the total heavenliness of pop: why does it just go on about love, heartbreak and loneliness and not humiliation, abortion and death? Heartbreak, loneliness and love are enjoyment, and humiliation, abortion and death are the only true stuff of life. To sing of them though would be hellish, so no one does.

I forget when it was that I suddenly recognized some kids learning to paint and mentioned it to Manzi, who took a particular fancy to it, bought a full set of brushes and paints and produced a daub which, when she showed it to me, I found particularly objectionable. I, who had no interest in the painters, told her she shouldn't paint. All at once she was in tears, saying it was because I didn't want her to see them and wanted them all to myself. I wrote a letter that ran to forty pages to verify that I meant nothing of the sort, which made it up between us, but she never painted again. If I spent the whole recording fee on the finest materials for you, Manzi, would you come back and paint?

I lie down on the floor again in a denim suit, no respecter of places. I always dressed as a boy at middle school and in the evenings when I walked in the park with Manzi, for fear that two girls would attract undesirables. I dressed as a boy and swaggered along with my arm around her shoulder. We always felt like laughing but maintained a respectable silence when we saw anyone coming. When we really were approached by dubious lads I was so scared my calves just flexed. We would have liked our husbands and us to make a foursome — the word was always on our lips — but Lu Sheng ignored the other man. Neither of them was the first to speak when we did drag them together. The four of us went to the park once, and Manzi and I gabbled on together while they actually followed behind us not saying a word. It was so awkward that I felt guilty towards her, though in fact if she really had had a husband it would have made a mockery of everything we stood for. Perhaps a foursome isn't an acceptable state to anyone.

You scramble out of bed first thing, Manzi, and go into the kitchen to boil your husband an egg and put the kettle on, then wake him up. You debate the day's menu over breakfast: "The price of tomatoes is up again." "We won't have any, then." "Shall we have cucumber?" "Up to you." Then you bustle off to work, where you wonder what to buy for dinner afterwards, what new clothes to get him, how to budget, how to arrange the room. You leave work with a big net shopping bag on your bicycle and a bunch of veg clamped on the rack. You go upstairs and in through the door, take off your coat and put on an apron, give your hands a brisk wash and start washing vegetables, cooking, sweeping up and tipping rubbish. You've begun putting on weight, the skin on your fingers is turning coarse and dry, and there are in-grained black marks in your palm lines. "Are your happy?" "He's considerate." They won't sneer when you're pregnant this time. People will give up their seats to you on the bus, and it'll be such an easy birth. You want to hold her and kiss her every day: no time to bother about figure or clothes; you scarcely sing any more, and you don't go blank. Sud-denly one day you think of me, and you bustle round to see me, chatter about the family and bustle off again. You talk jubilantly about your child in minute detail, not caring whether or not I want to hear. You sing if I beg you, listlessly and off key. You tell me your child is going to be a musician.

You scrimp and save to buy her a piano so that she can take over where you left off. A chip off the old block, you call her, a thing of greater perfection than you. You force her to play from the age of five; she won't, she cries, and you hit her and drag her by the arm up on to the piano stool. She plays and exercises by Beyor and Czerny with tears in her eyes, and the minute you're gone she runs off to play jump-rope. She hates you and your piano and your sheet music. She brings a boy home secretly one day to break the piano strings for her with pliers. That worries you, and you get a repairer in. At the very least it gets her out of practising for a couple of days or months, de-pending how good you are at getting one. You have her sit for music primary school, music middle school and music college, and she comes out of college a pianist, who sits on stage dignified and cultivated and plays things you've never heard before. You're proud of her; you're moved by her; you love her more than you love yourself. But I know that if I asked her to write a song for you she'd never manage one decent line. She couldn't throw herself into *My Heart Belongs to Me* the way you could. She couldn't stare blankly at the sky the way you could. What kind of a chip of the old block is that? You're all sitting round, the whole family, one day with your daughter at the piano, and you're so happy you get carried away and sing one of your songs, and she just says, "You're quite off key, mum." It brings you up short, and secretly you start to cry. What kind of a chip of the old block is that?

15

"Phone call for you!"

"For me?" Who could be calling me? Manzi? I go to the phone booth.

"It's me." It's Mr Ding's daughter.

"Anything up?"

"I heard you were recording, and I wanted to tell you what to sing."

"What?"

"*Let it be.*"

"Why that particularly?"

"I hate that man and woman stuff."

"Why?"

"I just do."

"Why do you just do?"

"Just me."

" It' s not in my repertoire ."

" Why not?"

" It just isn' t ."

" You do talk nonsense ."

" You should tell that to your dad ."

" Do you think I haven' t? He doesn' t even listen to his wife ."

" Who is your mother ."

" Well she' s his wife ."

" Fine, then, you little horror: first you sing something to me ."

" All right . Listen ." She sings into the phone: " Love is in the air; I see it everywhere — "

" Get knotted!" I bang the receiver down. And I want to hear her sing it through and to talk to her .

I feel dirty, dirtier the more ancient I get; I won' t wash clean. I like talking to this girl because she' s young and as clean as a bowl of water . I stir up no end of shit for myself when the blasted mood takes hard enough hold of me . I create too much trouble for myself, which itself makes a mess of reality . Lots of people seem to like to listen to us sing, but they laugh at us when they find out the motives behind the songs, not that that stops them wanting to know what gave rise to the lyrics, as if that would let them in on secrets . The laughter gives way to heaped praise, alien grief to personal illumination . Once when I was performing the old lady in charge of the programme kept tagging along behind me asking what had made me write *Come On*, *Let' s Go* for Manzi . There must be some secret behind it, she said . I said there wasn' t, and she pointed at Lu Sheng and said, " Quarrelled, had you?" All I could do was nod agreement, caught between tears and laughter. " I was right, then," she crowed. " You couldn' t have written a song like that if you hadn' t." The relationship was the handiest explanation of the lyric, I thought, satisfying her curiosity as it spared me the need for words. Eventually she said to the stage manager, " She stands up there singing about a scrap with her boyfriend." And she shook her head. The information made her intrigued by everything I sang, and she would sit alone in a corner mulling over my lyrics word by word and line by line whenever she had nothing to do. For all I know she analysed them by date and location and worked them up into diverting stories to tell her husband when she got home.

" Look, mate, do you have to make the rhythms as hard as that?" the electric guitarist flares at the synthesizer guy as he rehearses along with the electronic drums and synthesizer. " It' s going to be the death of me!" The electric guitar squeals. " No, it' s not. Try it again." " I bloody won' t. Up yours!" " Oh come on!" " We' ll get by without the electric guitar." " Oh no, we won' t." " I' m not playing." " Come on. Go through it one more time." " Do it on your synthesizer." " It wouldn' t be the same." " You' ll get by. Anyway, I' m not playing." " Not if I' m begging you?" " Not unless you get rid of that programme of yours." " Oh come on, after all I put into it?" " Then I' m not playing." " Well fucking don' t. You lot think there' s nothing doing without you, don' t you? I could synthesize the whole lot of you and be done with it!"

I lie on the carpet and turn face down. There' s a suspicion of a draught, and I can smell soil. It' s a very long time since I sang lying on soil. I close my eyes in a sunset blaze, and Manzi's lying beside me singing on and on. She could sing from dawn on into the afternoon without getting tired at noon, where I got sleepy just lying in the sun. We wouldn't get up and go home till the soil was freezing. Once she sang all day from dawn till dusk, twelve hours. She collapsed when she went to bed and woke up the next day drenched in sweat with a sweat stain the shape of her in the bed. Later when I performed until I dropped I could always think of the state she was in when she crawled out of bed first thing. I wrote a song for a low, regular voice going over and over what I felt about her, and it's always brought thoughts of prostration to people's minds.

It's not as if nobody thought anything of Manzi as a performer. There was a man came with an assistant once to negotiate quite seriously with us about making a tape. Instead of listening to us sing he looked all around the room. We stopped. "You're just not listening," said Manzi. "How do you know?" he said, coming over the great man with too much business acumen to have to keep his head still while he listened. Now if you want to listen to music while you scan the room, what you want is a tape deck, I'd have thought, not the two of us as large as life. We clammed up. "Go on," he said. "Sing, why don't you?" We stayed clammed up. "Your songs are fine, for what that's worth," he told us. "I just wonder if you're what the public wants. Ever tested that?" "Everybody loves it when we sing," said Manzi. "What do you mean by everybody? Your friends, that's all. Why don't you perform?" "We've never had the chance." "There's a family planning campaign on: why don't you do songs about that?" Manzi went white as a sheet, and I could feel my lips freeze. "If that's your attitude," she said, "I don't think we have anything further to discuss. Thank you." "Revolution!" he said, slapping the table as hard as he could. "There's going to be a revolution in song, understand? And who will you rely on but us?" Manzi, lips atremble, wrenched open the door and stood in the doorway to show that she wanted no more of this. Some days after this unpleasant breach he took us to dinner, where Manzi quarrelled with him at table, picked up her bag and left in tears, not entirely because we were being asked to do family planning songs: there were personal reasons too. Singers like us were still few and far between, and managers wanted money, limelight and our gratitude into the bargain.

16

The synthesizer guy is still in tireless dispute with everyone. The band leader says to the drummer see if you can't do without the synthesized programme, the synthesizer guy shouts there's a whole day wasted you can't just take it out come on, and the electric guitarist says look kid if you think we're going to be made a laughing stock of just because a pedant like you out of the goodness of his heart shoves every accompaniment in the world willy-nilly into one song you've got another think coming. The drummer goes to the drums and bashes out an endless rhythm that confuses even him and is actually more complicated than the synthesizer guy's programme the synthesizer guy says wouldn't it be less effort to just use my programme anyway well the drummer's not having that he says he does it with more feeling than the electronics do, the synthesizer guy keeps on playing his drum programme so loud that everyone's nerves are frayed and the drummer can't play try as he will and the electric bass player with the sweat dripping off his nose has been through it so often that he knows it better than the programme does.

"Hey," the synthesizer guy calls to me, "come on over here and join in."

"A hundred!" I laugh and hold up one finger.

"Sixty?"

"A hundred!"

"Eighty."

"A hundred."

He breaks off, silent, adjusts his glasses and pulls a face at me.

I've got more and more used to coming out and asking for money since Mr Ding put me on the stage. It amuses even me when I make myself blush, but I certainly wouldn't sell myself by taking money to do material I didn't like. I sometimes thought I'd sunk low to grub money for my songs, until the show where I saw a woman put on a record backstage and mime to it out front. Now that if you like is low. And the nauseating songs you do come across, lyrics, melody and accompaniment: the day I'm forced to sing them for a living I will have sunk low.

There's a Taiwan pop song I'm fond of that goes, "Have we changed the world, or has the world changed you and me?" I wonder, if Manzi were alive, whether she'd have refused contract after contract and recordings and fees. I think she'd either be a global sensation or shut herself away where no one would get her name on a contract. I'm certain she'd be too sensitive not to break down in tears at the shock of an applauding house. She'd be absolutely incapable of going out there and introducing herself or waving at the fans the way some do. "Don't take it seriously," she used to say, yet she led the most conscientious of lives. That's how people are: some things you can just swallow, but wrenching out every nerve for detailed inspection is a sure way to suicide. Look at some of the comic characters you see in the street: women of all heights who will get themselves up like judges in great rabbit skin hats; the songwriter who only has to see a girl to be signing an autograph; the man who does business out of a suitcase quietly choking in a big hotel; not daring to run fast for fear you'll slip on the snow; having to smile brazenly at people when you've broken your word.

The synthesizer guy's drum programme has finally been messed up by someone or other, and he's yelling furiously. All right, says the band leader, this time the drummer can play it. The synthesizer guy is not having this. He insists on the song being done to his programme, which he'll reprogramme even better than it was. I've heard a well-known story about him. He spent twenty-four hours working out a programme that eventually only the vocalist would perform to then spent all night jubilantly immersed in it, until the vocalist was tired out of his wits. At seven the next morning he adjusted his glasses, sat down at his equipment and announced to the vocalist with subdued excitement,

"Right, you're ready to record," at which the vocalist burst into tears and said, "I'm too tired to dream, let alone sing."

I clamber up, rush to the phone and get through to Mr Ding. If I don't say what I mean this time I am a fool.

"Hello! Hello!" I call as soon as I hear someone pick up the receiver.

"What is it now?" Mr Ding recognizes my voice.

"Uh — ."

"I'd sing along while they're recording the band if I were you and get you used to each other rather than moon around."

"Um — "

"They'd do better spending more time and keeping up quality, tell them. I've just been sent a sample tape by another band. Shoddy, quite shoddy."

"Yes."

"He's too easily led, that leader of yours."

"Mm."

"Tell your band leader not to use that copyist any more."

"I will."

"Don't drink too much water while you're singing."

"— "

"The tape'll be a big seller. Work hard on it."

"— "

"My daughter says you could do with some more forceful songs."

"— "

"Are you still there?"

"— "

"Do your best, now."

"— "

I listlessly replace the receiver. I'll never be able to say what I mean.

I go to the corner of the studio where I left my music case, take out the music and leaf through it, wanting to make a sound.

Manzi, what are you doing here?

I hear them all in confused discussion, saying you are going to be a success. I'm frightened you're too tired to want to talk, and that's wrong. You take things too much to heart. You must laugh them off. It's taking things to extremes to keep saying Manzi Manzi to everybody. Try to talk. You're too tired to want to, that's what I'm frightened of. They say you're a stickler about friendship, just saying "Manzi" and forgetting about Manzi in the yellow top. Manzi's not worth a damn, no more than the songs that accompany you are. Living people want to be your songs too, like me. Must you say nothing? Must you mouth Manzi Manzi?

What is it you actually want? To get something? To be rid of something? Can't you think? Daren't you say? Couldn't you do it? Do you plan to go on and sing stark naked? Be on a tape cover stark naked? On stage your songs are lit green and red, red and green. On stage they can use gas to make you look like a goddess standing there. Can you see your Bach yet? You insist he didn't exist: have you made up your mind whether he did or not? Why do you think on and on about Manzi Manzi and whether or not you'll actually sing? You might as well toss a coin and let it decide heads or tails. What is it you actually want? To get something? To be rid of something? Can't you think? Daren't you say? Couldn't you do it? Go and put on the yellow top and go back to where you and I went that year, will you?

I open my compact, and there I am like a lioness in the mirror. I put blue eyeshadow on my eyelids till my eyes gleam like a demon's, and the gleam explains that I want to sing and when I do I'll never stop. The accompaniment will sound twice as loud in my ears, and the strings and the guitar will make my blood course. Electronic drum programme or live impromptu, I don't care how they do it, I'll sing to it, I'll keep on singing and never stop. I can be honest or I can be a fraud. I hate long-distance running more than any sport on earth, God knows why. I adore the gleam in the eyes for itself. I'll sing about the person in the mirror and not about me.

Manzi in the yellow top, the yellow top Manzi wore. I've never worn one since. I burnt mine along with hers. I happened upon them one day when I was turning out the chest I'd locked them in, snatched them away from the girl beside me who wanted to try them on, took them into the kitchen, lit the gas and burnt them. What did it smell like? The fire got so big it nearly set fire to the kitchen. I snatched them up by an unburnt corner and threw them into the tub in the bathroom, and the blaze blackened the tub and the bathroom wall. My whole family said I was crazy, and I just couldn't find any way to scrub the bathroom clean, and now whenever Mother goes in there she mutters.

I go for another cup of hot water. My back hurts from lying too long, and so does my stomach. I imagine the street lights are glaring by now. One night Manzi and I cycled out into the country and sang till twelve o'clock, all the way back and on till five in the morning without even a dog for an audience. Coming back into town we bumped into a policeman, who made us get off our bikes and asked us what we were doing, where we lived, if we had jobs and whether the bikes were stolen. He went on and on at us until a great horse and cart came along, when he let us go and started on the carter. Mister policeman must be bored, said Manzi, and wants somebody to talk to. We were sprawled on a park bench in the city centre at five when I felt this lad on a bike circle the bench, look at us and ride off. At the time I just didn't have time to be frightened. When we woke up we ran to a natural swimming pool, and when we'd washed our faces I said Manzi you're ever so pretty, and she said I was too, which boosted our self-confidence, and we pedalled home singing and looking straight ahead of us. When we got there she and I lay on my bed and chattered on about her boyfriend and love, and I fell asleep half way through the first sentence but woke up a sentence later and grunted agreement to her question. I'm sure she thinks I was awake to this day. The street lights are glaring now. I should be there, not here singing. I should be standing on a police rostrum with a guitar. I'd like to write a song, something about a man made of water frozen into ice who weeps so much he melts himself. Yes, that's where I should be, directing the traffic with songs, telling them to go this way or that or round the town or away and never come back, and all of them having to go where I sent them.

17

I go out of the studio, right outside into the street, which isn't in a busy part of town and has hardly any traffic or shops on it. Night hasn't quite fallen as I walk on down. A woman's peddling roast sweet potatoes. I pick out three, and she weighs them then says, "Should be fifty fen, but give me forty-nine." I give her fifty and pick them up and bite into one, and it's bad, and bite into another one, and it's bad too, and I run my eye over the third one before I break it open, and it's all black inside. I throw them into the ditch one by one. Why did I forget to tell Manzi about the yellow tops when she was here just now, and that it wasn't me but Lu Sheng who's not talking, and about Mr Ding and his daughter, and all the other things I'm not happy about?

I discover I'm not warmly enough dressed for the chill there still is in the air. All I have in my jeans pocket is some small change and a face tissue. I'm not wearing lipstick or rouge, simply blue eyeshadow. The hems of my trousers are frayed and covered in mud. They're out at the knee, and I've patched it inside and stitched circles of black thread on with the sewing machine. Some people suggest I put a sailboat cutout there, but I think I'll go for a bright red patch instead. That'll look great. I can't imagine how those oil spots on the thigh got there. I seem to have rubbed water on and got rid of them until the mudstains and the sun brought them right out again. It'll be too dark to see mud or oil in a bit, just trousers that need washing with two bags at the knee. The leather belt's old and scuffed white. How can you wear that with your trousers, they say. I don't mind. A belt's a belt, though I suppose a pop star's ought to be flashier. For that matter, these trousers don't need a belt. I've not given enough thought to having one or not and if so what sort. The cream shirt, however, which is a man's, is perfectly clean. I was always a one for shirts, but the wind goes straight through them. I'll have to put this creased, filthy denim jacket over it and turn the collar up too. I'm not wearing nearly enough.

I once went to see a real thriller writer I know, and there he was as white as a sheet and his lips trembling away. I asked him if he was ill, and he pointed to his manuscript and said, "I've got a dozen people dead, no villain and no sign of the police." I wonder how far it is till you see the crossroads. There are no police on this street.

February 5, 1985

Translated by Simon Johnstone

Liu Suola was born in Beijing in 1955. She became a teacher at the Central Institute of Minority Nationalities after graduating from the composing department of the Central Conservatoire in 1983. In 1985 she published her first novella *You Have No Choice*, followed by the novellas "Blue Sky and Green Sea", "Looking for the King of Song", the short story "Track" and the Sanwen "The Rocking Road". *You Have No Choice* won a national prize for one of the best novels of 1985-1986. "Blue Sky and Green Sea" was made into a rock opera, with Liu Suola doing the scenario, music, singing and recording. The same year her fiction collection *You Have No Choice* was published both on the mainland and in Taiwan. In 1988 she went to England to continue her education, during which period she wrote "Showaddy Chaos" and other pieces. She is now a member of the Chinese Writers' Association.

Hopes Worn Away

Peng Xiaolian

I tuck the quilt tightly around my shoulders again, but I can still feel a cold draft snaking its way from my neck downwards. I curl up into a ball, hardly daring to move. I can't hear the wind outside the window, but the window is rattling as though it's muffled by something. There's an oppressive buzzing noise all around which is only broken when a firework soars skywards, its shriek still as ear-rending as ever. A moment later, the windowpane flashes white, leaving me dazzled. As I stare into the darkness of my room, black and white shapes lock together like on the face of a ringworm patient, and creep towards me trembling. I shut my eyes and turn over, but the sound of laughter and voices comes through the wall, together with the noise of spitting oil in the pan. Everyone in the house is rushing around, busy with something or other. "Bride" is yelling to my younger brother: "Help me turn the light on in the kitchen." "Isn't the light on downstairs?" "Weiqing's finished cooking: they'll turn the light off in a moment." "I know."

My little brother — I grew used to conversations like this long ago. However, when a colleague from another town came and stood at the foot of the little flight of stairs, she was really puzzled: "I've never seen anything like it — so many lights and wires and light cords on such a tiny flight of stairs, and they're all covered in dust. What's it supposed to be, a mechanized stage set?'' When I passed the comment on to my younger brother, I couldn't help laughing. Whenever I caught sight of those filth-covered wires winding their worm-like way into each of the small flats, it never failed to amuse me. "It's you who make me laugh, not those wires. All houses are like that. That's nothing to be surprised at.'' Little Brother gave me a contemptuous look over his shoulder.

The glass flashes again momentarily as another firework races into the sky. Some children are shouting in the alley. Normally at this time I hear an ancient clock chime — I don't know who it belongs to — and start counting from the first stroke up to the twelfth. After the last stroke I hear the lingering sound spreading out and strolling into the darkness — But today I haven't heard it. Maybe it's because tomorrow's New Year, and everyone's too busy. New Year. New Year. I don't get it: isn't just another day like any other, just another twenty-four hours? Calling it New Year is symbolic, a symbol to distinguish it from other symbols and nothing else. Why do we save up all our good food for this one day? Why do we work ourselves into a froth for this one day? Why do we spend all our money on this one day? Why — too many whys. I'm getting confused myself. There are never any reasons behind the things we do everyday: don't we just do them because that's what everyone else does?

I can't work it out. Anyway, my days are all the same: not much thinking, just padding the day out with English. New Year. How old am I? Thirty-what? Where will I be when spring comes? All of a sudden, I shrink towards the bottom end of the quilt. It's really cold; a shaft of cold is moving up from my feet. I tremble and tug at the quilt urgently, clinging on like grim death. The joints in my fingers are starting to ache, and I don't know what to do, which is agitating. Every day, every single day, I wish I could get to sleep — I'm really tired, so tired I can't go on. I read those foreign language books time and again, even looking things up in the dictionary; but the moment I shut the books, my mind's a blank, as though I haven't read them at all, not a trace of them left. In the darkness, I feel like this little room has been enveloped in a huge net, and that the net is drawing tighter and tighter. This doesn't upset me though, because the net doesn't seem to be tying me up: I'm clutching a book and shrinking smaller and smaller — I long for the moment to pass, for eleven o'clock when I can escape into dreams. But the moment I dive under the quilt I just wait for the dawn to come again. I'm scared. Scared of what? When I went to work in the production team in the countryside that time and spent the night shift alone in the grain store, a rat had scurried over my shoulder and I didn't move an inch. So what's the matter with me now? Fidgety, I dive completely under the quilt and can at last shout out: Nothing!

I think it's probably me that's mucked up my life. Why can't I go downstairs and chat and laugh with the neighbours? Why can't I go and fry melon seeds with Little Brother? But Little Brother and I never eat together, because he always gets things on the cheap — He's very economical, and I really don't think badly of him because of it. To tell the truth, I even admire him a tiny bit. He's told me how he haggled the price down, tapping away at his pocket calculator as he talks. When he's pleased with himself, he presses down the hair on his temples, flattening it down into a spiral shape. The only trouble is, he's always talking about the same things, in the same old way — even the tone he uses when he's pleased with himself is exactly the same. I'm sick and tired of it.

One day Little Brother came over to me holding a cake of soap. "Where did you buy this, sis?" "That little shop in the alley." "Is it some sort of special product or something?" "No." "Then how come it's still so big when you've been using it for half a month?" Hearing I'd fallen for it, I didn't dare look in his direction. Little Sister rushed over: "I told Big Sis to use your soap. So what? It's the first time you and your wife have actually bought some soap, and you're still nicking our toothpaste. And what about every time she has a period? She uses enough of our toilet paper then!" "Don't you feel ashamed, saying things like that?" "It's true: why should I keep quiet about it?" "But we have to support a whole family!" "No one forced you to get married!"

From then on the toilet was really clean, with everyone taking their own things out of there. What a family — Haggling over every penny! Little Brother would keep his door shut, and every time he went out he would lock it. Things came to a head, and whenever we came home, we each went to our own room.

The cold air around my feet is still working its way up and chilling me to the bone. If that's what marriage is like, it's a bit scary. I'd be trapped in this tiny room, buried under those pieces of toilet paper and slowly suffocating.

Now I hear the heavy tramp of male feet on the stairs, followed by the thud of a woman's high heels. They aren't talking to each other, just hurrying up the stairs. Now they're on my floor. They don't stop, just make a practised turn in the dark, and a moment later there's the sound of keys being fumbled and a door being closed. Little Brother and "Bride" have entered their room. The kitchen downstairs has quietened down too, the nighttime silence developing. Then a frightening wheezing noise comes through the flimsy wooden partition: the sound of Little Brother making love. "Bride" gives a suppressed shriek. I turn over and bury my head under the pillow, trying my hardest not to listen, but my limbs are all going soft, and I feel like my whole body is burning, so hot that I cling desperately on to the pillow as I shake. I despise the two of them. No, that's a lie. I don't despise them at all. When Little Brother decided to get married, Little Sister and I immediately gave up the big room and squeezed into the garret. But it's true that they're making me feel extremely uncomfortable. Maybe I despise myself. Why should I listen in on them like this? Turning my head the other way, I feel wronged.... I'm really not doing it deliberately.

When the groans and sighs next door peter out, I'll still be feeling jumpy. Apart from those English books and the broken old bits of furniture, there is nothing around me but the flaking old wall. Weekends and holidays — the whole business only goes on for a few minutes, but it makes me feel physically exhausted like

I've climbed a hill. I'm single and I want to distance myself a bit from all that — But there seems no end to it all. I seem to see an even higher hill ahead. I'm desperate for a companion. It doesn't matter at all who it is — I've never had anyone particular in mind — just as long as he's sincere. Perhaps — my companion can be male or female, young or old, I don't mind. I'm exhausted, hoping against hope that someone will come and knock on my door, then come in and chat with me about anything. I don't want to pick up that frigid English book again.

I'm missing my younger sister —

That younger sister of mine who looked so horrible when she was asleep and who always stuck her feet on top of me. Her hair would always be in curlers, and if one of them fell out, even if it was in the dead of night, she would get out of bed and fix it before she went back to sleep. The day before yesterday she got married to a boy who had been in the same year as her at middle school. She's just a cheerful big baby. She was always asking me: "Is that book of yours interesting?" "No!" "You're lying. Why do you carry it about all day then?" "If I don't read it, what else is there for me to do?" "Go out with me. We'll go dancing. That's a lot of fun." I was tongue-tied and didn't say a word. Am I getting old or something? How is it that I'm so utterly uninterested in something that my little sister finds so exciting? If you watch my little sister you'll see that whenever she says anything, her hands are always waving and gesticulating in a very ungainly way: it makes you think that just about anything can make her boil over with excitement. She's very young!

I used to be disappointed with my little sister. When I came back from the countryside, I found her really boring. Her greatest pleasure was apparently going to the toilet. She would go in and stay there for ages. The neighbours would get impatient and start swearing violently, but she couldn't care less. Suddenly the door would open, a fragrant smell would waft out, and she would emerge, her lips painted bright red. She would pull a face at them before she flounced off. She didn't let it bother her: she could be quite thick-skinned at times. Intriguingly, she had always despised my younger brother for his thick skin. "That open university student! He hasn't even learned how to use a calculator to add up a two-cent bill. What's he actually learned, eh? How to lock his door when he goes out. What a load of crap __ "

How could I not prefer Little Sister? She's such an innocent person. I'd like to be as happy as she is, and be able to push Little Brother to the back of my mind. Really, who cares whether someone's a university student or not? What about personality? What about heart and emotions? But Little Sister wants to broaden her knowledge. One day, instead of going shopping and browsing as she usually did when she finished at work, she came back early and lay on her bed, reading a book under the little lamp and sighing now and then. When I discovered that she was reading a collection of Pushkin's love poetry, I turned my face away quickly so that she wouldn't see my mood. She was Little Sister after all.

"He's also a university student, but he's not always holding a book like you," she started. "He can ride a racing bike, and when we went to the little reservoir in the suburbs he made me teach him the butterfly. He learned it straightaway virtually, and he really splashed about." She became serious. "He's still studying, so he can't get married, but I'll wait as long as he wants — for love!" When she said the word "love", it sounded quite sacred. I stared at her uncomprehendingly: "What are you sighing for then?"

"I don't know." Little Sister's voice went very quiet. "I've never met anyone like him before. I never know what he's thinking."

As Little Sister's voice petered out, I thought to myself: love is a simple word, but no one escapes it. When a person's life really begins, when they become mature, they all search for it and make sacrifices for it — When I remember it, it feels like a scar, a thick wrinkled scab, and so I avoid it — Little Sister's skin is still so smooth and fine. I brushed it with the tip of my fingers, stroking her. Little Sister's big, innocent eyes had something else in them now, they were not as simple as they had been, and they were no longer always sparkling.

Suddenly she burst out: "Can you teach me some philosophy, sis?"

"What?" This time I really couldn't help laughing out loud.

"Don't laugh at me." Her hands were clasped tightly together, her head hanging low. "He was talking about me — and I couldn't understand what he was saying."

"If you don't understand, you should make him repeat it. You're supposed to be talking about love, not philosophy.''

"I don't dare. He's changed — '' She gave me an imploring look. "Will you go and talk with him — please?''

"How can I?''

"You're both university students, sis — '' She couldn't go on, just threw herself on the bed and started to sob loudly. Her whole body was shaking, one foot on the bed, the other dangling in mid-air. A moment later there was a thump as her shoe fell to the ground, but she ignored it. What could I do for her? Go and talk about philosophy in her place? Little Sister's hair was sticking up messily as though she hadn't bothered with it for several days, and the roots were covered with a light layer of dust. In an instant she had turned shabby and ugly. Hearing her snivels and wails of utter despair, you would have thought it was the end of the world. Little Sister was naive, but serious and honest too, her shallow agony filled with vitality.

Although the whole idea was crazy, I eventually went to talk with her young man. When I saw him, I was puzzled. His face was as hairless as a baby's, and he was that skinny and pale-skinned type you see everywhere in southern Chinese cities. How could Little Sister be in such a state over him? The boys she'd dumped before had all been more attractive than him. His only plus point was the shabbiness of his clothes, which seemed to imply a confidence that he didn't have to go out of his way to get girls. Or maybe that was just part of his unconventional style.

"You've been going out with my little sister for almost two years now. What are you going to do about it?''

''I'm going to make her dump me.''

What sort of answer was that? I decided to get to the bottom of it.

''All it means is that I want her to be the one who suggests we stop seeing each other. That way she won't get hurt.''

What a ''nice'' guy. Shirking all responsibility and still trying to look like the victim. Don't give me that. I felt angry on my little sister's behalf. Little Sister had been painting herself a very rosy dream, ignoring the very long boundary that existed between them: a boundary that she couldn't hope to cross. He had certainly never thought of sacrificing anything. He had just been all talk — But that's not illegal or even dangerous. Even when you're married you can get a divorce — What's wrong with playing the field a bit to find the right person? He made Little Sister happy too, so what's there to criticize? He was staring at me as though I was a bit simple, a retard, not even understanding this most basic of truths.

''I understand. I'll tell my little sister.''

''What'll you tell her?''

''What do you care? Once you've dumped her you won't have to worry. Being selfish isn't illegal. That's all there is to it.''

''Leave it out: I was just being honest. You'll go on about how she's so upset; what about me? You hate me because of your sister. You like her not only because she's your little sister but because she's young and honest. So do I. As I'm a man, I also like her because she's pretty.'' He got stirred up. ''Now she tells me all her worries and troubles — so l get no happiness from her any more. Why should I bear all her troubles? When you get upset, don't you bear it all yourself? I've had enough. I don't want to turn into a romantic novel creep.'' As he spoke, he fished out a pair of glasses from his pocket, put them on, and then turned his bag upside down looking for something or other. The thing he was looking for wasn't important at all. Maybe it was something of· my sister's that he wanted to give to me. I can't remember. I just remember that he changed after he put those glasses on — he didn't look as handsome as before, and when he pushed them on more firmly, he really did look unhappy. "Maybe I am selfish like you say, but I'm not a hypocrite. Everyone's so overcautious these days, and they never say what they really think. They conceal their real selves all their lives, right up to when they die — How can you stand it?''

I didn't answer. I didn't know how brave I was when it came to facing myself either. I'd thought of telling people everything honestly: it was too much of a burden on me. But who would understand? Who would even want to listen? I suddenly became aware of the young man's aggressive stare and heard him saying: ''Why don't you say something? You're the same as me; you've got a miserable life too.''

He was right, but very few people would guess it. I always throw up barriers around myself so that people can't see the real me, scared that they'll laugh at me and even more scared that they'll pity me. In my immediate circle of acquaintances there isn't a single person who is willing to face up to themselves (apart from Xiao Yan, always Xiao Yan —). He was quite right. I really wanted to look at him and see just what sort of person he really was. I wanted to talk to him about any old thing. Really putting myself down would be a good way of venting my spleen, and he'd be sure to understand — But now there was a bicycle between us, so I didn't turn back. What did I need to see him for anyway? Our eyes would meet, then we'd stare at each other for ages, then we'd talk openly and honestly — and then it would be the same old thing, the order quite unchanged. I stared ahead and said, "I'll tell Little Sis." I walked off, ignoring him. Life's just like that: you just have to take it one step at a time. I'd been as unhapy as Little Sister before, worse in fact, that time by the hill behind the village when I'd wept my heart out. So what? I'm old now, and I can deal with anything. Maybe I should stop a moment and think over what he said. Just being friends would be okay. At least he would understand what you were saying and wouldn't think you were some sort of freak. As I realized that there is no truth in reality, I felt very sad.

What should I be doing? I feel like I'm a paralysed old woman, lying on the bed unable to move, my twisted mouth unable to speak, only able to slobber a long stream of saliva when I want to convey something. But I'm not dead. My brain is still working, and a heart still beats in the shell of my body. How can I pluck up the courage to stare in the mirror and look at the sad remains of my life? I'm alive, truly alive, but most of the time it's only the fact that I can feel myself gradually dying that makes me aware of it.

But there are still people of our generation who have the courage to face themselves and face reality. Xiao Yan is one of them. Her life is far from smooth, but she never gives up. She's always rushing back and forth, that cascading hair of hers trembling in the wind like a black flame.

She stood before my lonely little room. Suddenly she held out a pack of Peony brand cigarettes: "Su Ning, try one!" "Aren't you worried about wrecking your complexion?" She flung the pack on to the table and lay down on my bed, facing upwards. Suddenly she turned over and started grumbling at the wall. "My complexion can go to hell. All I want is to have a cigarette, draw it in, puff it out again, make it really smoky and fumigate this awful city. Get married, look for a partner, save a bit of money — what's it all for?" She gave a long sigh, turned over and stared at me. "Shit, country people have it much better than we do! If they want to do something, they just go ahead and do it. They don't have time to get depressed or lonely out there. You remember how when we were there we just spent our whole time longing to come back to the city, as though it was heaven or something. And when we got allocated work, there wasn't one of us who didn't fight like crazy to get work here. We didn't know until we got back that we'd fought our way into a grave." She hung her head and closed her eyes. "I should just go back — go back to the production team I worked in. These days we don't have to apply to the local authorities to change our domicile — I can become a teacher and get three times more money. We can have a house, a space and can live our own life — "

I shift my body and lie flat on my back. A light moves across the ceiling, the reflection of a car light in the street. My mind often goes blank, and when I'm discussing serious subjects with others I often catch myself humming a tune. I'm too tired. My trains of thought often break down. That sort of thing happens fairly often, and it quite frightens me. Thinking about it now, my stupidity lies in the fact that I'm too earnest. Earnestness is a very outmoded attitude. That's why I've been manipulated time and again (it's always been my own fault). Why did I take that outburst of Xiao Yan's so seriously? The expression she wore when she entered my little room didn't change on the spur of the moment. She was exposing herself completely as if she was torn to pieces and hung up for people to see.

"The head of the county where we school leavers went into agriculture came to make an investigation in south China. He gathered us together for information and gave us a feast after it. I suddenly discover that people like him live above the ground. What about us? We are buried deeply under the ground. The country folk are quite amazing when they talk. They cite figures the moment they open their mouths to speak, so accurate that they even can speak out the figures behind the decimal point. They can actually count their happiness. Why don't we go back and work there? Do you think we ought to just stick it out and get rotten here?"

I was really moved by what she was saying. Really, I ought to go there with her.

The next day, before it was fully light, I stepped out. The streets were still empty, and wisps of steam and fragrant breakfast smells were spiralling out of the little shop on the corner. In the triangular park fenced with iron railings, old men and women were practising their sword play, and there were already quite a few people practising *qigong*. For some reason, when I saw the old people doing their exercises, it all seemed very familiar, and I was reminded of something; it was as though I'd stood there before, had stopped there before. It felt the same as when I used to set out at this hour for the fields in the countryside. Subconsciously, I started walking faster towards Xiao Yan's house —

It's really cold! My whole body curls up, and I clutch the bottoms of my feet as hard as I can. I still can't forget how I was insulted. I start reciting English, trying my hardest to get back to sleep. But no matter how hard I try to stuff the thick honeycomb of jumbled and fragmented letters into my brain, it's all a waste of time. I just see Xiao Yan's calm gaze. She came up behind me at the end of the alley and all of a sudden tapped me on the shoulder in a friendly way. "Don't hurry. I deliberately came outside to talk with you. I'm fed up with my family." I looked up, but I didn't see Xiao Yan, my eyes were rivetted to the little strip of black cloth on her pocket — I didn't know whether it was a trade mark or supposed to be some sort of decoration. I waited. Her affectionate gestures weren't really those of someone our age, and I began to get a vague feeling of foreboding. I can't just retreat or give up; at our age, chances to go all out for something are few and far between — But if Xiao Yan pulled out, I wouldn't be able to go it alone. When you get old, it's like when you cross the street; you support me, and I'll help you by the arm — you be my crutch, and I'll be your walking stick.

"Listen to me," Xiao Yan was very depressed. "My family won't let me go. And anyway, the thing is that I'm not really sure myself that I want to go. I've seen people who've transferred before. Thinking about it rationally, there's nowhere else that can compare with here for convenience — of course — "

I couldn't take in a single thing she was saying. I didn't need her to tell me all this. The first time I left this city, getting back here was the only thing worth struggling for. Wasn't it you, Xiao Yan, who was saying that the city was like a tomb yesterday evening? How was it that one night later she contradicted everything she'd just said? What's happening here? I couldn't answer, and I walked off quietly. No, it wasn't those slippery paved streets that I was yearning for, nor was it those French- and Japanese-style gardened foreign houses, much less those high-rise buildings — I yearned for some sort of turbulence, crazy impulses and changes that would at least make me feel alive. That's exactly it. So why was it then — even bearing in mind the fact that I would have to do it alone — that I didn't dare rush blindly ahead one more time? I turned to face Xiao Yan: "Er, maybe you should take me there and recommend me to them."

Xiao Yan stood there for ages before opening her mouth: "Is it worth it?" She really didn't mean it nastily at all. But I felt that those four words condensed everything that she particularly disliked about me. In my fright I began questioning my yearning.

"You seem so normal most of the time, but when it comes down to it you're really weird."

"Am I?" I asked timidly. "Weird?"

"I'll say you are! Here you are, in your thirties __ you ought to think of something practical. Find someone and get married. Be more down to earth; face yourself__ Neither of us are Van Gogh or Modigliani. When you come down to it you'll find that all roads are the same; they don't really mean anything. If you let your mind run wild and don't get married, you're bound to end up __ "

"Xiao Yan, look __ They're selling fried turnip dumplings." I was so terrified that I butted in quickly and cut her off so that I wouldn't hear the last half of her sentence. I bet she was going to say I'd end up a ghastly old maid. I'd made a fairy tale for myself but now found that I'd entered a nightmare, with me as the fairy tale's old hag __ an old hag that everyone called "Old Maid". I felt a chill spreading over me.

Xiao Yan stopped walking and turned on me with unconcealed fury: "I'm going home. What's the matter with you? I try and hold a serious conversation with you, and you start talking about fried turnip dumplings. I don't get it. You really disappoint me." Shaking her head, she gave her neat, long hair a quick flick, then turned and walked off. Then there was just me left on the dark streets, standing there like a block of wood. I didn't turn round, just felt a twinge of despair, as though I'd messed up something really important. I was really sad. Why had I disappointed Xiao Yan? She was a genuinely nice person, and people who were as nice to me as her were few and far between. I knew that. Yet, hadn't I disappointed myself too? Was I really a cracked old maid? Maybe I shouldn't have said anything about wanting to leave this city in the first place __ But does that mean that normal people are like plants, staying where they're planted until they die of old age or go rotten?

God, where do all these ideas come from? I felt my steps getting heavier; I was just too tired. I walked back following the stone wall, then crossed the little alley, the noise of a nightstool being scrubbed coming over like someone in a little band playing the drums with a wire brush. Scrub, scrub — the beats were very regular. That much wouldn't change, it would always remain part of my life. No wonder — no wonder even Xiao Yan looks at me like everyone else. All the well-intentioned and ill-intentioned gazes and comments chased after me, piling up on top of me and making my breathing difficult. Old Maid — what an ugly name!

I felt I was finished. Purely in order to rid myself of the "Old Maid" tag and to prove my normality to everyone, I started actively looking for a partner. No, it wasn't exactly like that. If I examined my conscience, I knew that behind all those excuses there was a tiny part of me that was longing for a partner.

But who? I had no idea. Anyway, it wouldn't be the prince I dreamed of in childhood; nor would it be the movie-star real man I yearned for in my adolescence. The things that mature people ask for are realistic — boring even — altogether lacking in vanity and idealism.

As my sister put it: "University graduates aren't worth anything, especially girls. What have you got? You haven't even got a house. And everyone wants someone young and pretty."

I didn't say anything. It's really hard, I thought to

myself; my demands are still too high. The only thing I longed for was sincerity. It seemed there was something almost farcical in someone of my age speaking the word. But was there really no one like that? Xiao Lu — I tear off the quilt that's weighing on my neck. My throat starts to tickle. I want to cough but find I can't. I can only feel a noiseless trembling in my throat that reaches down to my stomach. If I could cry, if I were still able to cry, I would feel a lot better.

Little Sister introduced Xiao Lu from her factory to me. At long last I stepped over the threshold and went round to his house for "normal social contact". On the way there I wasn't really thinking of anything in particular, and even as I stood before the front door of his one-storey house, my mind was still a blank. All sorts of noises were coming from inside: the bang, bang, bang of something being hit; a popular tune was blaring out of a tape recorder, the lyrics very muffled, as though the singer was making a deliberate effort not to be understood. The woman was singing in a husky, gravelly-throated sort of voice, wailing like an invalid trying to vindicate herself just before she died, "I'm in pain, my heart is torn...." I got fed up and pounded the door twice. When the door opened and Xiao Lu appeared, the banging stopped. The singing "I'm in pain, my heart is torn...." immediately increased in volume and rushed at me with a roar. My heart contracted, and I wanted to ward off the attack, but I was quite powerless; I stood there feeling very awkward. Xiao Lu stared back into the darkness, narrowed his eyes and said nothing. Although it was really just an instant, it seemed like ages, and I could feel my courage waning until I really wanted to run away. But then Xiao Lu spoke: "Ah, Su Ning: I thought it was someone else. Please come in and sit down."

The house had just been thrown up temporarily by the side of the road, and the traces of a sewer were still there. All around there were planks of wood and half-finished pieces of furniture. I stood in a space I found between furniture, looked up at Xiao Lu and smiled: "You're busy."

"Not really. I'm fine. How about you? You've got thin."

"I'm okay, I — " I looked at my wizened and scrawny fingers, nervously rubbing back and forth on the unvarnished furniture. "Oh, my sister made a mistake when she said I was thirty. Actually, I'm thirty-three — "

"You mean you and I are the same age?" As Xiao Lu blurted it out, his voice sounded louder than usual. He immediately shut his mouth tight as though he wanted to cover up something. His slightly thick lips pouted, he looked round, then he swivelled his stocky body and clumsily turned off the tape recorder. He stood there with his back to me and his head hung low.

The world suddenly became very quiet, unnaturally quiet. I saw him raise his hands, plant them on his thickset hips, let them drop again, and then finally cross them in front of his chest. I was very familiar with each of his movements and they made me feel a surge of warmth. I wanted to say something, but didn't know where to start. I looked at the corner of the room and the heap of broken old furniture stacked there; the set-out was very shabby, and the floor was covered in curly wood shavings and scraps of wood that gave off a faint smell of timber. I really wanted to leave. Just then, Xiao Lu seemed to relax, and he politely pulled over a chair for me to sit on, putting a coarse cloth cushion on it first. In the dim light, his face looked really kind and gentle.

I took the chair but didn't sit down. I watched him bending over and straightening the cushion and noticed he had some wood shavings in his hair. I felt like stretching out my hand and gently brushing them off, but in the end my hand stayed where it was; inside it felt like I'd done it though, and a feeling of warmth flooded me. I saw him look up and laugh good-naturedly, and I felt comforted. When our eyes met, I laughed a sincere laugh.

I didn't think there was anything to be scared of, I was not sure why. Could it have been the concern he displayed with his attentive observation, "You've got thin", or could it have been the good-natured grin or the way he hadn't made a fuss about my age? I was just aware that I didn't find this little house as oppressive and restrictive as my own small room. I said, "My little sister had a go at me. She said I ought to be more friendly, not spend the whole day with my nose stuck in a book."

"Please, don't say anything else. Your little sister had a go at me too. I — " He looked away. "I thought she was just joking. I never imagined you'd actually come. Please, have something to drink!" Then he was silent. I was silent too. Whenever I really want to do something for myself, I always have no sense of propriety, not knowing how to do it.

But that time Little Sister had asked me to mediate for her I had been able to make the correct inference and make the correct judgement for every sentence, every movement, and every pause that my opponent had made. To others, I'm simply a sophisticated and experienced person. In fact, I'm very obtuse and can't express myself, or I say inappropriate things. Every time I make an "appropriate" remark, it's always a real effort, as though I've literally wrung it out of my brain. The fact that I was able to sit here now, quietly and very relaxed, with a sincere person for company, made me experience a great peace of mind. After a moment, the silence seemed to bring us closer and closer. In this little room I felt that there was no subject that was taboo. "Xiao Lu, do you find me difficult to understand?" "No, you're like your little sister. You're just a nice person."

Honestly, it really is just as simple as that; I want a partner, just like the majority of people, and an ordinary family — even if everyone else thinks he's very lowly and dull, it doesn't matter to me, just as long as he's honest. I'd like to sense that person's smell, get close to his body and fight for my breath in his close embrace, never pushing him away. I don't know whether I've just started getting coarse or just started to understand life and people. Are there other things that people yearn for more than honesty and trust?

It's been a long time now since I've experienced that feeling. The feeling where my heart is like the village well: very still and very deep, the water smooth and rippleless, reflecting not only the azure sky but your face too, under the rays of the sun, when you look down; then the golden light draws you in silhouette, and you look like you're surrounded by a halo. The night becomes warmer and envelopes the little room —

At this point, my heart feels as though it's just been clawed, and I shrink back. I don't dare do any more thinking. I'm scared. I don't know what my problem is, why everything that starts off so nicely always turns out to be just a dream. Why did I go and see Xiao Lu? It was all just wishful thinking on my part. How should I punish myself? I toss and turn, desperate to get to sleep as quickly as possible. But in the dead of night I start picking at my scab again, looking at the tender pink flesh underneath and the tiny drops of blood that are oozing out. The flesh is ridged and damp, so that I don't dare touch it.

But is it really my fault? When I got the admission notice from an American university, I was afraid of losing everything here. I'll never forget that day. When I saw a row of mysterious Arabic numerals in the scholarship space on the form I felt like my brain was falling apart, bored through by these letters and numbers. I held my breath and gripped the admission notice tightly. I was about to stride out at long last: people would look at me with new eyes, and no one would sneer that I was weird. I had powerful evidence to challenge people with, and I felt my vanity sated for the first time in my adult life. I wanted to pray for myself, but I had no idea what to pray. Gradually I became aware of the beating of my heart, thump, thump, beating wildly. I did my best to calm down, and not get too happy, as though I was scared of losing everything through premature excitement.

Gusts of autumn wind swept the land. The skies become dry and cool, surrounding the little room and making me feel suffocated. I feel as though all my internal organs have leapt into my throat and are palpitating there. I stand up and try to look as though I don't care, but it is no good. I need to find someone to talk to; we can talk about anything. I haven't felt that happiness for long. I almost forget what it is like.

Little Brother and Bride's room is quiet now. Little Sister is still doing overtime. Who can I go and talk to? Of course, Xiao Yan — She understands me.

I rushed out on to the street. The street was really crowded with people rushing to buy things — from leather shoes to cotton padding — in the wake of price-hike rumours. The length of the street was bursting with people, like when a cinema discharges its audience, people clinging, shoving, moving step by step. The street was filled with the stench of human bodies. But price hikes didn't mean anything to me, and I hurried to cross the street and find Xiao Yan for a chat.

But the little iron gate outside Xiao Yan's house was shut. I was just toying with the idea of forcing my way in when suddenly there was a shriek like two panes of glass rubbing against each other. The screech clawed at my innards, and I couldn't help trembling. "What gave you the right to go through my drawer?" yelled Xiao Yan.

There was the heavy thump of a fist angrily slamming on a table. "I'm your father. Of course I've got the right. How dare you talk to me like that? I want to see what kind of friends you're keeping."

"Now you're retired, you've got nothing better to

do all day. That's it, isn't it? You can't just trample
over my rights!''

"You — Get out!''

"I haven't got a house. Do you think I like living
here? I've had enough!''

"Do you think it's my fault you haven't got your
own house? I'm not the head of the Housing Department — Get out — I disown you!''

All the windows upstairs and in the neighbouring
houses clacked open. Then people started coming outside into the alley to listen. Terrified, I began to retreat
step by step, the racket still unfolding. I reached the
end of the alley, where there was a hill-like pile of rubbish; a dirty path ran through the centre of the rubbish, and I made my way over the stinking fruit peels
and cinders, just like a burglar escaping from the scene
of the crime.

Once I was a long way off, I turned back and saw
that Xiao Yan's house was now surrounded by a
large crowd, like an army of ants clustering around an
open wound. They seemed to be sucking the blood
and pus that were seeping out and increasing in number, pressing even nearer, gathering at the centre of the
wound. I turned and fled.

I stood in the long queue of people outside the public telephone booth, fumbled in my pocket for some
change, smoothed out the crumpled and torn little note
and handed it over to the old woman who was in charge of the telephone. The bottom of the receiver was still
moist with someone else's spittle; little bubbles could
be clearly seen oozing out of the grooves. Grey filth.
Impatient as I was in my nausea, the dialing tone took
ages to come. The person behind me in the queue rat-

tled his keys and kept sighing loudly. I wanted to ring
up Xiao Lu, but what should I say to him? Tell him
that I was going to leave the country? Would he want
to share that piece of good news? I hesitated — The
old woman was already rapping the desk with her
knuckles: "Come on, come on, there are other people
waiting."

I got flustered. I lost track of what I was doing for a
moment, and when I finished dialling, I found that it
was my Little Sister's name that I was yelling down
the receiver. "I've got no time to explain now, but
can you come home early this evening?"

"What is it?" Little Sister's loud voice and the various machine noises boomed through the receiver; Little
Sister talking fast like a gramophone set on the wrong
speed. "I can't come back early, I'm really busy.
Our group leader is a 'thief': he got two hundred
yuan last month, and I only got ninety-seven — I
can't come home early."

"Forget it then."

"In the future, if there's nothing urgent, don't ring
me at work." She nimbly cut off as the last word
trailed off.

I stood there stupidly holding the receiver until the
old woman rapped the table again, and I put it back
in its cradle. Happiness, which had hardly even arrived, disappeared again leaving me clutching vainly at
its shadow. I can't even remember how I felt when the
letter arrived. It really wasn't anything urgent — Why had I rung up Little Sister? Fortunately
I hadn't disturbed Xiao Lu. Otherwise — I walked
home the same way. The shops were already closed,
and there were no people left on the streets now. Just

the flashing neon lights above my head remained. "Happy Home Brand Radios": the green neon went out, then dazzling red characters appeared in the darkness: "Happy Home Brand Electrical Appliances for the Happy Home". The line of characters flashed twice and then fell into darkness. Almost immediately the green characters leapt out again: "Happy Home Brand Washing Machines", "Happy Home Brand Record Players," "Happy Home Brand Radios" —

I stared at them for ages and suddenly felt a wave of dizziness, as though my head was swelling up; everything started to spin before my eyes, and when I shut them, I felt as though I was standing on a turntable and out of control, the things in my stomach churning too and surging for my throat. I didn't know how, but I felt my gums go all soft and saliva flooding outwards from either side of my tongue. I quickly clutched at a nearby tree and stood still a moment. When I opened my eyes and saw the world again, it was still those trembling characters that came into view: "Happy Home Brand Electrical Appliances for the Happy Home". I quickly looked away. In the cold night wind, scraps of paper hung down from a multi-coloured wall covered with all sorts of posters: "Good faith house swap". "Good faith exchange: Beijing— Shanghai". One poster had a picture of a ballet-dancer on it: "Quick Method of Teaching". The paste on the back of the posters was oozing down the wall; some of the posters were old and already torn, and under my gaze they shrank smaller and smaller, trembling their way into the distance.

Feeling drunk, I made my way along, step by step, using the wall for support until I reached some steps in front of a building. Here I sat down, unable to go any further. Right next to me was a young couple. The girl was quite openly sitting on her boyfriend's knees, her feet swaying in mid-air, the boy cuddling her and clumsily rocking her. To any passers-by — including me sitting right next to them — they paid not the slightest attention. I buried my head deep between my knees, oblivious to everything. For a long while I even forgot myself and couldn't remember a thing. I was only aware of the existence of the couple next to me. What they were actually doing or saying was beyond me too. I was just vaguely aware of the girl's affected voice, which sounded wrong for someone of her age; it was a spoilt child's whiny voice — Were they coarse? Were they disgusting? I had no idea. All my dazed brain was registering was the fact that they were pressed so tightly together and must be very warm — A damp chill spread up from my bottom. My hands gripped my shoulders as I leaned on my knees. I really envied the two of them.

America, the scholarship and those neon lights were dazzling me and making my heart beat wildly. But when daylight came, they would all just disappear like a dream without a trace. America's no paradise; there was still a harsh reality advancing towards me. Working, working (if it isn't washing dishes, then its acting as an au pair), rushing around to earn a living, to read those frigid books, just me on my own, no Little Sister, no Xiao Yan, no Xiao Lu, not even this couple pressing next to me. I wouldn't be able to smell the stench of a crowd of jostling people again. Why do I still want to go then? Now that you're about to start another life at your age, what have you got planned, I asked myself time and again. What's America got for you? I yearn for change, I yearn for honesty, I yearn to leave all my frustrations behind, I yearn to broaden my horizons. That's probably the answer. But I still can't convince myself. When I think about leaving, I suddenly feel a lightness caused by the knowledge that the burden I've born for several decades is about to fall off. It's as if when I take one stride, the whole of my body will tumble headlong. In America, what will it matter — my frustrations, my agonies, my joys even, and with whom will I share them?

God, why didn't I think of all this sooner?

Late at night, Little Sister turned to me and mumbled as though she were talking in her sleep: "When you go, can you get me some nice clothes and make-up?"

"Er — "

"Really, please don't forget. I'm just worried that once you've got lots of money I'll never see you again." As she spoke, she stretched out an arm and squeezed me affectionately. But when Little Sister talks like that, I never know how to reply.

Little Sister slipped hazily back to sleep. Her arm pressed heavier and heavier against me, and her hot little palm shook as she breathed in and out. But I just couldn't get to sleep. Those neon lights were fixed now, hanging in the darkness and twisting into strange shapes, stretching out one claw after another to stab me. I shrunk backwards and discovered that I had fallen into a desolate and uninhabited zone. It was as though I had lost myself. I suddenly twitched and woke myself up. Scared, I turned over and sat up, which woke up Little Sister again. I didn't care. I pulled up my knees and, resting my head in my hands, tried to calm down. I felt Little Sister's warm hand brushing my dry waist. "Get to sleep, sis. What's the matter?" "Nothing, something startled me. I thought I was lost." "Don't go to America. I wouldn't want all that hardship." "It's not that I'm worried about." "What is it then?" "I can't really say __ I, I want to get married." "Who to?" "A man."

"Sis?" Little Sister was shaking me. "You're talking in your sleep."

"No, I'm not." I knew that I'd never been more awake. In the dark room, it was almost as though the sound hadn't issued from my lips. It was too steady. My wizened fingers thrust deep into my hair, the tips scratching the roots.

"I want to marry Xiao Lu. Don't laugh at me."

"Of course not." Little Sister started to cry. "Why are you in such a hurry? You've only known each other two months. Is it wise?"

"You don't understand. It's actually very simple. When I go to America, I can't be a rootless person __ In America, I think I'll always be an outsider."

"Well, write and tell me everything."

Little Sister, when your impulsiveness leaves you, how long will your patience and interest in me last? When you're far away, how do you preserve this fragile thread? Little Sister tugged the quilt upwards with both hands and burst into tears in spite of herself. I gave her the pillow cover to dry her eyes.

... I turn over and get out of bed. I daren't think back to the terrible humiliation. I haven't even put on my shoes, and the freezing cold floor is making my whole body shiver. Who can I blame? No one. No one forces me to go. Let me freeze. That's called reaping what you sow. I should carve the humiliation into my heart, and that way I won't make the same mistake twice.

But I don't have any faith in myself. It's all thanks to damned America. Why do I try so hard to get to that dump? It's like when I was in the village, and I was desperately yearning to come back to the city. I always forget that if I'm in a place that I don't belong to, even if I'm planted there like a tree, I'll be thirsty, I'll wither, and then I'll die.

I dive back under the quilt again and curl up into a ball, shivering.

I've had it; I'm finished. I must just be a good-for-nothing. Otherwise, why would Xiao Lu have gone back on his word at a time like that?

I asked him: "Have you got all the marriage documents sorted out?"

"Here they are." He hung his head and started looking through his pocket. "I've been really busy just lately, everything's in a mess."

Chatting together, the two of us entered the building. But Xiao Lu kept looking around him, really nervous. I stared at him and was dense enough not to notice anything amiss. We strode along the long corridor of the District Committee building. The office doors on each side all had rectangular plaques, but owing to the fact that there were windows only at the ends of the corridor, it was too dark to get anything more than the basic gist of what was written on them.

"Su Ning, will you wait a minute. I — " Xiao Lu plucked up all his courage and said. "Everyone keeps saying I — I'm not good enough for you — "

The corridor was so quiet and so narrow that after Xiao Lu had finished speaking, there was almost a little echo. I was really scared that someone would have heard; it sounded so deafening. I shivered uncontrollably and stopped walking but didn't dare look up at Xiao Lu. Almost as though I was mumbling to myself, I said, "Why do you listen to others? Do you still not understand me?"

He didn't answer, just carried on walking. I could hear he was holding his breath and breathing in tiny little gasps. It's so difficult to be sure what people are really thinking. How is it that such simple questions are suddenly made so complicated that they can apparently never be solved? We'd already got to the end of the corridor but still hadn't seen any plaque that referred specifically to a marriage registry. The two of us looked round at the same time and saw a fat middle-aged woman walking up; she was tidying her hair with one hand and using the other to bring a hair clip up to her mouth, where she was about to prise it open with her teeth and put it in her hair.

"Excuse me, comrade, where's the Registry Office?"

"Over there, over there — " She mumbled the answer as she struggled with the hair clip. "Over there, but up a floor. Oh, I think it's changed now. Go and ask upstairs."

She disappeared like a shadow. However, her appearance and the pause she created seemed to have snapped a thread between the two of us. Anyhow, from this point onwards Xiao Lu seemed to have changed his mind completely: "Su Ning — " "What?" He rubbed his face hard with his big hand, despite the fact that it wasn't cold at all. He obviously wanted to say something but couldn't quite get the words out. He hesitated and started walking up the stairs in the corner. He was staring into nothingness and was still rubbing himself. I stayed where I was, two steps away from him, and looked up at his strong back. He arched his back and laboriously lifted his foot, and then for some reason he caught it on the next step and stumbled forward; in the confusion, he stretched out his hand to grab something, but before he actually got hold of anything he regained his balance, and the hand was left flailing about in mid-air in a very ugly posture. In spite of myself I called out: "Watch it!"

It's all over. I was just about to go up the stairs when he suddenly turned round. We were very close, so close that we couldn't see each other's faces clearly. I wanted to know why he had stopped, what he was thinking, but in the end I learned nothing, because when I looked into his eyes, I just saw myself. A me that had changed shape in the pupils of his small eyes. My head was oval, and my cheekbones stuck out alarmingly, making me look really ugly. The little freckles under my eyes seemed magnified too. Was this me?

"Su Ning, I — " Xiao Lu finally slipped into the plural: "We — Let's go home!"

I was prepared for it but still couldn't say a word.

"I've got some other things to attend to. I've been really busy recently. I, really, I'm not making this up. If you don't believe me, ask your sister."

"Oh — "

"I — I, I, let me go home and think about it, okay?"

"Oh." Again that was all I could get out. After a while, I added: "You still haven't decided?" As I said it, I finally woke up. I finally realized where we were standing and what we were talking about. I was sorry that I'd said it, as it would look like I was being sarcastic; in fact, reality had just caught me unprepared.

"I'm sure — " He looked very nervous. "I'm sure you won't blame me. Why did you want someone like me anyway?" He looked puzzled. "I'm just a nobody, and you — you're a university graduate, you're about to go abroad — why did you want someone like me?"

Honest and kind. He really was both of those things, and maybe his honesty and kindness were prompting him to ask this question. It was true that most people would think in those terms. But during the period we'd been seeing each other, he'd been asking that question all along: had we really made no progress after all this time? Had we just been walking in circles? I looked at Xiao Lu and saw that he was waiting for me to reply, his face bright red in his nervousness. I had unconsciously turned him into a worried man; I had made him less simple, less at peace, and I had made his life a turmoil. How could I explain all that?

What could I say? I almost felt apologetic.

"So I'm a university graduate. So I'm about to go abroad. So what? What does all that prove? Does that make me someone different?" In my anger, I really wanted to come back with something like that, but when I opened my mouth I said something else instead: "Okay. Let's go home then!"

I stepped off the steps and went to stand by the window at the end of the corridor. I looked out. Outside, the sunshine was very strong, and I was dazzled; then I looked again, and it was okay. Out on the street, as I mingled with the dense stream of people and bikes, my thoughts abandoned the shadows I'd fabricated for my own happiness, and I decided not to indulge in beautiful dreams again. I would throw myself into real life once more and make my way through the jostling crowd —

I really ought to sleep. I've got a really bad headache, and there's no point in thinking about all this anyway. A new day and a new year have just begun, and this spring I'll be going to America. I look at my little room again, wanting to carve it all into my heart for the last time. But the window is as black as pitch, and so is the room. I shut my eyes, and the America I see is also dark, the tall buildings blocking out the sun. There are so many things I yearn for; behind the darkness there must be so much — But now the only thing I really hope is that if I'm reincarnated, my life won't be like this; I'd like to be someone like Little Sister or Xiao Lu — Even someone like my younger brother would be better than what I am now. I've managed to ruin everything, but I'm afraid I'll never find out where my problem really lies. Anyway, there's no such thing as reincarnation.

I'm freezing. I pull up the quilt again and start counting, 1,2,3,4.... I dive under the quilt, and it's dark there too. Maybe if there is no light at all I'll get to sleep quickly.

Translated by Christopher Smith

Peng Xiaolian was born in Shanghai in 1953 and went to live and work in a production team in Jiangxi after leaving junior middle school in 1969. In 1979 she passed the entrance examination for the Directing Department of the Beijing Film Institute and on graduation went to work as a director in the Shanghai Film Studio. Two of her films, *Me and My Classmates,* and *Women's Story*, have won prizes both in China and abroad. In her spare time she writes novels and film scripts. Her principal works include the short stories "On My Back", "Night and Day" and "Movie Dream".

Crucible

Jiang Yun

HE had never expected to take on a female apprentice this late in his career. And she did not dream that her dark-complexioned master would be so womanish.

1

It wasn't really a factory. Its full name was the Water and Electricity Installation Brigade of the Housing Commission. They did all kinds of welding and riveting. For instance when small chemical fertilizer factories sprang up all over the country the yard was suddenly littered with all types of tanks and columns for welding.

Where tanks and columns stood, weeds grew in profusion despite being trodden on and scorched by the welding torch.

There were more men than women in the workshop, and the men really spoilt them. Although the women were past their prime they still dressed up and flirted. For ten years the workshop had not taken on any new employees, and the men still called the women Gui'er, Zhenzhen, Aiai or Little Qi and Little Li as though they were young girls.

Then they took on a batch of proper apprentices,

and among them were quite a few sweet young things.

From then on the Gui'ers and the Zhenzhens and Aiais became "boss ladies".

Even so the feelings remained. Before the "boss ladies" had outgrown their Zhenzhen-Aiai era, the men had their moment of glory, which they never forgot. In those days the workshop had just been established. A few old masters and a handful of young men and women went about picking up as much piece work as they could. Making money was all that mattered. Everybody worked like a demon, and the workshop did wrest quite a sizable chunk of business from state-owned enterprises with lots of capital. They worked their fingers to the bone, but they acquired skill, strength, confidence and pride in the process. In those days everyone had a name-brand watch on their wrists, their bicycles were brand spanking new, and their shoes were always shined. There was a camaraderie too. If one wore boots, they all wore boots. When they walked into a cinema, the clicking of their heels was enough to shake down the walls of Taiyuan town.

Time passed. The Gui'ers , the Zhenzhens and the Aiais grew old, and so did the men.

They had stopped doing piecework long ago and stuck to an unchanging fixed wage. The shiny new bicycles had rusted, and the name-brand watches were on the wrists of wives. But vestiges of the glorious days remained and were passed on as legend from one generation to the next. They still held their heads high among the bricklayers and plasterers. They were not ordinary. They had a welding gun, and a skill.

Most of all they had tasted the glory and the hardship of pioneers. They loved to squat in the shade and flirt with the young girls, regaling them with tales of the past; of the shiny knee-high boots that clicked, and how they stomped about in them. Now they mostly wore tattered work shoes. The days seemed longer, but time flew by, day in day out. Even the criticism board in front of the workshop took on a new look.

He wasn't what they called home grown. He was brought in from the outside. People hated outsiders. He was like an intruder at a wedding feast, in the group but not a part of it.

He was often lonely.

He came from a poverty-stricken place called Linxian in Henan, a place that produced oesophagus cancer and beggars. The family was very poor. He left home when he was very young to learn a trade. Then, by some miracle, the Red Flag Canal was built, and a popular song about it came out. He managed to find a song sheet and learnt it, moving his lips but not actually singing. When he thought he had it down pat, he sang out loud — and found he couldn't carry a tune. He gave up singing after that.

They called him the man from Linxian.

He was a lathe operator in a large factory. During the three hard years he quit and joined the house-renovating brigade and moonlighted for extra money on the side. His father died when he was young, and he had a mother and brothers to support. They lived in East Bridge Street, which was lined with low, shabby, dun-coloured adobe houses. The inhabitants were as drab as the street. Somehow his mother found him a wife in his native place, so he went back and forth. He had four daughters. In spite of running back and forth, he felt he did not belong to anywhere.

He did not have much schooling, but he was sensitive. He had read quite a few classics and acquired a world-weariness from them. He pitied himself and vilified himself by turns. At times he felt he was no better than an ant, but then he also felt he ought not to be an ant. He was constantly torn by these conflicting emotions. He was dark-complexioned and stockily built, not at all a romantic figure. Yet there was always a vague sadness about him that people called "sourness" for lack of a better word.

He had few friends, except Old Wu. Old Wu was also a character. He had been a bricklayer. Because he belonged to the faction that was in power at the time, suddenly he was transferred to the workshop as head of the machine shop. Old Wu knew nothing about machines, but he was smart enough to see that the situation wasn't a simple one, so he brought a friend along for courage, not realizing he was even more timid than himself. He felt the others looked upon him as some kind of threat.

When he laid down his trowel and took up the ruler, he found his fingers were not as nimble as they had been. Long ago there had been another female apprentice. She had been young and worn her hair in a long braid and called him "master". He had not been quite as dark then, nor had his waist thickened. His glossy hair had been parted down the middle and smelled of pomade. His whole body had smelled of it. She had been as pale and cool as a stream. On her days off she had worn a jacket with simple patterns and carried a matching knapsack. And the last character in her name had been the faminine "mei".

He had never thought he would take another female apprentice when she left. He thought they were more trouble than they were worth.

But here was Old Wu with another one. This one was thin. A long neck rested on prominent collar bones. Her eyes were wide, and her brows were thick. Her mouth seemed to take up most of her narrow face. It was late spring and dry, and her lips were chapped and flaking. She was ugly. But the way she addressed him as Master Zhao struck a chord. Also she had an unusual name — Pu — which probably meant she came from a cultured family. And she was talkative. "I'm rather dumb," she told him.

"I don't think so," he replied.

"I really am." She was quite definite about it.

"Then you'll have to learn slowly," he said matter-of-factly. "It's not that hard."

"I'll never get the hang of it." Her mind was quite made up. "Not in a hundred years."

"Then you might as well quit." There seemed nothing more to say.

"But you mustn't send me back." She seemed to look upon him as an accomplice. "I beg you."

She had a high forehead. She was anything but dumb.

"Who said anything about sending you back?" he smiled.

She smiled too. When she smiled she was quite pretty.

"I've been given several copies of *Machine Layouts*. Please don't give me another," she said.

He smiled awkwardly and said nothing. He could not fathom this strange new apprentice.

"Don't you want to be a worker?" he asked.

"No." She was emphatic.

"What do you want?"

"To wander," she said. "To go to the ends of the earth and do what I want."

Her answer took him by surprise. He sensed she had not led an easy life and that she was probably very unhappy. He asked her what she meant by doing what she liked.

"Just doing whatever I fancy, on the spur of the moment," she said.

He said, "Here you can do as you please. I won't interfere."

She had seen the song sheet sticking out of his jacket pocket. It was the old song about the rolling waters of the Zhang River and the mighty Taihang Mountains. To show her gratitude she said, "I'll teach you the song."

2

The B665 shaping machine had stood against the southwest wall beside his tool cupboard. He moved it a smidgen to make space for a locker room. There was no locker, so the clothes that came off were thrown in a heap in the tool cupboard. He propped a few boards on some bricks, and that served as a rest bench.

She thought it was quite luxurious, a perfect place to read, but kept her thoughts to herself. He kept asking her to teach him songs. She taught him the one about the rolling Zhang River, and went on to one about wild geese and the brigade marching forth. But he was tone deaf, and he could never stay on key, and she was bored.

"Did I get it right that time?" he asked anxiously.

"Perfect," she said to mollify him.

He never put on airs with her. If anything, he was anxious to please, and she was grateful in her way. When she said she hated sharpening tools, he did it himself. Then she was embarrassed.

"I'm allergic to the sharpener," she explained. "When the sharpener starts turning I break out in goose bumps."

"I understand," he said quickly.

"Have you ever heard of anything so silly?" she asked.

He had to admit that he had not.

"I had a schoolmate who broke out in bumps the minute she was assigned to farm in the countryside. They were everywhere, even in her eyes, nose and throat. They tried everything on her, but nothing worked. They sent her home, and she got over it right away, but when she went back to the village, back they came. The doctors finally thought she had an allergy. Do you know what she was allergic to?"

"What?"

"It was the adobe sleeping platform!" she giggled.

"It takes all kinds," he sighed. "You have the frail bodies of ladies but have to lead the life of maids."

"That's right," she smiled coldly. "The heart wants to fly, but the body is rooted to the ground."

He glanced at the wistful, lonely curve of her wide mouth with a hint of haughtiness in it. She must come from a well-to-do family that has fallen from grace, he thought.

She didn't mind the heavy work: moving half-finished products, dumping metal shavings, swabbing the floor and such. She knew what was expected of an apprentice. She would really put her back into working the bench vice. She would insert a length of pipe, grasp it and press down. For a moment the effort lifted her off the ground. But the vice held. She could do it as well as he. Strangely enough she preferred the heavy work. On the other hand work that required skill didn't interest her. Other apprentices would butter up their master, anxious to look at blueprints, careful to pick up any little tricks of the trade. But she was not interested. She could not read blueprints.

"This is a cross section," he explained.

"You tell me what to do, and I'll do it," she cut him off. "I'll never learn all that."

He was worried. "If you can't read a blueprint, how are you going to do the job?"

"You'll tell me."

"What if I'm not around?"

"Where can you go?"

"What if I die?"

"There'll always be a way," she said.

There was nothing to do but let her carry on with the heavy work.

Once he remarked that she had strong hands. She lifted up a pair of gnarled and calloused hands and said ruefully as Ke Xiang in *Azalea Mountain* did, "What does one get working? Shoulders of iron and thick strong hands."

They laughed companionably. She had a loud, open laugh, and she didn't mind the curious glances it attracted.

He said, "I want you to do something for me."

"What is it?"

"I want you to jot down all the phrases and idioms you use each day in a notebook for me."

Her face went blank. What did he expect her to do? Scribble every phrase down as she uttered them? How was anyone to carry on a conversation that way?

"Will you do it for me?" he asked again.

"I'll try," she said, not knowing what else to say.

But the request perplexed her. He really got a notebook for her and put it in the tool cupboard. First he asked her to try and remember all the expressions she used. She wracked her brain and came up with things like "do as I please", "wandering to the ends of the earth" and "the heart wants to fly, but the body is rooted to the ground". And she told herself to stop using expressions like that.

He leafed through the notebook and muttered, "Here you can do as you please."

She sighed. The last of the daylight struggled through the grimy window and flooded them with pale light. His dark face was haggard. The bench vice groaned, planing a large sheet of metal. The shavings flying off in sizzling blue curls struck his arm.

He was oblivious to the smell of scorched flesh, but her gorge rose.

3

Gradually people took a dislike to her. She was ugly, proud and affected, and she had the sour man wrapped around her finger.

The weather turned warm. Spring was over quickly

in this town. The winds of spring stirred up dust that cut off the sun. When the wind fell off, the sun blazed, and it was summer. As usual tea and sugar were distributed to fend off the heat, but the tea was stale, and if it was made strong, it burned the throat and looked murky. The workers became lethargic in the heat. They sat around most of the day, hiding in empty rooms or behind the tanks and columns away from the searching eyes of the bosses. They chatted or played poker, and somehow the day passed. The regulation one hour lunch break stretched into two and three hours. They emerged from a comfortable nap and groggily quaffed a cup of cool tea, which sent a warm surge through their bodies. The machine shop was silent.

Not a sound came from it. Everyone seemed to avoid it.

As long as they were together, no one else came near, but the others watched the two of them huddled by the tool cupboard, talking and singing. He sounded like a cat in heat. They made faces and said it was "sickening".

They disapproved of his flirting. The man from Linxian, with his dark face and his thick body, was behaving like a romantic matinée idol, when everyone knew he had a wife in his home town.

These were down-to-earth people. When you're thirsty you drink; when you're hungry you eat. That was their creed. All this sentimental mumbo-jumbo grated on their nerves. Men were supposed to be straightforward and women passionate. A prank had to be bawdy to be good. To be sure, there were matinée idol types among them, who were handsome and dashing and had many affairs.

Although these fellows played the sentimental lover, in the end it was still a matter of slaking a certain thirst.

It was all a game. Lao Yuan was that sort.

Lao Yuan was a machinist of about thirty. He was fair-skinned and tall and wore horn-rimmed glasses. In the winter he was always in a silver grey or blue suit of padded cotton, cut in the Chinese style. A long, wine-red scarf was drawn around his neck, half of it carelessly flung over a shoulder, as dashing as a movie star. In the summer it was either a blue or a snow-white shirt and carefully creased pants. He could sing bawdy songs, play a bit of accordion, catch fish, play poker and recite a bit of poetry that made women wild. He was always after fresh prey.

When it came to women Lao Yuan was usually gallant. But for some reason he despised her. He was constantly running her down. He once remarked, "She's got the mouth of a hippo! Who'd want to kiss a hippo!"

Everyone laughed.

"To each his own," they chortled.

"Right. Get desperate enough, and you'll have it off with a pig or a dog."

The women smiled knowingly and spat on the ground. "Sickening beast!"

In the southwest corner the lathe was huffing and puffing, smoothing out some object. They stood on either side, she scraping away the metal shavings with a wire hook and he intently watching the blade glide back and forth.

"They're talking about me," he remarked.

She looked up. "What are they saying?"

"They're talking about me, that's all."

"Let them," she chuckled coldly. "They can't hurt you."

"Don't you care?"

"Me?" she was amused. "Why should I?"

"Once I had a friend who said if someone spat in his face, he wouldn't wipe it off. He'd leave it to dry," he said.

She was suddenly uncomfortable. That was going too far. She couldn't imagine what it would be like to have someone spit in her face. Spittle left to dry must surely smell. She felt dirtied.

"Life is meaningless," he remarked.

"It's hard," she agreed.

Maybe it had to do with the passing of spring. She seemed to bloom. The dryness went out of her, and even the flakes of dried skin on her lips disappeared and they became red and lustrous. She seemed fairer too. It was as if she had been reborn. When he looked at her, heat suffused him. They talked about all sorts of things. Mostly they talked about the books they'd read. She read mostly Western books; he read Chinese classics. He told her his favourite was *Er Du Mei*. It was a sad story, he told her, and the character "*mei*" in his daughters' names came from it, but he did not tell her the other reason for that "*mei*".

In his speech there was a hint of a Linxian accent. Most people from there had an accent. The difference with him was that he was soft-spoken, and there was always a tragic undertone in his voice. He was diffident and shy like a girl. The longer you knew him the more you came to recognize his womanishness.

That was a quality she disliked. She recognized the tragic quality in him, and she wondered where it stemmed from. Gradually she stopped thinking of him as a teacher, just as he had never thought of her as an apprentice. He pitied her. She was like a puppy that had fallen into water. She was just a helpless, wet puppy scratching at his heart. Only she wouldn't stop until she unearthed something soft, like a larva. His heart felt like a larva, wriggling slowly, uncomfortably. He listened to her endless chatter, and there was a clean, tender feeling in him. But at night his dreams were confused, dirty and shameful. When he woke his sheets were wet. Yet he never harboured an indecent thought during the day. Finally he had to admit that he was despicable and dirty like the rest.

When he met her the next day he felt awkward. It was as though he had sullied her.

Of all things, she had to talk about a dream she had had and went on to describe it in graphic detail.

She said, "I dreamt I gave birth to a hundred and twenty-seven frogs."

He was bathed in cold, clammy sweat. His flesh crawled.

"Really. I remember it vividly. One, two, three, four ... a hundred and twenty-seven frogs. Strange. Why not a hundred and twenty-five?" she looked up at him and sighed. "It was disgusting."

He was bewitched, restless. Each night before he dropped off, he begged himself not to have another of those exhausting dreams, but from time to time they came unbidden. During the day he felt guilty, afraid she might somehow sense his betrayal. She became more attractive by the day. It was her wide mouth that fascinated him the most. Her smile tugged at his heart. Her long, thin body became supple and yielding. She had taken on the shape of a woman, and she enjoyed the dumb admiration in his eyes. Yet it made her uncomfortable too. Although she was accustomed to the informality between them, and she was grateful for a master who did not put on airs, she was suddenly aware that he was a man. The new awareness made her suddenly awkward.

She thought a master ought to be aloof. And then she noticed there was a subtle change in the atmosphere.

4

She was sensitive. It did not take her long to recognize the looks she was getting, and she was dismayed.

"They're talking about us," she told him.

"I know," he replied.

"Beasts," she chuckled, "measuring everyone by their own standards."

He did not know how to respond, so he kept silent.

No one greeted her. No one asked her help in private chores, share a joke, have a chat or go out shopping. No one noticed when she put on a new dress. They were only interested in examining him and her under a microscope. At first she was aloof. Finally when she understood she was being isolated, she was angry.

Do I care? she asked herself. Do their tricks bother me? She was used to loneliness. There was something almost noble in that. She went through the yard and the workshop with her head high, looking neither right nor left. She did not want to speak to or be bothered by anyone. She buried herself in books. She became irritable.

Once he asked her to measure something that had just been planed. She slammed the calipers on the work bench viciously and said, "I told you I don't like the work, and I don't want to learn. Why force me!"

The machines were stopped just then, and she was shrill. Everyone heard. She looked around and saw them whispering with their heads together and burst into tears. He was silent all that afternoon. He was distracted. His hand trembled so, he could barely hold the calipers. He did not notice the cutting edge was going too deep until, with a crunch, it went through the lathe. The machines shrieked, and still he did not react. Fortunately Lao Wu heard the noise and came running to shut off the power. "Idiot!" Lao Wu shouted.

He said nothing.

She shot a nervous glance at his blank face and wondered what to do. Why couldn't he put on the airs of a master, just this once? If only he would rage and rant and behave the way he was supposed to. She could bear anything but this blandness. He was beyond help, she decided. She sighed. She made up her mind not to behave like a spoilt brat from then on. She couldn't stand his look of dumb hurt. She had discovered he liked the theme song from *Green Pine Hill*, for she had seen the slip of paper on which he had copied the lyrics sticking out of his pocket. She knew he wanted to learn it but was too shy to ask. She was feeling guilty and resolved to teach him as a peace offering. She taught him the song line by line, mustering all the patience she had. She was aware of the amused glances of the others, and that depressed her. He was in a daze, and the tune wandered all over the place. He sensed the others giggling in the corner, but when he saw the look of utter resignation on her face, he could not utter another sound. He was sad and embarrassed. She was numb. She held a metal hook used for scraping metal filings in her hand. She lifted it sharply and shattered the light bulb over the lathe. With a loud pop, the work bench was plunged in darkness. It was an odd reflex. The sudden darkness stunned them both.

Finally, still dazed, she said plaintively, "Why don't you yell at me? Why are you so easy to bully?"

He just looked at her without a word.

5

They went on like that. When she was in a good mood, she chattered merrily. She always had a lot to say, and in her loneliness she needed an audience. He gradually got used to her unpredictable moods. When she smiled, the sun shone in the little corner. When she did not, the whole world sank into gloom.

It was a long, hot summer. When it was over he felt he had aged ten years. The autumn rains of September began, and he asked leave to go home for the harvest. He did not tell her until the date of his departure was fixed.

"But what will I do?" she asked in a panic.

Suddenly she was the helpless puppy again. He was

soft. He actually thought of not going home. But then
the thin yellow face of his wife flashed before his eyes.
His wife had given him four daughters and ended with
a list of illnesses as long as your arm. She had chronic
back aches and heavy menstruations. He couldn't
leave his wife to her own devices at harvest time. On
the other hand he couldn't leave her either, since she
couldn't even sharpen tools. So he spent the night in
the workshop sharpening a whole range of tools,
which he laid in the tool cupboard for her.

He told her, "Select the things that you can do,
things that are easy. And take your time. Leave the
other stuff to me."

She said she would. She looked so lost and abandoned that he felt guilty for leaving her.

" Come back quickly," she said.

He promised he would be back as soon as possible.
He forgot her arrogance and unreasonableness. He
only thought of her good points, her helplessness and
her cleverness. Her pitiful look haunted him and made
him think of his wife as the hateful perpetrator of this
unchivalrous thing he was doing. He blamed himself
for her predicament and worried she might not be able
to cope with a heavy and dangerous machine.

In fact she could not cope. She was unusually clumsy and nervous. In the mornings when she had
changed into her coveralls, she hesitated to throw the
electric switch, afraid the machines might catch fire and
explode. Her imagination ran riot. She stood in front
of the switch shifting her weight from one foot to the
other, unable to touch it. In the end she shut her eyes,
gritted her teeth and reached for it. It went on with a
snap, and there was no explosion. Then she breathed

a sigh of relief. But the palms of her hands were sweating. She realized how much she needed him. In this tiny corner of the earth, he was her brain, her backbone, her eyes and her limbs. He was the jar she kept in the corner, into which she dropped whatever she fancied.

It happened that work was heavy just then, and everything came marked urgent. She could not read blueprints. Though she turned them this way and that, she might have been reading horoscopes for all the sense she made of them.

Fortunately a lot of the work she had done before. Although she could not read the blueprints, she at least knew what needed to be done, and nothing went terribly wrong. Also he had asked Lao Wu to keep an eye on her, and Lao Wu was as good as his word, dropping by and giving her pointers. She endured, counting the days to his return. She dreamed of looking up and seeing his smiling face beside her. She forgot her boredom, forgot his irritating womanish ways, his sentimentality and his sour ways. She brushed all that aside. It was as though she had never been annoyed by him. She was unsure of herself and nervous, and she missed him.

Before long all the tools were blunt. She tried to sharpen a planer blade herself, but the minute she turned on the sharpener, the blade began to jump in her hand. She held on, though her hand hurt. The blade was almost worn away but still had no cutting edge. She took it to the forge and begged the blacksmith for help. She leaned on the door jamb and watched the two men hammering a lump of golden-red metal on the anvil. One had a thin, dark face, and the other was fat. The smithy was dark and cramped. Its dun-coloured adobe walls, the gloom and the two taciturn men lent the place an air of mystery. She heard the sizzle of the water, and the steam that billowed was acrid. The blacksmith threw the blade at her feet: "Take it away."

After that she tried sharpening them herself again. The handle got hotter and hotter, until she could not hold it and broke out in a sweat. Someone shoved her aside roughly and said, "Give it to me."

It was Lao Yuan.

Instantly the sharpener wheel hummed. Lao Yuan was in his element. The blade was sharpened in a trice. He mounted the blade on the planer. "Now let's try it," Lao Yuan said. She switched on the machine, which made a swishing sound, and the metal shavings that flew off were silver-blue crystals. She had never seen anything quite as beautiful.

"Thank you," she said. The words slipped out before she could stop them.

People were not used to thanking one another.

"Don't thank me," Lao Yuan said. He grinned, showing a neat row of pearly teeth. "Your master hasn't even shown you how to sharpen blades."

She quickly went to his defence. "It's my fault. I'm too stupid to learn."

"The man from Linxian is careless."

"No. I am stupid."

"Not at all," said Lao Yuan, "in fact you're the cleverest of the lot."

Lao Yuan laid flattery on with a trowel, and there was no gainsaying him, for it just made you sound pretentious.

"I really am stupid. My mother used to feed me chicken wings to make me clever, but it didn't work."

Lao Yuan flashed her a smile. They were relaxed. She saw him in a new light, not as an enemy. In fact she thought he wasn't a bad sort.

"I know you read a lot. What do you like the most?"

"Oh, just anything I can lay my hands on."

"I like reading too."

"What do you like?"

"The classics," he said, and named Zola's *Nana* and several others. "I've read them all."

He was tall and handsome and wore a pair of scholarly-looking spectacles. He dressed like a student leader of the May Fourth Movement. He was well read, and talking to him was a joy. It was before the time of the Japanese film star Takakura Ken, who seldom smiled. In troubled times women preferred the smiling, romantic, matinee idol type. He was the sort that would appeal to a woman such as her.

6

Actually Lao Yuan also had a female apprentice, called Jilian.

Jilian was a coquette. When she walked she seemed to float. She had big, wide eyes set in a rosy, heart-shaped face. Jilian glowed. Jilian was simple. It only took a few kind words to have her eating out of your hand. People took advantage of her good nature. If you stole a kiss or a feel, she would never complain or make a scene. The others said Jilian was cheap and that her mother was a fallen woman.

Jilian's mother had three daughters. Within a month of giving birth, she started binding her waist, so tight she hardly breathed. Now she was over forty, and her waist was still like a young girl's.

Jilian had her mother's figure but her father's eyebrows and eyes. She was attractive but not brassy. She was modish. Her work pants were a bit faded and shrunken, showing a trim ankle clad in light brown stockings. She had had several love affairs, none of them serious. They had caused neither much joy nor sadness. At the moment she was involved with a young thug from west of the river around Xiayuan. It didn't take the young thug long to have Jilian completely mesmerized. Her parents were violently against it, and Jilian was often sporting bruises on her face and body. Everyone knew her father was beating her. But it didn't dampen her spirits. Jilian was as cheerful as ever.

The only person that intimidated Jilian was her master. Lao Yuan had time to laugh and chat with the women. He was friendly with everyone but her.

When his work was done, she had to fetch water for him to wash his greasy hands. He would frown angrily if she was slow. He was full of the master's airs and graces. Although he had a reputation as a ladies' man, he never laid a finger on Jilian.

7

Lao Yuan started going around to the southwest corner of the workshop to chat with her.

"It's quiet here," Lao Yuan remarked.

"That's because no one ever comes here," she

replied.

"Your master is a strange man," said Lao Yuan.

She agreed and immediately regretted it. "But he's a good man," she added lamely.

Lao Yuan sensed he had touched a nerve and said no more, but he was spending more and more time with her talking about books. He lent her *The Red and the Black*, *Nana* and *The Small Hotel*. She lent him *Eugene Onegin* and *Jean Christophe*. Lao Yuan knew some bawdy songs. She brought a collection of 200 folk songs from around the world, and they found they knew most of the same ones. They started singing together. Sometimes he sang the lead, and sometimes she did. Their voices blended well and attracted quite a following of youngsters. Suddenly the southwest corner became very popular. Young people such as Jilian, Erbao, Xiao Jiao and Xianxian gathered there to listen.

Sometimes they played a game matching titles of films, old and new, locally made and foreign. One person would think of a title and the other would quickly have to come up with another. She and Lao Yuan always lasted the longest.

She knew a lot of foreign films, and Lao Yuan had the names of a number of films made in Hongkong.

"How old are you, that you've seen all those films?" asked Lao Yuan.

"I guess I've seen them all, but all I remember are the titles," she replied.

They both felt a nameless melancholy. At such times they felt very close to one another. Melancholy suited Lao Yuan, with his pale face and burning black eyes.

She no longer missed him, and the days flew by.

Lao Yuan, watching her fumbling with the blue-prints, soon realized she could not read them.

"Can't you read them?"

She shook her head and reddened.

"It's easy," said Lao Yuan.

"I can't seem to get the knack of it."

"That's because you refuse to learn."

They sighed. Lao Yuan looked at her curiously pale face and said comfortingly, "A monk has to ring the temple bell. It's inevitable." Lao Yuan made sense. It seemed that no one else had ever spoken to her so simply and directly before. She forgot how her master had tried to reason with her time and again. Lao Yuan traced a fingertip across the drawings, and everything became perfectly clear.

Finally Lao Yuan was finished.

There was no sound in the machine shop except the rain falling on the weeds and drumming on the tanks and columns outside. It rained miserably till nightfall.

"Thank you," she said.

Lao Yuan smiled wistfully. She did not know what was on Lao Yuan's mind, but she sensed whatever it was, she needed it. She felt almost transparent in her need.

"We seem destined to meet," was all he said.

8

Lao Yuan came from a family that had fallen on hard times. His father and grandfather had been in positions of power when the warlord Yan Xishan was a name to reckon with, but he had never shared any of their glory. Instead he endured a great deal of hardship as a result of that connection.

Still, he enjoyed talking about those times. He spoke of his family with regret but also a certain pride.

"You'd be surprised what a lot of fallen nobility this rough place harbours," he told her.

Lao Yuan pointed out that this one had been the head of broadcasting under the Kuomintang; that one was the scion of a wealthy overseas Chinese who had made his fortune in rubber in Indonesia; and the father of another was currently a member of congress in Taiwan. But she saw them only as dull nonentities indistinguishable from the grey masses. Lao Yuan was different.

There was a touching romanticism about him, as though he carried some secret burden. In their silent moments she seemed to reach for something, at once bitter and warm, just beyond her grasp. Lao Yuan had a dainty wife, whom people said was the perfect mate for him. Yet he never spoke of her and often sighed at the unfairness of life. He was fond of Lu Fangweng's *The Phoenix Comb* and sometimes sang bits of it to her.

"That's the way life is," sighed Lao Yuan.

It made her heartsore.

9

She had almost forgotten there was anyone else in the world, unaware that one was hurrying back as fast as he could.

One morning as she came out of the locker room, there he was, as though he had fallen from the sky.

"Master, you're back!" she cried excitedly.

He was glad to be back, but there was also a trace

of sadness in his face. So many emotions churned within him. He was darker and thinner, standing there like a shadow.

There was a womanish tenderness in his eyes that was disturbing.

Lao Wu came over. "You're back early. Is the harvest done?" he asked.

He mumbled something and blushed as though a secret had been exposed. Actually he had been restless at home and bored with his country wife. The place where he had grown up tending cattle and playing in the mud had become alien to him. He had been lost. He had left before the harvest was really over and hurried back to the town as though a hundred devils were on his heels. He had been eager to be back in the town that enticed him, yet he was a fish out of water there too.

"You're tanned," she observed.

She too had changed. When he left she had had the eyes of a frightened mouse, but now her eyes flashed like a cat's. She had been a pitiful little thing wondering how to cope. Her helplessness had haunted him and compelled him to hurry back, but she had changed into a pert little cat. She glowed, asking him this and that, making him feel awkward. He was expecting a mess: work piled everywhere, waste needing to be dumped, blunt tools left helter-skelter, the machinery gathering dust, and her at her wits' end, waiting for him to put things right. But everything was shipshape. Finished work was neatly arranged on the shelves. Unfinished work was laid out on the work bench. There was no sign of disorder.

"You've never done this work before," he remarked.

"That's right."

"Do you know how?"

"I just followed the blueprints," she said, unable to disguise the pride in her voice.

"Can you read them?"

"Sort of — "

She had performed a sleight of hand. He could not fathom her, and she enjoyed the effect. There was a time when she thought it would be such fun to be able to wave a piece of red cloth and produce a snake or a bowl of goldfish, but she didn't really want to be a magician. It was just that it would add a dash of excitement to her drab life. She tilted her head to one side and watched the strange expression on his face.

"Oh! Oh," he said.

She wondered what the exclamation meant. Although she didn't bother to think about it, the moment was spoilt.

"Not being able to read blueprints was a handicap, but Master Wu and Master Yuan gave me some pointers. The rest I muddled through."

She had unintentionally brought Master Wu into the picture and given Lao Yuan a back seat. She tried to sound light and cheerful, but her words were still a clap of thunder over his head. She saw the dumb look in his face and knew what he was thinking. He had a suspicious nature, and he felt betrayed.

People were factional here. None should poke a finger in anybody else's pie. Still she considered him really shallow and such a peasant. She didn't want to quarrel on his first day back. She tried to sound casual, but it came out sounding defensive.

"What's the matter? It's almost impossible to work without reading the blue-prints."

"Oh! Oh!" he muttered distractedly. He thought she was being self-righteous and putting the blame on him, when all along it was he who had been trying to convince her of that simple fact.

She felt a helpless rage against his silence. If only he would rant at her, scold her for shaming him, rail at the others for their interference: anything except his "Oh! Oh", which infuriated her and meant nothing.

The other apprentices, Xiao Jiao, Jilian and Xianxian, drifted in. They all greeted him. Even Lao Yuan shouted a greeting to him. He was amazed. It had never happened before. He was sure it had nothing to do with him. It was her, and she was full of guile. He was the last to leave after work that day. Lao Wu was waiting outside the gate and engaged him in gossip. He listened with growing impatience.

Finally Lao Wu said, "That apprentice of yours is unreliable. Sooner or later Lao Yuan's bunch will lure her away."

His temper flared. "What's it to you?" he shouted.

10

The southwest corner of the workshop was silent again.

They stood on opposite sides of the work bench, he watching the planer glide back and forth, she listlessly scraping the shavings off with a hook.

The lathe hummed. Everything was as it had been, but he knew nothing would ever be the same.

No one came into their corner. Xiao Jiao, Jilian and

Xianxian made faces at her from across the room. She grinned back. He could not see what was happening behind his back. He only saw her grin, and he was overcome with loneliness. His hangdog look irritated her. Often she would slip away to read in the locker room. At other times she went to another part of the workshop to gossip with Xiao Jiao and the other young people. She felt justified slacking off under his nose. Sometimes Lao Yuan would saunter over and join them. Everybody talked at once. Lao Yuan regaled them with stories of the past and the antics of the famous ones among them. He told how two people had made a wager whereby the loser would have to call the winner father, but the loser had turned the tables on the victor by treating himself as a child. He had started demanding food and drink, cigarettes and spending money from his make-believe dad. The thing had got so out of hand that the winner had had to concede defeat. Lao Yuan had the knack of spinning a yarn, and listening to him, she wondered if some hurt lay hidden under his jollity.

She and Lao Yuan lived in the same part of town. Often they rode their bicycles home together. They rode slowly, chatting companionably. She saved a great many things to tell Lao Yuan, just as she had done with him. It did not occur to her that she was casting about for a new audience. She and Lao Yuan began to look like lovers.

One time Xiao Jiao overtook them and mischievously shouted, "A pair of prawns, a pair of prawns, worth one yuan twenty-eight," and sped off.

She blushed, but he shrugged it off. "Rascal," he said casually.

She relaxed. She liked a man who could conceal his inner turmoil.

"Will one yuan twenty-eight buy a catty or a pair?" he asked chuckling.

"You'd be lucky to get the small shrimps at that price," she countered.

They laughed, but their laughter was laced with sadness. Neither knew where the sadness stemmed from, except that it ran deep. They became self-conscious and talked of inconsequential things. He said he liked prawns, and she admitted she liked them too, but she couldn't find them in the market. He named several other things he liked to eat, and she thought he had refined taste.

"I am a born gentleman," he said archly.

He was showing off when he said that, and she realized it helped him survive.

11

Jilian was pregnant, but no one knew.

She bound her waist like her mother had, and she wore loose-fitting clothes, so that even in the fifth and sixth months no one noticed.

But the "boss ladies" were shrewd enough to detect some subtle changes in her. They remarked that hers were no longer the buttocks of a virgin. They said that pregnant women craved hot, spicy foods. Jilian did not exhibit any such tendency. She was as active as ever, trying to shake loose the unwanted lump of flesh growing within her. But it was firmly anchored. She moved loads of half-finished products, but still it clung. She remembered her grandmother saying once that unhingeing old-fashioned doors caused abortions. but there was no such door in the town. She did not know what to do. Her man was the responsible type.

"We'll get married," he said without hesitation.

"But I haven't finished my apprenticeship," Jilian worried.

Finally, when her condition was beyond concealment, her mother wept, and her father threatened to kill her.

Eventually they calmed down. Her parents prepared good wine, cigarettes and fancy cakes, and when the marriage certificate was obtained, a wedding date was set. The boy's family cleared a room and gave them some furniture. It was a happy occasion, although it was close to the date when the baby would be due. The brigade was naturally less than pleased. Jilian had not finished her apprenticeship, and this would create an undesirable precedent.

However, she was pregnant, and in the end their objections were only on paper. Lao Yuan was humiliated. None of the other masters had encountered anything like it. Jilian had let him down. He wore a long face, and Jilian cowered and did her best to keep out of his way. Jilian invited all the apprentices to her wedding and included the masters too, although she knew they would not come.

Xiao Jiao, Xianxian and the others scrubbed their faces clean and went with a sense of high adventure. Afterwards they talked of nothing but the sumptuousness of the feast and the beauty of the wedding chamber.

Jilian wore a short jacket of red silk, her little round belly protruding in front of her. Everyone agreed the short jacket was a mistake. The older women cornered the young ones and made them describe Jilian's dress and headgear down to the smallest detail. They wanted to know what the groom wore and what Jilian's parents wore. Were they happy or were they glum? How did the young couple entertain their guests? What was on the menu, and was the meat cooked in fresh oil and the chicken done to a turn? When they had heard all they wanted, they clucked and shook their heads.

"Apparently it went well. Someone on our street gave birth at the wedding," said one of the "boss ladies".

"Really, what is the world coming to!"

"They say, 'you may have seen the world, but have you seen your mother's wedding?'" The women hunched their shoulders and tittered. The young people blushed to the roots of their hair.

In the small hours, three days later Jilian was rushed to the hospital and gave birth to a strong baby girl.

The brigade marked Jilian for a serious breach of conduct and put her on probation for a year. Jilian thought nothing of it, but Lao Yuan's nose was seriously out of joint.

12

His wife came and left their eldest daughter with him.

Actually it was his idea. He thought the girl was clever.

"Let her go to school in the city," he suggested.

And because she loved him, his wife said to the girl, "Go look after your father."

He did not like being called "dad". He insisted on "father". He did not want his daughter to cook and wash for him. After school he wanted her to learn to play the pipa.

In those days five children out of ten were made to learn a musical instrument. It was thought that having some musical skill would open doors to better jobs. Anyone with musical skill could get out of the farming brigades and become a factory worker or a soldier and be guaranteed an "iron rice bowl".

Therefore all the little girls in the town, no matter how tone-deaf, struggled with a violin or a pipa. His eldest daughter was no exception. He shared a courtyard with a younger brother whose daughter had progressed quite well with the pipa. She knew a few tricks and could pick out a tune quite creditably, so he decided his daughter should take lessons as well. He got his brother to find him a second-hand pipa, which swallowed up all his savings. He and his daughter lived on cereals for two months, without so much as a blade of greens.

His daughter, clutching the pipa, was all hands and feet. Her small face became sallower by the day. She was listless, drooping like a frostbitten flower. She was afraid of her father, who loomed over her, glaring, as stern as a judge. But once she put down the pipa, the girl came alive. She was an active and vivacious child, and living in the same courtyard with Aunt and Uncle there was always something happening. But like him, she was tone-deaf. He couldn't tell the difference, and so he would not give up. The girl became wan and pale, but all he dreamt of was the future. She would grow up to be a young lady of the city, her face half hidden behind a pipa.

Her fingers would be supple and white. Perhaps she

would marry a refined young man who wore horn-rimmed glasses. On Saturday evenings they would stroll together in the park. He would whisper sweet nothings to her, and she would be romantic and coquettish.

13

A month after she had given birth, several people went to visit Jilian. Then the gossip started.

"Strange, the baby resembles him!"

"What a disaster!"

"The shape of the face, the eyes and the nose: the perfect image of him."

"How strange!"

"Anything is possible these days!"

They had been suspicious all along. Now someone remembered seeing him kiss Jilian. Someone else said she had seen Jilian in a cinema whispering and cracking melon seeds with a man, and she thought it was him. Gradually their doubts turned into iron-clad facts. They had gleefully unearthed a secret. A ladies' man like him with an apprentice like her: what could you expect? It had taken an infant to expose them, and suddenly everyone was filled with righteous indignation.

The stern face he had once pulled had been nothing more than a mask. That gave them another uneasy thought. They decided he was not the gallant they had thought he was. After all, there were so many older women who were willing and able. But he had had to pick a virgin. That was the greatest sin of all. Of course she wouldn't believe it when Xiao Jiao told her the story. She bawled him out and called him a liar and a gossip-monger who had nothing better to do.

But afterwards she began to doubt. Lao Yuan had not been seen for many days. Rumour had it that he had taken sick leave. It seemed too much of a coincidence. She was restless, and her thoughts raced around her brain like a squirrel in a cage. She became so absent-minded she put machine oil in her teacup. Afterwards, no matter how she scrubbed it, she could not remove the smell of the oil. In the end she tossed the cup out. He noticed but said nothing. He only sighed. That annoyed her. I bet he's going to run Lao Yuan down too, she thought. I bet he's really happy. She thought he must hate Lao Yuan, and she knew why. She knew he thought ill of them both. But she could do nothing about it. That hurt look on his face told her there was nothing she could say to change his mind, and so she said nothing and left him to think whatever he chose.

In the end he couldn't help himself. He had to ask her, "Have you heard what they're saying?"

"What are they saying?" she asked deliberately.

"About that incident."

"What incident?"

"Everybody's talking about it."

"I don't know," she said. "I hate gossiping behind people's backs. If you have something to say, say it to their faces."

She had given him what he deserved. His face darkened, and hers did too. He worked in dogged silence. She had to bang around and make a noise. She wished Lao Yuan would come back to work. She longed for his steady gaze; she longed to see him standing there before the lot of them, proud, unafraid with nothing to hide. She did not get her wish. Instead a sick-leave notice came saying Lao Yuan had come down with hepatitis B.

Her doubts grew. She had to know for sure. One day she bought a couple of tins of baby formula and a tiny suit of clothes and went to visit Jilian. She hated herself for doing it, but she couldn't help herself. Jilian was happy to see her, pleased with her gifts, and praised her good taste. The baby was asleep. She glanced at it quickly, feeling guilty, afraid Jilian might discover her despicable motive. In fact she saw nothing but a blur of pink and white flesh, but Jilian insisted she have a good look.

"Look at my daughter. When she was born she was as red and wrinkled as an old man, but the doctor said she would grow up to be a beauty, that she alone glowed in the nursery." Jilian poked the tender cheek with the tip of her finger and added proudly, "The silly girl is actually quite pretty. With eyebrows like willow leaves, almond eyes and a tiny mouth, who do you think she resembles? Her father says she looks like me." Jilian oozed the pride and joy of young motherhood. She was quite something. She had had her own way and produced a child without a shred of embarrassment or secretiveness.

You couldn't tell whether she was callous or simple and honest. Jilian urged the child on her, and finally she screwed up enough courage to look at her carefully. The baby was becoming a real person. Her skin was fair, and her hair was black. Her mouth puckered like the petals of a flower.

She was dumbfounded.

It was true. The baby resembled him somewhere — was it the eyes, the nose or the mouth?

Finally Lao Yuan came back to work. He was still dashing and handsome in his silver grey jacket and his long, wine-red scarf, one length hanging down his chest and the other carelessly flung over one shoulder. They greeted him with smiles.

"Are you really recovered?" They were full of concern.

He passed around cigarettes, and a match went the rounds lighting them. They stood smoking, laughing and chatting about illness and medicines. They were the best of friends. All the buzzing about Jilian and her child was forgotten. He acted as though there had been nothing more than a serious illness. He seemed more talkative now and laughed more readily. He was always offering cigarettes and was particularly generous with youngsters like Xiao Jiao, jabbing them with playful punches as though the physical contact was a measure of their friendship.

Illness seemed to have given him a new perspective on life, and he was determined to live it to the hilt. Only she recognized the change in him. His smile had become weak and false. He was too anxious to please when he offered his cigarettes. He seemed to beg for something. Although he did his best to conceal his weakness — and for the most part he succeeded — he could not escape her scrutiny.

So he took refuge in a crowd and left her alone.

When they met they greeted each other, talked and even cracked the odd joke, but they both understood that something between them was dead. They drifted further and further apart. In the process he lost something he had never perhaps really possessed. Though she still looked at him through rose-coloured lenses, he was gone from her.

14

She learnt to smile.

She smiled at whoever spoke to her. She even smiled when they did not speak to her. Sometimes her smile was a trifle mechanical. Then she would remind herself of the ancient adage: art will not crush.

She taught herself to co-exist with her master. She was no longer shrewish. She became gentle. She smiled softly and listened patiently to him talking about his daughter and the pipa. They both became adept at skirting unpleasant topics. She was haggard and wan. All he saw in her face was the bland and turbid flow of years. He wondered about her.

He supposed she was out of love. She had been strongly attracted to Lao Yuan, but the gossip had been a rude awakening. He felt a keen sense of loss, for the joy and pain of it belonged in another sphere of which he had no part and never would. His heart contracted with grief when he faced her gentle, bland smile. He longed for the brief, stormy days they had shared and that were no more.

He wanted to comfort her but didn't know how and was afraid she would laugh at him. He believed she needed people around her; she lived and died in a crowd; she suffered in a crowd. She would always need an audience. He realized that was all he had been to her. He lost interest in songs. He understood now that she had only been humouring him. Now and then they talked, mostly about practical things of everyday life. Once they drifted onto the subject of marriage.

"You've had a hard life," he said.

She was surprised.

"You can't cope with hard times, but you sure have a capacity for suffering," he continued. "You need a husband who'll treat you badly: because unless he does, you won't respect him."

It didn't make sense at first, but when she thought about it, what he said was true. She smiled, because he made it sound so simple. Life was like that.

Sometimes he was more profound than a fortune-teller. Palmistry wasn't as popular then, although there were a few fortune-tellers in the town.

Most people took it as a game, though some fervently believed in it. Someone found a fortune-telling manual, which was passed quickly from one person to another. People copied bits of it that related to themselves. In time it became less a manual than answers to the riddle of life couched in mysterious sentences preceded by a number. The number was the result of a simple calculation. You took the total number of brush-strokes in a person's name and multiplied it by four. Then you looked up the same number in the manual. They consulted the book together.

He drew "The boat capsizes in an angry sea", and hers was "He who picks flowers is happy". She smiled bitterly.

15

Finally she left. She took the university entrance exam and became a student again.

He thought it was the best thing for her. She would be in a clean, neat place where she could discourse on lofty things.

The others in the brigade commented tartly that talent had been wasted. During the years she had been there, they could have given her a desk job, let her write a few posters, draw a few plans, or at least do a bit of accounting.

Xiao Jiao, Xianxian, Jilian and the other young people borrowed a Seagull 203 and took her to the park for some souvenir photos. They posed on the grass beside the flower beds and archways.

Jilian had weathered the difficult months and filled out. Gone was the clinging smell of milk and wet diapers. She was wearing pretty clothes again, and she bloomed. She lay on the grass with her brightly coloured umbrella open beside her, shading her eyes with a languidly lifted hand. All the girls followed suit, using the umbrella as a prop.

She bade him goodbye. He tried not to be sentimental, but in the end he still could not hide the feeling that they would never meet again. He was reminded of Li Shangyin's line, "To meet is hard; to part is harder."

She was going to the mountains and sea of the south, from whence she came. Nothing would lure her back. His farewell gift was not the usual pen or souvenir album but a small meat grinder.

"Since you like dumplings, it might come in handy," he said.

She looked into his deeply furrowed face and saw the hurt in his eyes and realized she had caused him great pain. Instinctively she knew there would never be another who would love her as faithfully, unconditionally and hopelessly as he. She lingered, dumb with misery. She thought of the little notebook in his drawer, full of idioms she had jotted down, and all the lyrics of songs that were covered with greasy finger marks. They smiled.

Lao Yuan gave her an English-Chinese dictionary. He came by when no one else was around, put it on top of her tool-kit and left with a wave and a smile.

Later, leafing through it she found a note:

"I know you despise me. It's not so much whether I am guilty. In your eyes, my conduct afterwards was much worse, but to the others there are graver issues. I will not explain myself to you or anyone else. Perhaps you will never know the truth. A little mystery adds spice to life. Would you believe I regret nothing?"

She read those tear-blurred lines several times. She rushed from the workshop to find him, but he had gone. Tanks and columns stood among the wildflowers. Welding guns flashed in the distance. The sun rolled wearily toward the horizon, where the mountains rose and fell in endless undulations.

The city was a crucible.

Feb. '88, Taiyuan.

Translated by David Kwan

Jiang Yun is one of China's most popular women authors. She was born in Taiyuan, Shanxi Province in 1954. On completing her high school education in 1969, she worked as a common labourer in the Taiyuan Brick Factory and later became a machinist in the Water and Electricity Supply Brigade. In 1977 she was accepted by the Chinese Literature Department of Taiyuan Normal College. Upon graduation she remained at the college as a member of faculty. Jiang Yun made her publishing debut in 1979. Since then she has published many short stories and novellas. Today she is a member of the Chinese Writers' Association and lectures on fine arts at Taiyuan Normal College.

Purple Asters

Ding Xiaoqi

THE room is like a wok turned upside down, black and suffocating. The eyes are dyed black; whether they are open or closed makes no difference; it is impossible to see anything. The people on the *kang* are all fast asleep. There is only the sound of snoring, sometimes loud and coarse, sometimes soft and subtle, like the bubbling sound of boiling water. When you have made sure that no one knows your eyes are open, you just lie there and watch the darkness the whole night long.

You dare not turn around. It seems as if everyone on the *kang* is tied together by a rope. Should you happen to move you would wake everybody up. Even your man — you dare not pull the little tip of your braid out from under Big's shoulder blade. You are so close to each other that you can smell the warmth of his heavy chest. It flows into your face — now stronger now weaker — smelling like sun-dried mushrooms.

As afraid as you are of waking those asleep, you are even more afraid that those still awake might know that you are awake, too. It is already the seventh time that the old lady at the end of the *kang* has coughed; she uses the quilt to cover her mouth. Two bodies away from you is Second Brother. He still has not snored or turned around. "Second Brother, isn't your neck aching? Turn around a bit and hurry up falling asleep!" In your heart, you ask that this very long and black night may belong to you alone, that your weak body may be allowed to regain its strength, that the heavy pressure you still feel on your heart may be relieved a bit. If only the dense, stifling air in the room would escape through cracks in the window, through crevices in the door. That hand, which is not really huge but broad and hard, has already been moved to the other side of the *kang* as Big has turned around, but you still feel as if there is something real on your tiny breasts, and the tight feeling below your little belly.

Did you want to go with Uncle? Well, Dad and Mum did discuss it with you! That day, a man came to the house. He looked much younger than Dad, but Dad made you call him Uncle. Then Mum called you to the kitchen and told you that their home was in the Northeast, that they were very well-off, and very good people. You do not know why Mum did not call your older sister. In your family there were four girls. Only the fifth child was a little brother. You are number two, and because you were neither as clever as the oldest, nor as naughty as the youngest, and because you were not as pretty as number three, you were always the most obedient at home. You knew that if you did as Mum told you to, she would praise you for being sensible. She might smile — she smiled so seldom.

You remember it so clearly: the next morning Mum gave you a really fine, new pink gown, a pair of green nylons and a pair of new black velveteen shoes. The shoes had white plastic soles. They looked truly dazzling on your feet, just a little too large. In the early morning Dad said that Second Sister need not go to work in the field; she could stay at home and do as she pleased. Your two younger sisters gazed at you with envy; one said your dress was beautiful, the other said your shoes were lovely. As old as you were, this was the first time you had ever received so much attention at home. You felt very proud.

Around noon Uncle arrived, to take you with him. You did not feel sad as you left home; you did not cry either, despite having once planned that when you reached that day, you would do like your friends had done and wail hysterically. You only felt slightly uneasy after the excitement. It seemed as if it was only at night, when you climbed on to the train with Uncle, and you saw the shadows of the trees and mountains quickly passing by outside the wagon, that you finally realized the significance of your leaving home. Yet the most urgent question in your mind was whether the bamboo bed that you used to share with your oldest sister was now occupied by Third Sister? Long ago Third Sister had complained that she wanted to move out of Dad and Mum's big bed and squeeze into yours and Oldest Sister's little one. These thoughts made you feel like crying, but you hurriedly did like Uncle did, curled up in the train passageway and fell asleep quickly.

After travelling three days and four nights, by train, bus and tractor, Uncle finally brought you through this strong and solid wooden door. For quite a while you had been hoping that you would arrive soon. You honestly had no strength left to continue travelling with Uncle. In order to be able to climb up on that truck full of canvas bags, Uncle had pulled your arm so that it "cracked", and you still were afraid to move it backwards quickly. However, you dared not tell Uncle — mountain kids are not so precious; many of the illnesses they suffer are left to cure by themselves. Furthermore, you were lucky that Uncle had been taking care of you all the way, otherwise you would not have known how to get on the train or where to eat. You are such a foolish girl. This time you are really out in the big world. Never mind Mum and Dad; it would likely be difficult to find anyone from your village who had come this far.

Uncle took you over to that middle-aged couple, patted you on the shoulder and merely said these are your in-laws, now be good, and left. While the in-laws saw him to the door, you just stood in the middle of the room and looked at the stove by the wall. From underneath the lid of a pot, which was even bigger than the millstone at home, wafted a most delicious smell.

"Daughter-in-law, come in here!" An old lady's voice came from the inner room. Did you not realize whom she was calling? You looked around; there was nobody else in the room. At this moment out of the blue leaped up a filthy little person. Except for the whites of his eyes, from his head to his legs the only white things were two streaks of snot. "Snotty" pushed your arm, tilted his face and said: "She's calling you, daughter-in-law." You gave him a flustered look and felt like telling him that you were not called daughter-in-law. But you did not tell him. You were

afraid the old lady might hear you and think that you
were contradicting her. "She's calling you, daughter-
in-law," "Snotty" repeated it, only because it was a
novel form of address to him, then in a flash, while
looking at you, he sucked back the two streaks of snot
that looked like thick, boiled noodles. The only thing
heard was a "slurping" sound from his throat.

"Daughter-in-law! Is that you calling 'daughter-
in-law'?!" Following a very shrill voice,
"Snotty" stumbled and fell to the ground. The next
second a dirty foot appeared on either side of his
waist. The feet were covered by yellow rubber shoes
out of proportion with those skinny legs. "Yellow
Rubber Shoes" was sitting on top of "Snotty".
"Snotty" refused to give in and howled and fought
back. It was total chaos. You quickly escaped these
two combatants and went inside.

It was indeed a wealthy home. A huge *kang* reached
from one wall to the other. It was just enormous. It
took up four-fifths of the entire room. Bright and
colourful paper was pasted on to the *kang*, the type of
paper used for wrapping candy but which had not
been cut out. Perhaps because the *kang* was so huge,
you suddenly did not know where to look.
"Daughter-in-law, please sit down." The old lady
who spoke sat on the *kang* by the wall. You did not
know whether you ought to sit down or not. Your
rear end had not touched the edge of the *kang* yet
when another young fellow entered. "Grandma, I'm
back." Maybe it was the red sweat-shirt he was
wearing which made his neck appear very pale, so pale
that one could clearly see the light blue blood vessels.
He bent down, slapped the two rolling by the door

and just said "Don't be so noisy." The combatants did calm down and left the room. As he stood up and saw you by the edge of the *kang*, he turned red, but he still took the time to speak a few words. You did not quite catch what he said; you were too nervous. You quickly got up from the *kang*, but he had already turned around and gone outside. You were too stupid to say a word. You cursed yourself.

When suppertime came, you still had not figured out exactly how many people were in this family.

Grandma and Father-in-law sat with crossed legs on the *kang*. One side of the *kang*-table was reserved for you, another side was for Mother-in-law, who held the rice spoon and saw to the rice pot. The kids were all over, some inside, others outside in the courtyard; leaning against doors and windows, they each held a bowl, eating off in their own worlds. You kept your eyes on the bowl in your hands; you dared not lift your head, not to mention reaching for the dishes of meat and vegetables on the small table. You knew that you were embarrassingly clumsy in front of strangers. It was not the youngest in the family, but the oldest, who used the one and only aluminium spoon on the small table. As if it was a symbol of power, the old lady wielded the little spoon to dish out endless portions of stir-fried green onions and eggs' and took care of everybody in the family. She was like an old hen dividing the food evenly among her chickens — that included Father- and Mother-in-law, who were in their fifties.

"Please, daughter-in-law." This time you knew she was addressing you, and you held out your bowl just like Father-in-law. "And you, Big." The old lady went on. This made you even more nervous than when she addressed you. "No thanks." A curt, indistinct voice came from outside the window. You ventured to take a quick glance over there and saw the back of someone squatting, his shoulders broad and square. It was not the one in the red sweat-shirt. You wondered. The old lady took the egg that was meant for Big and put it in your bowl. Everyone in the room was watching; it made you ill at ease. "My brother is very fond of Sister-in-law." Second Brother walked in when the old lady called him in turn. The reflection of the red sweat-shirt made his sweaty forehead shine. You were so shy that your face was burning; it was doubtless very red. You felt scared, and happy too, because of Second Brother's words, and because of Big's egg, too.

After supper, Mother-in-law made Fourth Brother do the dishes. As it turned out, he was "Yellow Rubber shoes". This is my job, you thought, and said so, but no one in the whole family paid any attention to you; they were all busy rolling cigarettes, as if that was a very serious matter. The tobacco was packed in a small bamboo scoop placed on the *kang*, and they would push and pull it back and forth as if it had been greased. They used the small pieces of paper in the scoop to roll up the loose tobacco into cone-shaped cigarettes. Fifth Brother — "Snotty" — who leaning against Grandma, also began to smoke; he was faster at rolling cigarettes than the old lady herself. In no time the room was so full of smoke that it was impossible to keep one's eyes open.

That evening it was arranged for you to sleep between Mother-in-law and the old lady, and you all went to bed very early. The big, cosy *kang* was able to accommodate everyone's fatigue after a long day. You fell asleep as soon as your head hit the pillow and so had no idea how the others slept. When you opened your eyes the next morning, only you and Fifth Brother were still on the *kang*. The rays of the sun formed columns of light and dust that danced unbridled in between the two of you. Who knows how long Fifth Brother had been awake? He was staring at you with his brown eyes, spellbound, then he smiled and revealed two little yellow fangs. You felt very embarrassed and got up and dressed in a hurry. Just at this moment, Mother-in-law furiously pulled aside the door curtain, entered the room and without a word lifted up Fifth Brother's quilt and slapped him on the bum. The kid cried "ouch" and jumped up, then he quickly covered his private parts with his hands. Heavens, he was not wearing a single piece of clothing! You smiled at him, and recalled how every morning when you used to dress your little brother you would call him "water tap".

You finished washing up, and as soon as you came out, Mother-in-law handed you a bowl of porridge. You stirred in it with your chopsticks and found a large, slippery egg in the bottom, and you nearly dropped it on the ground. Before you had finished your porridge, Mother-in-law gave you thirty yuan. "Go to the commune and take a look around. If there is something you like, just go ahead and buy it." "No thanks." You had never before carried that much money. "Take it. Just look around and see what's going on. If you walk along the big dam it's not much further than twenty li." You still refused, but then Mother-in-law said, "They're very busy working in the field. Otherwise I'd have asked Big to accompany you." Only then did you take the money. Mother-in-law's hand was rough and warm. Just as you had gone outside, she called you again. "Don't forget to pick up two *jin* of soya bean paste. Tonight we'll have noodles for supper." Mother-in-law handed you a small clay jar. Now that you had been given such responsibility you felt really good inside.

The beginning of May just happened to be the blossoming season of the Chinese scholar tree. Oh, the scholar tree blossoms, so white and golden, blocking the clouds and covering the sun, and turning the long dam into a corridor of flowers. A light breeze blew from the fields and stirred up a refreshingly damp and sweet fragrance from each tree. Suddenly you felt short of breath. Heavens, what is that?! That is it, that is definitely it! You had never seen an aster before, but at first glance, the first time you saw this purple flower that made you quiver inside, you recognized it immediately! Don't be impatient; calm down; look ahead of you. Under each scholar tree these cone-shaped flowers were in full bloom. This discovery made you so excited that you felt your heart swell. Your fragile chest almost could not bear it. You had been searching for years, singing about it for years, it was just like you had imagined it to be, and yet not exactly as in your imagination. The colours were even more purple, the flowers even thicker and the stamen much more straight.

When you were eight years old, a girl around your age called Lili came to your village. She was the granddaughter of Madame Wang from the wine store and had come to spend her summer holidays. Several

times, as you returned from herding the cattle, you had
seen Lili in the courtyard behind Madame Wang's
bamboo fence, skipping over a thin elastic band which
could be stretched very far. As she skipped she would
sing some rhymes to the same beat. You would stand
outside the fence and stare your eyes out. Lili skipped
really gracefully. Her small, plump, white legs would
skilfully kick and twist, and her pretty dress would flap
like huge butterfly wings.

"Let m e teach you how to do rubber band
skipping, okay?" Every time Lili greeted you so enthu-
siastically, you would blush and refuse. Not that you
did not want to or did not know how to do
it — when you were all alone herding cattle you
would take the small rope for tying bundles of grass
and arrange it on the ground, then you would kick
and twist over it as you had seen Lili do it — but
you just could not skip together with Lili. You did not
have a dress with lace trimmings like hers; you did not
even have a pair of shoes. Your black, bare feet and
your thin legs were all covered with mud because you
had been looking after the old water buffalo. You hid
your feet in the grass and pricked yourself till it hurt
on the little "hedge-hoggy" balls.

"Aster flowers, aster flowers; they're not afraid of
stormy showers. When diligent people begin to discuss,
they come into bloom without any fuss." You had
learned this rhyme and so would stand in the grass outside the fence and help Lili sing, over and over again
without stopping. You had felt very happy. Later on
Lili had left, and just before leaving the village she had
given you the rubber band, so you could learn. She
had also said that she would come back the following

summer holiday and skip together with you. She had not been back since then. You also had not done any skipping since then, but the rhyme had stuck in your memory forever: "Aster flowers, aster flowers; they're not afraid of stormy showers. When diligent people begin to discuss, they come into bloom without any fuss." Whether you were herding cattle or cutting grass, you would sing patiently and endlessly to the mountains, to the trees and to all the wild flowers. At home they did not have that kind of flower, but you trusted that some day you would eventually find one — and now, no, at this very moment, right next to you bunch after bunch of these purple flowers so abundantly and generously bloomed for you, as if they knew that the girl in front of them, now called Daughter-in-law, had sung about them for so many years.

You counted them as you walked. You got confused but continued counting. In any case, you did not miss a single flower; you did not want any of them to feel left out.

The commune streets were truly lively. People were selling all sorts of things. The vendors, shouting out loud or calling out softly, rattling their tambourines and banging little copper gongs, all racked their brains for a smart way to advertise their goods. At the sight of the golden-yellow fried pancake in the pot, a stream of saliva rose from underneath your tongue. Standing in front of the stove, with the dark smoke curling up around it, you hesitated again. At home, Dad always used to say that a ten-yuan note was worth nothing once you had broken it, so don't break the note for a fried pancake. You had better take a look around. You pulled yourself together and swallowed the saliva.

In this way you walked past one stall after another. You wanted to buy everything but ended up having bought nothing. You had better buy the soya bean paste for Mother-in-law first. You felt that this would be only fair to her.

The state-run grocery was almost empty. A few shop assistants stood together, bored, watching the doorway. Any customer was a potential conversation topic. A shop assistant with permed hair got up and warmly greeted you. Having supplied the bean paste she went on to ask you where you were from. "Chenge Village production brigade, over by the big dam." You were eager to tell "Perm" everything you knew, because later on you would be likely to see a lot of each other. "I mean, where did you grow up?" "Perm" asked sincerely. "Hunan. It's very far away." You shook your head; it seemed that place already belonged to someone else. "Oh, I know, you're the daughter-in-law they bought down there, right?" "Perm" got as excited as if she had eaten a sour apricot, and her amused smile made her fat face so tight it was on the point of bursting at the seams. "It's true, isn't it? What's your in-law's family name? You...." You really felt like smashing the jar of bean paste into her fat face. But you did not do it. Instead you fled the store and turned down the most lively street before you finally took a deep breath. You looked back and swore that you would never ever set foot in that store again.

An old fellow with a red nose, holding a small bottle of booze in one hand, cried out to sell his small river shrimps. He would shout, take a sip, then throw a little green shrimp into his mouth and chew it with the crunching sound of someone eating peanuts. The saliva that you had managed to hold down now welled up again. Go have a pancake, you thought to yourself. This time, though, it was not because the ten-yuan note had already been broken, but because you wanted to show off. You wanted to let "Perm" see. You were convinced that fat face was hiding somewhere and staring at you. Let them see that you had not been bought as a daughter-in-law, that you were one of the locals; just like them you could buy whatever you liked to eat in the streets.

"Ouch!" Suddenly, a shrill voice was heard from somewhere ahead of you. A woman ran like mad through the narrow, busy alley. You quickly jumped to one side and nearly pushed over the bowl of fried pancakes. "If you run any further I'll kill you, you greedy devil!" The roar was a male voice, so deep and resonant. Before you had figured out what was going on, the man and the woman had already begun fighting in front of you. The woman was tall and big. Half of a fresh, red cooked crab swung back and forth with her flailing arm. The little string that held one of her braids had long since disappeared, and her dishevelled, sweaty hair hid part of her face, so that one could not quite see what she looked like. The man, dark and skinny — not very tall but undoubtedly very strong — pulled the woman's arm so that the blue veins stood out clearly. "I'm going to eat it!" The woman continued shouting, and with much effort she pushed the man violently so he fell over. "I'm going to eat it. You won't give me the money you'd make on it anyway. What a misfortune to be married to you!" The crowd roared with laughter.

The man had lost face. His face in fact turned red as a cockscomb. The woman, for a moment, had the advantage, and she forgot to be careful. She just stood there munching her crab. Who would have thought the man would grab the little stool next to him and smash it against the woman? As the stool fell upon the woman's legs, she cried out in agony, and she stumbled towards the side where you stood, scared stiff, as if she was begging you to help her up. You did not know whether to help her or to disappear. When you finally reacted, the jar of bean paste in your hand had already joined the woman on the ground.

The jar broke into several pieces. The bean paste quickly melted into a frankly diarrhoeic puddle. The man threw himself on the woman, and soon they were rolling around in the bean paste. The spectators formed a solid wall around the two of them, but nobody noticed you or your bean-paste puddle.

Empty-handed and with an empty belly, you walked along the big dam, and upon seeing the asters still blooming so unselfconsciously, you felt extremely sad.

"Dong!" sounds the bell again, and it is 4:30 a.m. The old grandma at the end of the *kang* has not covered her face to cough for a while now, and two bodies away, Second Brother has apparently also turned around. They are all asleep now — finally, nobody is paying attention to you any more. No one is pondering like you any more.

"It's time to get up and start working." You think that in this way you will feel less like you have done something wrong. You pull your little braid out from underneath Big's shoulder blade but dare not get dressed on the *kang*. If you wake up one of them, you will wake up all of them. Having escaped the dark clouds, the moon shines into the room, and the shadow of the book-sized window lattice falls upon the bodies and faces of the people on the *kang*, making them look a bit funny. You dare not watch any more, and holding your clothes in your arms, you tiptoe out of the room.

As you put on the five- or six-watt lamp, you can see the piece of bean cake that Mother-in-law placed in the large iron pot to soak yesterday evening. It has already swollen and looks all yellow-whitish. Half of it is under water, and half is floating on top. You almost use up all your strength to fish the bean cake out of the pot. You must not drop it on the ground. That might wake up everyone inside. Without a second thought, you dig all your fingers into the crust, and you feel a sharp pain between your nail and fingertip.

Just like Big, you sit down on a small stool and stand the bean cake between your heels. Then you use your hands to hold on to each end of the cutting knife. Using the weight of your upper body, you whittle the bean cake into little flakes the size of wood chips. Perhaps the bean cake has not soaked long enough. The core is harder than wood, and before long your collar-bone already hurts so much it makes you quite discouraged. How come when Big was doing it yesterday it seemed as if he was cutting beancurd?

Big — you cannot help thinking of what happened last night; that something on your chest starts pressing again. If you still had as much confidence in Big as on the first night, and if Second Brother would not continue smiling at you as on the first day, you might not agree to sleep at the end of the *kang* any more.

Two days ago on your way back from the commune, almost at the end of the dam, you saw a red spot moving in the distance. Sure enough, it was Second Brother. When he smiled, his dried lips were cracked and peeling. "Older Brother sent me to meet you." Without saying your name he asked, "Where are the things?" "The jar of bean paste broke." Your voice was extremely low. You were trying to control it so that it would not tremble. "What about the other things?" No reply. "How foolish you are! If you haven't bought anything, you'll have to return the money to Mum." He was already on your side. Your mouth was smiling, but tears began to fill your eyes. He pretended not to notice and walked ahead of you.

Mother-in-law did not say anything about the broken jar, and she also did not ask for the extra money back. That day Mother-in-law moved your quilt to the end of the *kang*. You noticed that yours was the only new quilt in the family. You were eager to please Mother-in-law. Now that you had broken the jar there was no opportunity to ingratiate yourself with her. Furthermore, you were only too happy to sleep at the end of the *kang*. When you lived with your oldest sister, you had slept by the wall. Underneath the mat by the wall you had kept many things — little clay dolls, a pair of purple cotton socks, those things girls use when they are grown up and which you were embarrassed even to show Mum. Then there had also been a small bundle of rubber bands — the one Lili had given you. You had given it to Third Sister before you left. Mum would not let you take it with you. She had been afraid Mother-in-law would laugh when she saw it.

The whole family had gone to bed. Only Big went out at some point. In fact he had not been inside since supper time. When Father-in-law had finished his very last cigarette, Big still had not returned. Mother-in-law had left an empty space between you and Fifth Brother, but there was no quilt there. It made you a little apprehensive, but no one in the entire family seemed to notice, and so you dared not ask.

Only when people on the *kang* started snoring, and you too had apparently dozed off, you heard someone tiptoe into the room. It was Big. Without turning on the light he felt his way to the empty space, then took off his shoes and crawled up on the *kang*, and in a second he had curled up between you and Fifth Brother — he had not even undressed. You could feel how he tried hard to hold his breath, as if he was afraid it would frighten someone.

The next day — that was yesterday morning — when you opened your eyes, Big was already outside cutting up pig feed. "Let me do that." You hurried out and spoke in a low voice. You felt this was your job. "You couldn't cut an inch." When Big spoke, he did not even lift his head. He is certainly not as jolly as Second Brother. You felt slightly regretful.

After breakfast, Father-in-law handed you a small hoe, so you went out into the field with all the guys. You did not mind hoeing up weeds. You worked together with Big and Second Brother, each of you taking two furrows. Father-in-law was not with you. Big was really good at it. In his hands the hoe seemed like a shaving knife, quick and precise; in a few minutes you were left far behind. But every time you moved forward you would discover that a large part of your furrow had already been thoroughly hoed. At first you thought you had moved into the wrong furrow, but soon you realized that Big was helping you, so that you could keep up with Second Brother. You liked working with Second Brother. He would talk about the village. He was a good talker, and he often made you laugh. Initially you were embarrassed to really laugh. You would close your lips and suppress your laughter, but later you forgot and just doubled up laughing. After all, you liked to laugh, you see. Second Brother seemed happy to see you laugh. Why else would he have gone on talking like that?

Mother-in-law brought lunch, green onion pancakes and lentil soup. She sat to one side and watched everybody eating. Whoever finished would get some more, just as at home. When she dished up soup for you she suddenly said: "Daughter-in-law, from now on our house belongs to you and Big. Second, Fourth and Fifth brothers will have to build houses elsewhere when they marry." You felt slightly embarrassed. Why was she talking about these things? You looked at Big, but he had buried his face in his bowl. Then you looked at Second Brother, and though he did smile, there was something weird about his smile.

At midday it was very hot. Like everyone else, you took off you jacket and threw it on the ground, then you went up to the furrows with Big and Second Brother. For some reason, Second Brother did not talk quite as much as in the morning. You wanted to explain, to tell him that you could still live together, that no one needed to go build another house. Then you did not know whether you ought to say this or not, or how to say it. You were somewhat annoyed. Probably you had not been careful and hit something hard in the ground. As you pulled hard the head of the hoe came off, and you were left holding the handle. As if he had expected it, Second Brother turned around, and his dry lips broadened into a smile. This made you feel as if you had just had a drink of spring water. As if by magic, Second Brother got hold of a large stone, and made you grasp the handle below while he hammered on top. For some reason, when Second Brother had just raised the stone, his hand stopped in mid-air his eyes stared straight down your neck, and the sides of his nose turned red. You thought there was some kind of monster crawling on you, and quickly looked down to see. My God, it was because your blouse was so loose, and there was no button at the neck, and you were leaning forward! From above, your breasts, not really big but still quite full, were completely exposed. Even the tiny drops of sweat and the little pink nipples were clearly visible. Completely flustered, you covered your neck with both hands, and dared not look up at Second Brother again. God, my God, you cried desperately inside you. When you finally lifted your head, Second Brother had already finished fixing the hoe and was far ahead of you. In fact he could work just as fast as Big. Now he will never notice me again — your sad heart trembled.

That evening, while everybody was smoking, you carried a basin of water from the vat into the courtyard and hid behind a pile of grain and firewood. There you took a wet towel and washed yourself inside your

shirt. That would have to do for a bath. Then you hurriedly changed into another shirt. What happened in
the field today had disturbed you so much that you
had no appetite for supper. The eyes of everybody in
the family made you feel nervous and uneasy. You
could not wait for the night to come; you wanted to
curl up underneath your quilt as soon as possible.
Only when everybody had closed their eyes would you
finally be able to relax. As you entered the room, you
noticed that Fourth and Fifth Brothers had in fact been
put to bed already. The grown-ups suddenly stopped
talking — what had they been talking about? They
did not want to look each other in the eyes. Were they
talking about Big? His hand, the one that held the cigarette, was trembling. That evening no one went out,
including Big and Second Brother, as if they all were
obeying some order.

Lying on the *kang*, you felt your body ache from the
day's work, but you were not sleepy. Fourth and
Fifth Brothers started fighting again but were brought
under control by Mother-in-law's palm, and in a short
while they were snoring evenly. Second Brother did not
take a book with him to bed and refuse to turn off the
light when Mother-in-law told him to as he used
to. He just crawled underneath the quilt and shut his
eyes firmly. Past nine o'clock, Father-in-law lay down.
Big was still in the courtyard, fiddling with something.
Not knowing why, you felt that except for Fourth and
Fifth Brothers, everyone on the *kang* was awake. No
one made any sound, as if they were waiting for
something. Waiting for what? Waiting for Big?

You were not sure how much time had gone by.
You only felt your eyelids getting heavier, then you

heard Big groping his way to the edge of the *kang*, where he sat down and undressed. His movements were light and very slow. Never in your life had you imagined that he would suddenly lift up your quilt and slip so resolutely underneath it. In an instant, you felt your whole body from top to bottom, even the root of your tongue, turn hard as a stone. You dared not utter a word. You could only pretend to be asleep. All you could do now was stubbornly hold down the corner of the quilt closest to the wall with the weight of your body, as if you were safe wrapped up in this way.

Was it half an hour yet? The clock had not struck even once. Why did it feel longer than a whole century? Your entire body was turning numb, especially the lower part. It felt as if countless little needles were pricking you, and your chest was so heavy you almost could not breathe. Big had not moved a bit either; the arm behind your back was as stiff as a stick. Had he fallen asleep? Trusting he had, you sighed with relief, lifted the corner of the quilt you had held down and moved your numbed body just a little bit. As if it had received some kind of signal, the moment you moved, a sturdy thing reached desperately inside your shirt and landed on your bosom — there was no way of resisting. It was Big's hand, rough and warm, caressing your smooth, small, yet full breasts. You could hear the sound of Big's panting suddenly grew faster. Somehow your stiff body turned soft, as if you had no bones, as if it was not your own body.

You did not have the strength to push away Big's hand, the strength to escape Big's body, the strength to prevent Big from doing what he was about to do; but you were still strong enough to sense how the people's hearts were throbbing on this long, huge *kang*, in this deadly quiet room — Oh, God!— a tearing pain in the lower part of your body, as if you had been pushed suddenly into an icy river on a burning hot summer's day; your whole body was bathed in a cold sweat. You could not tell whether the sweat was yours or Big's. Your body was like a piece of cloth: ripped apart, bit by bit, drifting away.

The piercing pain almost makes you cry out loud. When you raise your hand, you see dark red blood spilling out from underneath the broken nail on your middle finger, and dripping on to the uneven, yellow-whitish crust of the bean cake. You put your middle finger into your mouth. It has a salty taste. For a moment you cannot tell whether it is the blood or the taste of bean cake on your finger. You swallow it. You used to do that at home. Mum used to say that when you swallow blood from your own body, it will turn into your own blood again.

You start crying. The tears run steadily down your cheeks, down the furrows of your nose and into the corners of your mouth. It is not that you are afraid; it is not that your finger hurts, either. Your tears are running because you feel so lonely and so helpless, and there is no one to talk to. They keep running, but you do not wipe them away with your hand or your cuff. You let them run down to the corners of your mouth and stick out your tongue to receive them, so that you can lean back against the wall and savour the throbbing pain in your fingertip and the tears that run down your cheeks on to the tip of your tongue. "Still so foolish," you think slowly.

Not knowing how long it has been, you suddenly see Grandma standing in front of you. Father-in-law and Mother-in-law are there too, and Second Brother. What is it? You try hard to figure out what exactly has happened; why are they all standing in a circle around you, the look in their eyes so worried and uneasy? Oh, that face which is so dark and yet so red, the thick, short hair, and the short, rough hands sticking out from the sleeves! At sight of Big behind Grandma, you remember. You bury your face between your knees. No one but Grandma, pulling at your arm after having chased everybody away, could have made you lift your head again.

You do not go to work in the field. The old lady will not let you. She sends every one outside to eat breakfast by the stove, including Fourth and Fifth Brothers, who have to go to school, then she dresses your wounded finger for you. Second Brother has borrowed the mercurochrome from the neighbours. And Big — you discover that he has long disappeared, without even one mouthful of porridge — has taken his hoe and gone to work in the field.

The old lady makes you lie down on the *kang* to sleep. She also tells Mother-in-law to boil two large, brown eggs, and puts them beside your pillow. Except for yourself and the old lady, who is sitting on the *kang* making baskets, there is nobody at home. Even Mother-in-law has been sent out to do something. You just cannot sleep, so you get up from the *kang* and go outside to feed the chickens. Grandma does not stop you, but you can feel that she is watching you through the window over the *kang*. The sun has warmed the little courtyard, and the chickens go completely crazy over the feed that you throw down. They roll about on the ground, bumping into each other.

"Comrade, may I come in?" someone asks. You raise your head and look. It is a student in her twenties, carrying a big portfolio on her back. "I'm out here sketching from nature and just happened to be passing when I felt thirsty." The student speaks unaffectedly. You have no idea what it means to sketch from nature, but you do know that she wants some water. You take her inside, and full of confidence, she just sits down on the *kang* without being asked. She even starts talking to the old lady. "Grandma, how many people are there in your family?" the student asks as she drinks her water; she is being polite. "Eight; four grandsons," the old lady says with smiling eyes. "So what number are you?" The student turns to you. "I — " you do not know how you ought to answer her. "Oh, she is the wife of my oldest grandson," Grandma cuts in. "How old are you?" "Seventeen." "Ha, ha!" The student starts laughing as if she has heard something funny. "I am already twenty-seven, and so far no one has asked to marry me," she says so very honestly, without any sign of mocking you. "Has the family been divided up? So where do you live?" As she asks, she puts out her head towards the door. Except for the kitchen there are no other rooms. "Here?!" The student turns around. It seems as if she cannot imagine it. You nod frankly without feeling the least bit timid or embarrassed. You even think of telling her that because Big is the oldest grandson, Father- and Mother-in-law's oldest son, this house belongs to him and you, you do not need to move out, and when Second, Fourth and Fifth Brothers marry, they will build new houses. But you do not tell her anything. You just think about it, that is all. You are afraid that the student will ask more questions. She might ask how many years it will be till Fifth Brother leaves to build his own home. By that time, your son may be — oh, anyway, people like her are experts at asking questions, and you have always been afraid of answering them.

The student is about to leave. The old lady has you see her to the door. Actually, she is offering you some distraction. You quietly take the two eggs from beside your pillow and hide them in your clothes. "Will you be able to get used to living like this? Do you miss home?" See, the student really does start asking again, and she looks at you with knit eyebrows as if she knows you better than yourself. "Those are asters." You do not answer her but point along the big dam, underneath the scholar trees, to the purple asters that make your heart tremble. You do not know whether she knows how to sing that rhyme. You wonder.

The student has left. She is still waving at you though already far away. You do not go back in. The clusters of asters blooming so unselfconsciously in the sunshine on the big dam fill your heart with a purple radiance. If you follow the little road down along the big dam, you will get to your family's fields. Maybe you should give these two eggs to Big. He'll never be able to work the whole morning without anything to eat. Did Mum not always give two eggs to Dad when he was going out to work? You and Big will not be as poor as they were, and later, when you have a kid, you will not send her out to herd the cattle.

"Aster flowers, aster flowers; they're not afraid of stormy showers." You start singing the rhyme again, convinced that no one can sing it as well as you can.

Translated by Anne-Marie Traeholt

Ding Xiaoqi, born in 1957, went to farm in Liaoning Province after graduating from middle school in 1974. In 1977 she joined the Ensemble of the Navy Political Department as a lyricist. She has been publishing her work since 1980.

In the Vast Country of the North

Chi Zijian

CATKIN'S tears streamed down one by one like the snowflakes outside her window.

It was nine and she woke into a languid Sunday morning light. The pale blue curtains were no longer speckled with dancing spots of burning light, as they had been days before. Out of the dimness surrounding her, a thought crept into Catkin's mind, a thought that made her roll out of bed and rush to the nearby window, push open the curtains —

It was truly the snow falling. The schoolyard was white. Yesterday, a few dry leaves still clung to the tossing peak of each indomitable poplar, sloughing restless into the deep blue sky, and in the course of a single night the snowflakes had plucked them away, silencing their rustling autumn voices. On every twig, in every branch, tufts of snow were heaped like embroidery floss. From far off, they were like a flock of tiny, immaculate angels come to the world in a Christmas chorus.

Tranquillity everywhere. The atmosphere around Catkin, animated by the snowfall that whirled madly then calmly died away, invaded her soul. The weightlessness of the snowflakes carried her heavy heart up and far away to some bright, clear place. The lustrous tears rolled freely, drop by drop down her cheeks.

The snow fell ever more heavily. She put on her gosling yellow woollen pullover, wiped away the tearstains on her face, bent over the round mirror with its brown engraved frame on her desk and pointed at herself: you're a silly thing, a pitiful little Lin Daiyu.* Finally, after trying on a delicate smile that tucked into two shallow dimples, she felt a little better, opened a drawer and took out her diary. Her pen whispered against the page as she started to write:

Last night I dreamt about Dad again. He seemed to have changed his ways and stopped drinking so heavily. He looked much kinder. He lived in a distant and ancient desert, a world without people or the sound of birds. He had fallen on the ground, where he was surrounded by thorny brambles, spreading away as far as the eye could see, like an enormous net with him caught in the middle. I watched him struggle in it desparately; he reached out with his two great, oak-brown hands, raised all the way above his head. The hands suddenly grew larger and larger, and the fingers longer and longer, like red pines reaching into the sky, extending their sturdy branches upwards, remote and silent against the clear sky.

His big hands were too awful. What was he grasping for? The white clouds in the sky or the blue sky itself? The clouds are illusory and the sky is a sham; they appear immaculate and bright because of a trick of the sun. Dad, you don't have to grasp for them.

I woke up, and it was snowing. The first snow of the

---

*Lin Daiyu is the frail heroine of the Chinese classic novel, *A Dream of Red Mansions*, who is easily overcome by emotions and drop tears.

winter, and I cried. Was it only the emotions of my dream carried into waking, or the discovery of my heart, the draining of oppression, or because of some simple, natural cause?

I'm lost and don't know where I am. M, can you tell me?

She replaced the cap on her pen and jammed it back into the pen holder. It was packed tight, and she wondered where all the pens came from. So she pulled them out of the holder one at a time, and in a moment had reduced their number by five. With the pen holder looser, her spirit felt easier as well. So much easier she could almost smell the snow's chill exhalation and M's erratic moist odour.

Ma was always the same. The dusk of her years had gathered in the lines of her face. Across her forehead ran two deep brown scars, as though a sled were dragged over her brow all year long. M had more than once clambered up on her lap to taste the weariness in those scars with his pink, moist tongue. M's eyes were filled with tears, but Ma's eyes were always covered by mist, mist that clouded the eyes and never admitted the light. And M's eyes never stopped revolving, like the stars in the sky.

Catkin was seven, that's what Ma said once when Dad had gone beyond the mountains in driving snow carrying a load of goods on a pole over his shoulder. She and Ma collected firewood every day. That was when, for the first time, she realized that a human voice could be more lovely than those of birds: Ma sang a song that made her laugh and cry when she heard it:

> *One tiny flower on the mountainside blooms*
> *One narrow road in all directions leads*
> *Into the valley the tiny flower falls*
> *There is no road, and one drifts about.*

The dusk in Ma's face deepened. Everywhere Catkin turned, the trees, the wind, even the snow fell silent. She wept in broken sobs as Ma sighed and took her home by the hand. She never heard enough of that song, even to this day.

Dad brought back a load of things with him. For Catkin, a patterned cotton cloth and a red hair ribbon. Also a string of firecrackers that told her the New Year was on its way. That's when Ma explained to her that she was seven years old. She didn't understand what seven years old was and when she asked Ma, Ma answered, "It's all grown up." All grown up? What was that like? She couldn't imagine it. As her braid grew longer, Ma coiled it up in a little black butterfly. The hollows in Dad's face were just like depressions in the ground; Catkin imagined filling them up with little grains of rice. Perhaps then Dad's face might not be so ugly to look at.

As long as she could remember, Ma and Dad were always at odds when they began talking together, and Catkin had learned to be quiet and avoid trouble. At first Ma would yield tearfully, but eventually those tears had dried up for good. Catkin didn't like to see Dad get angry at Ma. So whenever they talked together she would try to make a quiet exit.

"The devil's to pay out there," said Dad. Catkin

was just on the point of slipping away, but hearing that, she stopped in her tracks and listened.

"What kind of trouble?" Ma asked softly.

"Arresting people and have them paraded in the streets. Streets full of students, boys and girls, all wanting to shake things up."

"Ah, the society's changing," sighed Ma.

The weather turned sluggish, and Catkin's heart turned sluggish with it. She wanted so much to know what was happening out there beyond the mountains. Ma said, after she had grown a few more years, they would send her outside; Ma also said the people out there were monstrous and wicked, and feared Catkin would get hurt. Catkin had been out there once, Dad told her that. When she was two, she fell ill for a long time with a burning fever, and Dad took her out and made her better. Unfortunately she couldn't remember any of it.

What's it like beyond the mountains?

Catching Catkin eavesdropping, Ma and Dad clammed up.

"What are you listening to?" asked Dad.

"To the wind," Catkin lied. "If the wind blows so fiercely, won't M's nose start to run?" Her eyes filled with tears as she forced herself not to cry.

"M?" Dad's pock-marked face wrinkled up like a bran dumpling.

"That dog," Ma quickly replied, "Catkin calls it M now."

"M, what the hell's a M?" Dad's thick eyebrows twisted together and curled like a garter snake. It scared Catkin so that her body trembled when she answered cautiously.

"M, that means he knows how to work."

"Oh, bullshit!" Dad grimaced irritably, but didn't ask anymore.

Ah, M! Catkin rushed outside and was at once blinded by the blowing snow. She rubbed her eyes, rubbed them until she cried.

The schoolyard was a sheet of pure white. And splashed there, who knows when, were several spots of red that were five girls building a snowman. He was tall, fat, sincere and dazzling white. One of the girls was unhappy with his nose and tried to fix his appearance with minute strokes, but in the end it wasn't quite what another girl thought it should be, and they fell together pinching and giggling. Not wanting to be left out, the others there joined the battle, and in a moment when they looked around, they found their snowman had collapsed in a heap. They fell on the ground laughing, opening like five cherry blossoms in full flower. And their eyelashes, noses, mouths and heaving chests were kissed by the waltzing snowflakes scattered by a delighted silent sky above them. The digital clock on Catkin's desk read 11:32. She put on her almond yellow eiderdown coat, her white woollen cap, white scarf and white gloves, then locked her door and left. She hurried through the dim corridors, then out into the schoolyard.

Free from worry, her spirits lifted. An expansive, sentient universe let drop a giant screen that floated like thin gauze woven from the snowflakes. And while the snow gently whispered as it drifted and filled in the spaces between the weaving, Catkin was reminded of the goddesses that danced and sang in the old stories.

She hesitated with each step, loath to mar that thick
field of white with her footprints. The five girls playing
in the snow peered over at her, then all at once stood
up, chiding each other to go on building their
snowman. Catkin gave them a smile and walked
straight on out of the schoolyard. Past the residences,
past the fields, down, out of the mountains she walked.

It was twenty years earlier, in just this weather, just
this season, she sat in this little room, with a restless
heart carrying so much unbearable loneliness and bitter
longing born of loneliness.

A piece of tough rope, braided from hemp. They
said it was her Ma's, now used to bind firewood. Catkin attached the rope around her body and sat in front
of the chimney tying knots. Dad had gone up the
mountain to hunt roebuck, while Ma squatted in front
of the cooking stove tanning a bear skin with ash.
Two days before, Dad had shot a big black bear. Ma
said it could be worth a lot of money, but Catkin
didn't know what money was.

Catkin tied a knot, judged the length remaining on
the rope, then, dissatisfied, untied it and tried again.
After several attempts she finally tied two knots on the
rope, dividing it into three sections.

"This is morning," she said to herself, pointing to
the first section. "Here's the afternoon," she pulled
again on the portion of rope between the two knots.
"And this is the long, long nighttime." Then she
sighed and propped her chin on her hands, thinking.

"Catkin, what are you doing making knots in a perfectly good rope?"

"Dividing the day," she said quietly, looking at

Ma. Ma draped the bearskin over the chimney flue and sighed too.

Every night the *kang** was heated until it became hot to the touch. Dad lit the bear-oil lamp and drank liquor, sending her to bed early. Obediently, Catkin slipped out of her clothes and let herself be tucked in. As soon as Dad started to drink, the muscles of his face would smooth out and the pits became a little shallower. And when he argued with Ma, his tone became a little softer, soft like a breeze in spring, wetly caressing the earth from which melted the last remaining snow. Ma bent down and lightly patted her to sleep, but although Catkin squinched up her eyes, she wasn't ready to sleep. She could sense the dusky flames flicker in the bear-oil lamp and the liquor in Dad piercing like a long silver needle. Soon, Dad finished drinking, cleared his nose and throat with an "uhuh ahah", went outside to pee and returned to blow out the oil lamp, then grope his way to the *kang*. At night they hung padded curtains at the windows and the room went black as death. Catkin grew terribly afraid, and imagined she had turned into a little black fly, ugly and tiny, unnoticed by everyone. Dad pulled Ma over. She listened to Dad murmuring to Ma and Ma responding reluctantly, and at that instant, Dad and Ma seemed to melt into one. She hoped they would always be like that, although deep down inside the terror still lurked.

Ratatatat, firecrackers exploded. The sweet redo-

---

*A *kang* is a large brick bed heated during the winter months in north China by warm air passing through pipes connected to a fireplace or oven.

lence of broiling pork was penetrated by a wave of thick, pungent smell of gunpowder. The room boasted an extra bear-oil lamp and their two rings of flame burned furiously. Catkin put on new clothes and pinned the red ribbon to her hair, then watched Dad and Ma go to the pine table to serve New Year's dinner.

The cold wind brayed like a donkey, each cry more shrill than the last, its ear-piercing wail echoing over the endless forest. There was no moon, only a few glimmering stars, shining wanly in the deep black screen of the sky. M reclined quietly beside her and, like her, looked searchingly at the sky.

Catkin couldn't make out the path that led down the mountain. Every time Dad went down, it was without anyone knowing at all. Every time he returned, it was always on the quiet. Once, hoping to find that path, she climbed up the high hill behind their cottage. But all she could make out were more mountains rising on all sides. Even though she was then barely seven, she had felt utterly without hope, utterly lonely and she had knelt on the hilltop and wept until her face was as pale as the snow. She wiped every tear away as it rolled out, as she always did. At last, it was Dad who came to carry her home. Dad did not thrash her for it, but his expression was twisted with fury. She never again dared go in search of that path down the mountain.

"Catkin, what are you staring at? Come inside and have your New Year's dinner," Ma came over and called. Catkin started to feel Ma's hand burn against her cold face. Her heart contracted.

"Ma, why does New Year happen in winter?"

"Winter is not so busy, and it's clean."

"Well, winter is cold," she answered back surlily, squatting and throwing her arms tightly around M's neck, her teeth chattering.

"Where Ma lived it's not so cold."

"Where was that? Where's Ma's home?"

"Ma hasn't any home. Catkin, now come in quickly. Kowtow to your Dad and wish him Happy New Year."

Ma pulled her inside. Dad was already waiting uneasily. His whole body shook up and down with impatience. Ma gave M a few scraps of venison and led him to a corner to enjoy it. Catkin kowtowed to Ma and Dad, and wished them Happy New Year. But she didn't eat her dinner. She said her teeth and her tummy ached. Dad was clearly displeased by this and he stared angrily at Ma, as if it were she inciting Catkin to feign illness. At last, he felt Catkin's forehead, shook his head and gave out a jeering laugh. Without warning, he pulled his belt from his waist and struck straight out at Ma with it. She didn't turn to run and hide, or cry. Dad extinguished the two lamps and plunged the room into well-bottom darkness. Catkin scrambled to the ground. Her mouth opened yet she dared not make any noise, scurried over to M and let him lead her outside through the door. A little starlight leaked into the room, and for a moment, Dad stayed his hand.

M demonstrated his valiance, bravery and perception. He was a great big, strong dog covered in mostly brown fur except for a snowy white muzzle, forehead and throat. His ears were thick and broad, but wouldn't stand up. Instead, they drooped on either side of his head and made his raven eyes gleam all the more. Dad always took M along hunting; time and again he dragged Dad back from the edge of death. But Dad didn't like M one bit. Once when he was drunk, Dad began yodelling some song and urinated on M's head. M, growling furiously and baring sharp rows of white fangs, started advancing wildly toward him. That scared Dad sober, and he pulled up his trousers in terror. Catkin was overjoyed; she really hoped M would take a bite at Dad's crotch. Afterward she had led M to a mountain spring and washed his head clean with crystal water, then woven a wildflower necklace to put around his neck. She climbed on his back, and grabbing his ears, they galloped about, M flying like the wind, Catkin laughing and gaily calling his name. In their excitement they ran into Dad who shouted out at M and cursed Catkin, "Dirty your pants riding a dog. Just look at your crotch, see how filthy it is, you little dog child."

It was as though M had been ready for this all along. Once they were out of the door, out of the darkened cottage, he carried Catkin straight into the deep forest. The sky was pitch black and the wind tossed the tops of the humming trees. What Dad might do to Ma after she ran away, Catkin simply couldn't imagine. Would he beat her to death? Her only thought now was to run, it didn't matter where. Whatever happened, she never wanted to see Dad and Ma ever again, never wanted to hear Dad's day-long cursing or smell that liquor wafting from his coarse face. She had to escape, and she trusted M would take her somewhere right and safe.

Barely conscious, Catkin wept. Her hands, feet, and face no longer felt as if they were her own. She had not worn her cotton padded mitts or rabbit fur scarf, and had only a pair of felt socks on her feet. "Huchihuchi" came M's odd, straining pants, and she kept thinking she ought to get off and let him catch his breath. But she couldn't move a muscle.

When she looked up and caught a glimpse of the sky, she realized all the crowding stars were rushing along with them as fast as they could go. She wept a little easier.

The snow fell thick and soft, and covered Catkin in snowflakes. She heaved a long breath and stuck out her tongue on which the snowflakes melted into tiny drops, and clear water trickled down her throat.

Suddenly M stopped. Wheezing brokenly as though he would drop, he arched his back and began to bark. Catkin realized how exhausted he was and she tried to wiggle off, but her legs had gone numb. They had travelled such a long way. The sky was still overcast and the cold wind blew pitilessly, making a sound that set her hair on end. For the first time she felt the enormity and terror of the black night. Suddenly she missed Ma, even her Dad, and then, nothing. Her mind was a blank. M shoved her into a hollow in the snow, and swooped on something five metres off.

Dimly she saw M claw at a black something. The black thing first wriggled in the snow and then very slowly rose to its full height and toppled onto M like an enormous tree struck by lightning. Catkin cried out, "M!" and lost consciousness. Her head, hands and feet seemed to fall away and her whole body was emptiness and light. A pale fog drifted in front of her eyes, thick and impenetrable. The fog was so suffocating that she almost choked. And however hard she tried she couldn't open her eyes. Later, when she did open them, she saw her Dad's stricken face, his porkmarks deeper than ever. She turned to look at Ma. Her hair was grey. So were her face, lips, eyes, and even her voice was grey. "She ... came to ... at last...." Her tears fell. They were grey too. Catkin felt an immense emptiness in her body as if all her insides has been taken away: she had nothing, and she couldn't move at all.

The sky darkened again and a limpid sun hid itself behind an ashen wall of shadowy cloud. She had lived through it. Weakly, she asked Ma, "Has my hair turned grey?"

"No, Catkin, your hair is still as black and shiny as a bearskin."

"M was crushed by a black ... a black bear." She began to remember what she had seen. The corners of her mouth twitched. She wanted to cry but no tears came.

"M didn't die, he's just fine." Ma looked away and gave a shout, "M, M...."

At her call, M bounded into the room and sat up nimbly, his forepaws on Catkin's shoulders, stretched out his tongue and doused her face and forehead in a shower of affectionate licks. The corners of her eyes turned warm and moist and a clear stream gurgled up inside her body's empty shell, and then she cried, cried like a drizzle on a sunny day, fresh and free of care.

"Can she get up?"

"She'll have to rest in bed a little longer." Who was Dad talking to? Catkin looked in the direction of the voice and saw a person, who owned a nose, a mouth, eyes and ears just like them, standing there in front of her like something in a fairy tale. Her whole body shook with fright. Besides Dad and Ma, no one else had ever come here as long as she could remember. She thought of all the stories Ma had told her, and it puzzled her even more. Could it be one of those people who eat other people? Look how wide his mouth opens — how could those teeth be as white as birch bark? How could Ma's and Dad's teeth be yellow as mud? She closed her eyes, and her temples throbbed. Over the *kang* hung a damp, earthy smell. Ma sprinkled water on the *kang* when it got too hot. Catkin felt that smell tingle in her nose as she drifted back to sleep.

The snow continued to fall through the dancing wind, crusting the iron grey door with white. Catkin stood in the doorway until her legs ached, so she let herself slide down and lay on the floor. The sky appeared at once far, far away and so very, very close. She was a tiny snowflake herself, swirling among the others, all drifting up and away together.

She was better very quickly. She was able to manage the tough venison and she could play with M on the floor of the front room. The newcomer was very kind to her, and he folded paper airplanes and boats for her, although he always looked so downcast. His face was white and blank as a snowy wasteland, with smallish but gentle eyes that sparkled like M's.

Ma said thank goodness for this person, or she would have frozen to death. Ma said he came to this part of the forest to die alone. He wanted to lie down peacefully in the wilderness and let the snow silently bury him, but then he came across Catkin. The newcomer rescued her. And when Dad went out the next day at dawn, he rescued them both.

Deep inside, Catkin resented this newcomer. If it weren't for him, she and Mmng would be long gone from this world, gone perhaps to a place far away from the dark. So if she came on him by accident, she would always disgustedly look the other way.

The little back room was given him to stay in. He and Dad often argued about things in there, Dad's voice was rough and gravelly, his was weak and soft, like a terrified little rabbit minded by a lion. Ma said, beyond the mountains, people were stirring up trouble, and he had gotten dragged in the middle. The poor "son of a bitch" was pushed to the edge and ready to die. Catkin didn't understand how he could be the "son of a bitch" since he didn't look a bit like M. Not even his voice was anything like M's. Apparently, unusual things happened to people who lived beyond the mountains.

The nights were still just as long as before. The bear-oil lamp had been extinguished who knows how many times by Dad. Yet it was still flickering with light. Since the newcomer had arrived, Ma wasn't as ashen-faced as before, and when she was busy doing things she even hummed a little tune, as though through him she recovered some part of her lost fortune and happiness. But unlike the first time, it didn't make Catkin cry; she had no tears for this kind of song.

The lovebirds drift in pairs
In pairs they drift on a watery face
Butterflies flutter two by two
Collecting nectar in two's they chase

Catkin filled the length of Ma's hemp rope with knots. She called the knots stars. She wanted the stars to be as numerous as the yellow flowers in the fields.

Dad went hunting up-mountain, taking M with him. Sometimes he took along the newcomer as well. But whenever he and Dad went out, they always returned empty-handed, having caught nothing so much as a rabbit. Dad would pull a long face and furiously scold M's uselessness. But eventually he stopped taking the newcomer with him. When Dad went out alone, he always told Catkin, "Don't go running about outside. Stay at home and help your Ma." Then his suspicious eyes would dart maliciously in the newcomer's direction. Catkin faintly sensed that some new unhappiness had arisen between Dad and Ma.

One day when the sun was so bright it hurt the eyes, Dad went out hunting. Catkin sat on the *kang* and cleaned the bear-oil lamp until her hands were caked with soot. Ma sat against the wall thinking about something with a blank expression on her face. Then Catkin heard the newcomer's voice call from his room, "Sister-in-law — "

Ma gave a start, and shot a quick glance in Catkin's direction with a strange expression on her face. Then she went to the back room, taking light, unhurried steps like autumn leaves drifting on the water.

For some reason she didn't understand, Catkin was suddenly very interested. She pricked up her ears trying to hear what they were saying. But all she could catch were half-phrases that sounded like, "When the catkins turned white ... and the bulrushes...." White? She didn't know there was a time when she was white. Maybe she grew pixie hair. Then had she once been a fairy? Her heart pounded fiercely. Gingerly, she let herself down off the *kang* and circled around on tip-toe to the back room door, and stood there listening without a sound.

"Then what?" the newcomer asked.

"I ... killed him. Afterwards I took a hemp rope and threw it over the old locust at the entrance of the village, to hang myself." Ma stopped talking. The oven flue rattled noisily and Catkin knew smoke would be belching from the chimney outside. The room was strangely hot, and her face felt like searing coals, but she hardly dared to breathe. She clasped her hands in a fist and with great effort swallow the spittle rising in her throat.

"I don't think I will ever again see a moonlit night so beautiful as that one. The leaves of the old locust cast a scattered shadow on the road like a flower. When I threw the rope over a branch, two lines were added to the flowery shadow, swaying back and forth, like two horrid snakes. Then I thought the shadow of someone who hung herself would be too terrifying for anyone to see. I pulled down the rope, tied it around my waist, and ran." It was Ma talking still, but her voice sounded like a stranger's to Catkin. What was an old locust? Could it have such a nice-looking shadow? Even more beautiful than the white shadows cast in their own forest?

"Where could I run? Even if I had killed him, I couldn't cleanse myself of what he had done to me. I couldn't stay in Shandong. I couldn't stand it, so I ran away to the Northeast by myself."

"So how did you come to be with Catkin's father?"

"When I got here, I didn't know a soul. I had nothing to eat, nowhere to live, I just wanted to die again." Whenever Ma got to the difficult parts, a nasal weepy sound invaded her voice. "I took that rope and found a place deep in the woods. But I never expected the deep woods to be filled with butterflies. There were gold, blue, white, even green ones, and they flew all around me, and I cried when so many tiny wings brushed against my face.

"The sun was bright that day, so when he came past that place on his way down the mountain and saw me crying there, he came over. I told him everything. He said since I'd killed a man I must never see anyone else ever again. He was afraid I wouldn't stay with him, so he branded me on the forehead with a red hot iron bar. When spring arrived the next year, I gave birth to Catkin. I counted the days. Catkin isn't his."

Ma sighed. Catkin sighed with her. It upset Catkin to discover so many secrets no one knew of, hidden away inside Ma.

"We have met, both sorry souls at the ends of our rope."

"Sister-in-law."

"Brother...."

Everything was silent. Ma didn't say anything else,

nor did the newcomer. Catkin's legs jerked in little spasms, and she moved back to the room with blurry eyes. Just then there came a great crash as the door leapt open, and Dad, covered in snow from head to foot, entered the cottage in a cloud of cold air. He must have been tracking large game all day but let it escape, for his whole face was filled with rancour and his eyes burned with resentment. He had vented his anger on M because she could see where the dog's forehead was clotted with dried blood. Crying, she ran over and put her arms around M. Dad tossed down his hunting rifle, and strode straight into the back room. Catkin knew something awful was about to happen.

The stars clashed noisily and a great ball of fire arose. Ma wept, Dad howled, and the newcomer groaned. M sniffed about Catkin's trouser-legs, pulling at them piteously. She held him as tight as she could, held him with all her might. The next moment, Dad stormed out. He picked up the rope on the floor where Catkin had tied her countless knots, and started striking her with it in a fury. "Bastard girl, little bitch," he cursed.

Catkin imagined that her dad had clutched a handful of chilling stars which were sinking their tiny teeth deep into her skin. She thought the room would collapse and they would all be crushed to death. Collapse! Please hurry up and collapse!

Suddenly, Dad let out a dreadful yell. Catkin blinked open her eyes and saw M's muzzle covered in blood. The rope Dad beat her with lay on the floor, and his hand was a mess of bleeding flesh. Dad grabbed a sharp knife and staggered after M, caught him and sat on him, pinning the dog between his legs. M barked frantically, and Catkin scrambled over on her knees to grab Dad's leg. But he raised his foot and gave her a kick that sent her sliding across the floor. Then he plunged the knife into the dog's stomach...."

Catkin ran out of the room and dashed in the direction of the pale sun just as it was about to dip out of view, yelling,

"M....
"M — M — M —
"M— "

Extraordinary silence. M was dead. His two beguiling, warm eyes closed forever. His attentive, rousing bark silenced forever. For several days it did not snow and the weather turned crackling cold. Ma didn't die. Dad didn't die. The newcomer didn't die either. Life breathed on. On that day, Dad drank two bowls of liquor, sweat beading his forehead and carrying M on his back left and went to his ravine in the mountains. Catkin, leaning against the door, watched him stagger away uncertainly into a silent splendour far in the distance where the sun sank beneath the western mountains and splattered crimson tears like blood, brilliantly staining the wide earth in majesty.

The days kept on going. There was still the same warmth falling asleep or waking next to Ma. These nights, it was always best to dream good dreams. One more locust stood in the mountain forest, its leaves the shape of M's ears. Overcome with feeling, Catkin touched them tenderly. The sky was unusually clear and the locust leaves pinwheeled in sunshine while she swayed in their shadow. Soon the sun disappeared and the moon rose. She seemed to see that charming moonlit night Ma had mentioned. In a trance, Catkin allowed her arms to drift upward, rising like the wings of a bird. Suddenly, a pair of ochre hands stopped her soaring in mid-flight and she fell to the ground with a "thump".

When she awoke, her mouth was gagged with a kerchief, and Dad had deftly wrapped her in a bearskin and bundled her outside. The sky was an inky pitch-black, vaulting a soundless creation. Dad put her down, struck a match, and lit a piece of birchbark. The firelight shone red on half his face, and buried the other half in the night's blackness. The eye on the firelit side was serious and fierce. Then he threw the birchbark into the cottage, and as the flaming light fell, Catkin could see bark, dried grass, branches and tinder piled on the floor. She struggled to pull out the gag and pleaded tearfully with Dad who was now busy nailing the door shut. "Nail it when the sun comes up! Please wait until the sun comes up!"

Perhaps her voice was too faint. Dad nailed that door, then scrambled onto the roof to throw down some burning pine torches. Inside the house Catkin heard noises and then something was beating loudly against the door. Dad picked her up firmly and without looking back, went down the path that led beyond the mountains. But now, she wasn't so eager to leave, and she kicked and pulled at Dad's face and neck, crying until she was hoarse, "Ma ... Ma will be ... burned to death!"

But the path down the mountain just kept disappearing beneath Dad's feet. Looking back, she saw

their home already become an enormous ball of fire,
burning brilliantly. The fireball was like the setting sun,
sinking into the murky dark of the mountain forest;
then like the rising sun just at the point of creeping
over the trees. When Dad couldn't go any further, he
dropped Catkin on the ground, and buried his face
deep in the snow and lay there crying, his shoulders violently heaving up and down. It was the first time she
had ever seen Dad cry.

A two-acre piece of forest was burned down that
night. Dad gave her into the care of an old widower
without children. Dad was finished as a forester, and
the last time she saw him was when he left with several
other labour reform prisoners for the Northwest. He
gazed at Catkin with a manic look, unwilling to leave
her. He grasped her hand and said in a trembling
voice, "I spoke with your new Dad, and told him he
could get a pup for you, so you can raise a
'M'." Then he lowered his head and his shoulder twitched uncontrollably. Catkin stared at him, without warmth or expression. Finally, with great effort, he
unlooped a rope tied around his waist and passed it to
her in his trembling hand. If she missed Ma, he said,
she had only to look at the rope. Catkin recognized it
as the one Ma tried to hang herself with, and on
which she had counted off the days. She didn't know
how it came that Dad had brought it with him.
Unfortunately, the little stars on it had all died long
ago.

When she was sixteen, Dad died. She heard that at
the festival of the Double Fifth, he stole several bottles
of liquor and drank them dry, then disappeared into

the swirling sands of the vast desert to close his eyes forever. Now that he was dead, a great weight lifted from her heart thinking that he had got his retributions. But one night she saw his ochry black face in her dream, and when she awoke, her eyes were damp with tears.

"Teacher Bai, you'll turn into a snowman before long!"

"Come mountain climbing with us!"

"How about a snowball battle!"

Somehow those five girls in red bundled in their eiderdown coats had run over to where she was standing. They surrounded Catkin, five radiant suns. Catkin sat up, then in a small voice said, "I've been dreaming in the snow."

"Really?"

"Yes."

"Who wants to go mountain climbing anyhow? Let's lie in the snow and dream dreams instead." They all fell down and cried,

"I'm going to dream about pear blossom petals blowing out of a flute."

"I'm going to dream about tramping through the snow in search of winter plum!"

"I'm going to dream about juicy crabs at Mid-Autumn Festival."

"I'm going to dream about a skyscraper rising on the snow."

"Oh, I'm not so grand as you, I'll just dream about a sound sleep!" Surrounded by a long peal of sweet laughter, Catkin stood up, brushed the snow off herself, then smiled at them and said, "You've got enough dreams already, go climb your mountain!"

"What about you?"

"With all your dreams, I'll just go and write a sequel to *A Dream of Red Mansions.*"

She walked away from the grassy field, her feet sinking in the snow, entered the schoolyard, went to her room then sitting down in front of her desk, and began to write. Her pen moved with an astonishing life of its own.

I can never forget those two scars across Ma's forehead. M tasted the bitterness there, and I drew in its sad tenderness. Oh! My twenty-one-year-old Ma, those should have been your years of flowers and precious youth. But you reported that the brigade leader was stealing corn because you were starving, and he got back at you. He drove dear grandpa and grandma to suicide, and then he took you, and…. Can I really be the daughter of the man Ma killed? How can I carry the unclean blood of that bastard in my veins?

M, my buddy, what are you up to in that solitary forest? Do you romp in the snow? Can you see Ma? When she was burned, her face must have blazed red, her hair and whole body, too. There's a holiness to being cremated so solemnly and cruelly in such a pure forest. But what a terrifying holiness it is!

I never spoke of Dad and Ma to anyone, never wanted to. The dead are all dead. But I survive and live my new life. How will I go on renewing myself to create lasting peace and happiness?

The snow falls endlessly outside. Another Sunday will pass by. The sky gradually darkens, but inwardly I still carry that silent snow-capped range and that boundless desert. Although he wasn't my own father, I miss him as if he were. His pockmarked visage, just like the ashen face Ma left in my memory, still brings a sour happiness.

Dad, You needn't grasp so desperately in my dreams. Sleep calmly. The thick yellow sands will bury you in rich, mellow dreams.

The girls have gone to climb their mountain. The top is high up but they will stand proudly in their blazing red on its peak. I think I will go out and build a snow girl. A snow girl just like myself, for Dad to look at, for Ma to see, for M to snuggle up to. Then I will take the rope Dad and Ma left me and tie it around the girl's neck, knotted with a billion little stars, glinting in blazing glory.

It looks as though the first snowfall of winter will not stop tonight. As they flow without end from my pen, these clamouring feelings are finally coalescing as well. I hope this snowflake-fed stream will flow around everyone I know well, so they rest a little more refreshed and renewed.

Sky and earth will melt into one. Misty snow, come cloak the world in a vigorous vastness.

Translated by Geoffrey Bonnycastle